SALTY KISSES

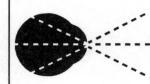

This Large Print Book carries the
Seal of Approval of N.A.V.H.

CHRISTY & TODD, THE BABY YEARS,
BOOK 2

SALTY KISSES

ROBIN JONES GUNN

THORNDIKE PRESS

A part of Gale, a Cengage Company

GALE
A Cengage Company

Farmington Hills, Mich • San Francisco • New York • Waterville, Maine
Meriden, Conn • Mason, Ohio • Chicago

LIBRARY OF CONGRESS CATALOGING-IN-PUBLICATION DATA

Names: Gunn, Robin Jones, 1955– author.
Title: Salty kisses / by Robin Jones Gunn.
Description: Large print edition. | Waterville, Maine : Thorndike Press, 2017. | Series: Christy & Todd, the baby years ; #2 | Series: Thorndike Press large print Christian fiction
Identifiers: LCCN 2017021530| ISBN 9781432838300 (hardcover) | ISBN 143283830X (hardcover)
Subjects: LCSH: Large type books. | GSAFD: Christian fiction.
Classification: LCC PS3557.U4866 S25 2017 | DDC 813/.54—dc23
LC record available at https://lccn.loc.gov/2017021530

Published in 2017 by arrangement with Robin's Nest Productions, Inc.

For Janet who is my Katie
and
For Ross who is my Todd
Forever

ONE

"Do you see her?" Christy leaned on the handles of her baby stroller in the airport baggage claim area and asked her husband once again, "Todd, can you see Katie anywhere?"

Their nineteen-month-old daughter, Hana, let out a wail from the stroller and twisted around, trying to get a glimpse of her parents. Christy pulled back the stroller's top cover so their blonde, blue-eyed little girl had a clear view of both of them.

"We're right here, sweetheart," Christy said. "I know you want out, but it's too crowded for you to walk with us."

The crush of international travelers surged around them as Christy and Todd stood in one place like a tiny island in a wind-tossed sea. Hana wailed again. The whining cry had become all too familiar over the past few days because Hana had another molar breaking through. Christy was lost in her own tangle of frustrations over being late to pick up her best friend who had flown by herself all the way from Africa.

"Did you bring any crackers for Hana?" Todd reached for the cloth shoulder bag in the basket underneath the stroller. The toddler recognized the familiar word cracker and turned up the volume on her cries.

Christy cringed. Even though she knew no one was paying attention to them, she still struggled with feeling embarrassed when Hana grew so loud in public. Christy imagined people looking at her and judging her mothering skills. She also was exasperated with the way Todd's solution to Hana's fussing was to shove something in her mouth — a cracker, a sippy cup, a pacifier.

Todd found a bag of crackers in the organized diaper bag and offered one to Hana, who eagerly snatched it and looked up adoringly at her daddy. Todd took the bait like the smitten father he was and smoothed his hand over Hana's feathery hair. It had taken months before hair had started growing on Hana's bald little head. Now that most of the strands were about an inch long she often resembled a dandelion that was ready for a wish.

"Is that better, Sunshine?" Todd gazed at Hana. His short hair was a lighter shade of blonde than Hana's but there was no mistaking that she'd gotten her daddy's memorable silver blue eyes.

Christy returned her focus to the bustling baggage claim area, seeking a glimpse of Katie. It had been almost five years since Katie had married Eli in Kenya and started to serve alongside him with outreach work that helped to bring clean water to remote parts of eastern Africa. Their African safari wedding was the last time Christy had seen Katie, and the major change to their friendship was something that had caused a deep ache in Christy.

She had never tried to express to Katie or Todd or even to herself the lonely sadness that had rested on her spirit like a quiet mist ever since Katie had moved to Africa. The regular video calls between Christy's home in Newport Beach and Katie's home near Nairobi, Kenya, had kept them connected all these years. But it was never the same as being together, face-to-face, heart-to-heart, laughing and crying in tandem over the daily moments of their lives.

All that was about to change because Katie was going to be in California for a little over a week. But the reason for her visit was not a happy one.

"Is that her?" Todd asked.

Christy stood on her tiptoes and tried to see the person Todd was pointing to.

"Over there. On the right."

Christy was aware that someone had come up beside her, unusually close, so she shifted her crossover shoulder bag in front of her where a pickpocket was less likely to gain access. She hated being paranoid, but she had traveled enough to know that in a huge, crowded airport like LAX, she was better off being protective.

"I don't think that's her," Christy told Todd.

"No," said the woman who was standing uncomfortably close to Christy. "That's definitely not her."

Christy spun quickly and bumped heads with her favorite redheaded Forever Friend. Katie's attempt at surprising Christy by quietly standing there until Christy noticed was met with a lopsided hug followed by squeals of joy and laughter that were so loud Hana burst into tears and let out a terrified wail.

"Hana, it's okay." Christy linked her arm through Katie's and leaned down. "It's your Auntie Katie."

"Hey!" Katie knelt in front of Hana and smiled. "Look at you! You're such a big girl, Hana."

Christy felt a sweet sort of comfort that Katie pronounced Hana's name correctly with both a's sounding like relaxing "ahh's." When Christy and Todd had spontaneously named their daughter after a very special place on Maui that meant a lot to both of them, they hadn't taken into consideration the number of people who would see the way it was spelled and assume her name was pronounced like *Hannah.*

Katie reached over to stroke Hana's dandelion hair. "You are such a cutie!"

Hana, who seemed to be trying to decide what she thought of buoyant Katie, pulled back and stretched out her arms with a loud wail, as if pleading with Christy to rescue her.

"It's okay, Hana. This is Auntie Katie. She's our friend."

Katie pulled back and gave Hana her space. "You'll get used to me, Hana. Most people do." With a grin, Katie added, "Eventually."

Katie's copper-red hair swished as she turned to Todd. "Hi to you, too! I hope I don't make you burst into tears." They hugged and Katie added, "Eli sends his love and really wishes he could have been here. Oh! I think that's my bag going by on the carousel."

The next half hour turned into a series of shuffles and bumps as they pulled Katie's beat-up suitcase off the belt, tried to keep Hana from wailing, and found their way to where they had parked their VW, Gussie the Bussie. With Hana in the security of her car seat and Christy next to her in the backseat to keep her entertained, Katie sat in the front. Todd jockeyed to join the tight line of cars inching their way toward the freeway. Rush hour in Los Angeles at the beginning of summer vacation was beastly.

"Katie," Christy ventured. "How are you doing? I mean, really?"

"Okay, I think." Katie took in a deep breath and leaned back. "I don't think anyone is ever prepared for the kind of phone call I got three days ago."

Christy reached forward and placed a comforting hand on Katie's shoulder.

"I mean, who's ever prepared to hear that their dad keeled over while moving his couch into a U-Haul trailer and died of a heart attack right then and there? It still seems unreal. Being here with you guys is unreal. It's like I'm inside this really long dream. I kind of don't want to wake up. But then, I kind of do."

Christy gave Katie's shoulder a squeeze. Todd glanced at Katie with a compassionate look and then returned his gaze to the road in front of them.

"We're glad you're here," he said in a calm voice. "Not for that reason, but we're glad you're here."

"Thanks, you guys." She turned to look at Christy. "Do you happen to have any water? I'm feeling kind of wrung out."

Christy quickly opened the lid of the small ice chest between the two front seats. "Sorry. I brought this and forgot to tell you. There's juice, soda, and water. I didn't know what you would like."

"Just water." Katie pulled out one of the bottles and drank the cold water slowly.

"I brought snacks, too." Christy pointed to the bag next to the ice chest. "Help yourself to whatever you would like."

"I'll pass. My stomach thinks it's still going through turbulence. I hope you don't mind if I konk out on you guys. I didn't sleep much on the plane."

"Of course we don't mind."

It took three hours to reach Todd and Christy's beach house, and blessedly, little Hana fell asleep after the first twenty minutes. Katie dozed off, too, with her head against the window.

Christy took in the smoggy view of the 405 freeway and tried to sort out all her mixed feelings. She knew that Katie needed to get down to her mom's in Escondido and spend as much time with her as possible. But Christy hoped to squeeze in as much time as possible as well. It would be a sad sort of torture if Katie's short visit didn't include catch-up time for the two of them.

The sun was setting in a blaze of orange and pink when Todd pulled into the garage. Hana awoke feverish and disinterested in food. Katie sounded coherent, but she looked flushed and disoriented.

"I'll get Hana into a bath." Christy headed upstairs with her squirming daughter in her arms. "Do you guys want to call for a pizza?"

"I'll take care of dinner," Todd called back.

As Christy climbed the stairs, she could hear Todd explain to Katie some of the changes they had made to the house, including the new tile floor they had installed a few months ago. She knew there would be time later to give Katie a grand tour and point out all the decorating changes she had made. For now, Hana was her top priority.

Christy had to make her way around a maze of boxes stacked up in their bedroom to reach the bathroom. The downstairs sewing room Christy used for her growing home business had been transformed back

14

into a guest room, and all the pieces of her messy workroom had been stuffed in boxes and toted upstairs. Christy ran the water in the tub, and Hana broke into a round of tears.

"You are just one unhappy little girl today, aren't you? Is it your teeth? Let Mama see."

Hana refused to cooperate with the tooth examination. She pulled away and wiggled as Christy tried to undress her.

"Come on, sweetie. Let's put you in the bath." Christy noticed a rash on her tummy and frowned. "What is this from? Your daddy didn't give you more strawberries, did he?"

Christy's best efforts to interest Hana in a calming bath were met with more tears. The evening routine that was usually filled with giggles and splashes was cut short. Hana had to be coaxed into her cuddly jammies and into bed. She clutched her stuffed bunny rabbit and reached for her pacifier.

Christy whispered a prayer over her and rested her hand on Hana's forehead, reciting the same blessing Todd always spoke over Hana when he put her to bed.

"Hana, the Lord bless you and keep you. The Lord make His face to shine upon you and give you His peace. And may you always love Jesus more than anything else."

The familiar words seemed to calm Hana. She let out a defeated sort of whimper as Christy softly closed the bedroom door.

Stepping gingerly on the squeaky floor, Christy returned to their master bedroom across from Hana's room and meandered through the stacks of boxes once again so she could tidy up the bathroom and drain the tub. Christy caught a glimpse of her frazzled-looking image in the mirror and pulled the clip out of her long, nutmeg-brown hair, letting it tumble like a waterfall down her back. It had been years since she'd had it trimmed. The ends were split and dried out, but since Hana was born Christy usually had worn it up in a braid or in a ponytail every day so Hana wouldn't pull on it.

I really need to do something with my hair one of these days.

She gave her mane a quick brushing and leaned in to the mirror. A dark shadow appeared under her left eye but not her right. She knew it wasn't mascara because she hadn't put any on that day. Then she remembered the episode earlier that afternoon when she had tried to maneuver Hana into her car seat to go to the airport. Hana had reared her head back and collided with Christy's cheekbone.

I am a walking train wreck.

Christy's eyes were a distinct shade of blue-green that seemed to change depending on what she was wearing. The white shirt she had on washed color from her skin and her eyes. She thought she looked as if she had been the one crying all day and not Hana.

In an effort to lift her mood, Christy rubbed some of her favorite coconut-and mango-scented lotion on her arms and headed downstairs. Katie was seated at the kitchen counter and was chatting with Eli on a video call.

Leaning in the way Eli always did whenever Katie was on a video call with her, Christy said, "Hi there! We sure wish you were here."

"I wish I could have come, too. Next time." Behind Eli was what looked like a papaya tree and the faces of a bunch of giggling children dressed in school uniforms. They took turns popping in and out of the view of the camera.

"I'll try to call tomorrow," Katie said. "Have fun with all my favorite little monkeys." She waved to the children, and one of them waved back, smiling broadly.

"Love you," Katie said to Eli.

"I love you, too."

As Katie ended the call, they could hear the children laughing in the background and mimicking Eli's "I love you." Katie smiled when she turned to Christy. "He's checking out the location where the first team of the summer will be staying. It's in one of our favorite villages near the Tanzanian border. The team is staying at a school so that means they'll have children following them wherever they go."

Seeing Eli in the field made it even more understandable why he couldn't come with Katie. Christy couldn't help but think that it would have been helpful for Katie if he had come. If nothing else, for emotional support.

But then, maybe Katie felt it was easier to deal with her family on her own. She's never really included me in her family stuff, either.

Christy looked around. Their house was small enough that when you stood in the center of the kitchen, you could look into the entire downstairs area, including the spare room, bathroom, and part of the deck. "Did Todd go for pizza?"

"He left about fifteen minutes ago. I helped myself to some watermelon I found in the fridge. Wow, Christy, your hair has really gotten long."

"I know. I need to get it trimmed. It's so

18

dried out."

"Do you have any aspirin?" Katie asked. "I have a screaming, jet-lag headache."

"Sure." Christy opened the cupboard closest to the back door and showed Katie her organized shelves lined with a variety of vitamins and herbs as well as healing oils.

"Whoa! When did you turn into the Queen Mother of All Things Homeopathic?"

"When I was pregnant with Hana. It started with an herbal tea for nausea."

"Ah yes. Herbal teas. The gateway drug."

Christy wasn't sure if she should laugh at Katie's quirky comment. Katie pulled out a small, dark vial marked, "Serenity" and held it up, waiting for an explanation.

"Essential oil," Christy said. "I have a lot of different ones. I bought them from a massage therapist at work who was starting a side business. The Chinese herb pills came from a guy Todd surfs with. And, of course, you can help yourself to any of the vitamins in there that you want."

Katie's green eyes carried a hint of marvel as she said, "Amazing! I never thought you would turn into the grown-up version of me — the organic me — from back in high school. Remember how I wanted to create a new save-the-planet blend of herbal tea?"

Christy nodded, smiling along with Katie

19

at the memory.

"It's so good to be here with you, Christy. You have no idea." Katie gave Christy a hug and then pulled a bottle of generic aspirin from the cupboard. She poured herself a glass of water, then downed it in one long dreg before she filled her glass again. "Maybe I'm just dehydrated. This water tastes so good."

"It does? Todd and I think it tastes like chlorine sometimes."

"Tastes great to me." Katie filled her glass a third time and sipped slowly. She paused to look at the clean water in the glass.

"It's moments like this that make me even more committed to do what we do. Clean water is such a luxury in most of Africa. Did you know that more than three hundred million people in Africa still live in water-stressed areas? The numbers are highest in sub-Sahara. I saw a new report last week that said 85 percent of all the diseases in African children under the age of five are caused by polluted water sources."

Christy tried to take in the magnitude of what Katie was saying.

"The area Eli is taking the team into this week has a village that lost 35 percent of the villagers over the last six months due to lack of water and polluted water."

Christy sat on one of the stools at the counter. She hadn't given much thought to what it would be like to not be able to give Hana a bath or a drink of fresh water right from the tap. Christy knew that what Eli and Katie did was important, but it had been a long time since she had heard details.

"Eli really wanted to come, you know," Katie said. "There isn't anyone else who can do what he does. He has to organize the well drilling with the short-term team and at the same time keep things peacefully on track with the village leaders. I'm constantly amazed at my husband's leadership abilities. He accomplishes so much through relationships. Everyone trusts him, and Eli has a lot of respect for being a relatively young man."

"You married a good one," Christy said with a smile.

"Yes, I did. Thanks to a little help from my friends." Katie raised her glass of water as if toasting Christy.

A flock of memories fluttered between Christy and Katie as they reminded each other of the way Christy and Todd had practically forced Katie to get together with Eli. Christy and Todd knew the two of them would make a great couple. Eli knew it. Katie just didn't see it until it was almost too late.

The back door opened just then, and Todd stepped into the kitchen with two extra-large pizza boxes in one hand and a grocery bag in the other. His car keys were clenched between his teeth.

"Speaking of the men of our dreams," Katie teased. "Yours comes bearing gifts of pepperoni-ness."

Two

Christy hopped up from the stool by the kitchen counter and took the pizza boxes from Todd. "Two-for-one night at Giannetti's?"

Todd nodded and took the keys from his mouth. "I didn't know what you wanted to drink, Katie, so I bought a bunch of different stuff." He put the grocery bag on the counter and turned to Christy. "Did Hana go to bed without a fuss?"

"Pretty much. She has a slight rash on her stomach. I hope she's not coming down with something."

"Didn't she get a rash when her first molar came in?"

Christy had to think a moment. "I think so. I know she was feverish then, and she was feverish tonight."

The truth was everything in her mind had been fragmented ever since Hana was born. She didn't remember details the way she used to. For the first six months she blamed it on sleep deprivation. Then she thought that nearly a year of breast-feeding Hana had depleted her of too many vitamins and left her with a foggy brain. That's when she stocked her cabinet with an arsenal of supplements. When Christy lamented to her friend Tracy, she had laughed. Tracy had a very active son and twins who were now toddlers. She told Christy that "bumble brain" comes with motherhood so she might as well get used to it.

"Go ahead and dig in, Katie," Todd said. "The one you requested is on top. I hope Christy told you we expect you to make yourself at home here. If you can't find something you want or need, let us know, and we'll get it for you."

"Thanks." Katie pulled a piece of the "everything" pizza from the box and took a bite. She closed her eyes, chewed slowly, and swallowed. Pointing to the wedge of cheesy, meaty, red-peppered, tomatoed, and mushroomed pizza she said, "I've missed this. Americans overdo everything in the nicest ways. Especially with food. This is amazing."

Christy pulled the bottom pizza box out and opened it to find a Hawaiian pizza with pineapple and Canadian bacon. Todd knew her preferences in pizza were much less elaborate. She took a bite and realized how hungry she was after the long trek to the airport and back.

"You know, since you offered, I do need one thing, Todd." Katie reached for a napkin and dabbed the tomato sauce from the side of her mouth. "I need you to do me a big favor Sunday."

"Sure. What do you need?"

"I need you to perform the service for my dad's funeral."

The kitchen seemed to grow smaller around them as Christy let the words, "my father's funeral," sink in.

Todd reached over and put his muscular arm around Katie's shoulders. In a gentle voice he said, "I'll do the funeral service. You tell me what you think would work best, and I'll take care of it."

Katie leaned her head on Todd's shoulder. In a small voice she said, "Thank you."

"Of course." Todd rested his head against the top of Katie's head.

The sight of her husband's tender expression toward her best friend made Christy tear up. Todd's wind-and-waves surfer boy look with his blond hair and blue eyes had slowly changed ever since he became a teacher. He kept his hair very short and his expressions seemed to be weighted around the corner of his eyes with a look of deeper empathy. He seemed older to Christy and she felt more secure with him than she ever had before.

"We're here for you, Katie," Todd said. "You know that."

"Yes, I do." She straightened and looked at her slice of pizza as if it had suddenly turned into a belly-up cockroach. "You know what? I think I could use a long, hot shower and one of your herbal sleepy teas, Christy. Then I'd like to go to bed."

"Sure," Christy said. "Towels are in the bathroom, and I put shampoo and some other shower stuff in there, too."

Katie headed to the guest room. She stopped in the kitchen doorway and turned to look at them. "Save that piece of pizza for me in the fridge. I might need a midnight snack once my stomach catches up with the rest of my body."

Katie never did return to her piece of pizza. She left fairly early the next morning to drive down to Escondido. She took Christy's car or, rather, the Subaru Katie had named Clover and had sold to Christy for one dollar when Katie left for Africa. It only seemed right to Christy and Todd that Katie have full use of the car while she was here, so Todd added Katie to their insurance policy and handed over the keys, telling her it was useless to protest.

Christy didn't miss having the use of Clover on Friday or Saturday, but when it came time to drive to Escondido on Sunday morning for the funeral, Christy wished they had the smaller car instead of their VW van. It was easier to reach Hana in the backseat in Clover.

Christy checked over her shoulder and could see that Hana was contentedly looking at books in her car seat. The last two days had been doozies. Hana's two lower molars had both come in, and so far today she had been in a much better mood and drooling far less.

"The traffic seems heavy for a Sunday," Christy said.

"Probably because it's Father's Day."

Christy felt as if a dart had gone into her stomach. "Oh, Todd, I'm so sorry. I had a little present and a card for you, but I completely forgot when we were hurrying to get out the door."

"Don't worry about it. I was thinking more of Katie. Rough day for her dad's funeral."

Christy's phone buzzed. She saw a text from her brother, David, who had just graduated from college last month.

HAVE YOU GUYS DECIDED YET ABOUT THE TRIP? THEY HAVE A FAMILY CABIN OPEN HERE AT CAMP FOR NEXT WEEK JUNE 25 TO JULY 1.

Christy bit her lower lip and thought about whether she should bring up the topic of their planned vacation with Todd right now. It seemed better to wait. Plus, she had a sinking feeling this was going to turn into yet another summer when she and Todd would end up forfeiting any sort of getaway.

Two summers ago their plans to drive up the California coast were postponed when Todd was hired for a teaching job and had to take summer classes to earn his credential. Last summer their finances were too low since Christy hadn't returned to her receptionist job at the spa after Hana was born. Todd had taken on a variety of summer side jobs to supplement their income, and they tried to spend as many hours on the beach as they could, pretending they were on vacation as they watched Hana wiggle her toes in the sand.

This summer, with the help of Christy's income from her sewing business, they set the goal of taking a two-week road trip to Glenbrooke, Oregon, to visit friends. The need to make good on their plans intensified when Christy's brother started to work at an outdoor adventure camp located just outside Glenbrooke. Four days ago Christy and Todd decided to leave as soon as Todd was done with school on June 23. But then Katie called, and everything went on hold.

Christy replied to her brother's text without discussing any of the details with Todd. SORRY I DIDN'T GET BACK TO YOU EARLIER. KATIE'S DAD PASSED AWAY SO SHE'S HERE UNTIL JUNE 26. WE NEED TO STAY HERE FOR NOW. LET US KNOW IF THE CABIN IS AVAILABLE ANY OTHER TIMES IN JULY.

Christy noticed another text she had missed earlier. Aunt Marti had texted that she and Uncle Bob had decided to attend the funeral, and they were bringing Christy's parents.

Christy read the text to Todd, including Marti's final line: WE WANT TO DO THIS FOR KATIE.

"That's nice of them," Todd said. "I'm glad they're coming."

Christy wasn't sure their appearance would be a good thing. She knew her aunt and uncle had developed a fondness for Katie over the years and that their affection grew when they accompanied Christy and Todd to Kenya for Eli and Katie's wedding.

What concerned Christy was that Katie didn't have a close relationship with any of her relatives so it might be uncomfortable for her "adopted" family of Christy's relatives to all show up. Christy hoped her clan would blend in and that Katie would appreciate the support.

Christy and Todd arrived at the cemetery before anyone else. Hana had fallen asleep so Todd parked under one of the tall, shady trees and pulled out his Bible and the notes he had written for the service to go over them one more time.

Christy leaned her head back and quickly fell into the familiar sort of half-nap state she had perfected when she became a mother. The daytime dosing allowed her weary body to snatch a little rest while her mommy ears still were tuned in to hear Hana's every squeak.

The sound of approaching cars brought Christy to attention about twenty minutes later. Hana woke as well and let it be known that she was ready to get out of her car seat.

"You okay if I leave you two?" Todd asked. "I thought I'd go over to where they've set up for the service. It's to the right. Do you see it? Where all the chairs are set up?"

"Sounds good. I'll get her changed, and we'll be over there in a few minutes."

Christy spotted Katie's unmistakable red hair as she was getting out of the backseat of a classic-style black Cadillac parked close to the gravesite. Katie was dressed in all black. Her mother was dressed in black as well and wore a scarf over her head. One of Katie's older brothers, whom Christy remembered was a mechanic and car buff, got out on the driver's side wearing a black suit and dark sunglasses. It seemed unreal, as if Christy was watching a scene from an old Mafia movie.

After changing Hana, Christy made sure she had plenty of juice, snacks, and toys in the baby bag and locked the car. Then she pushed the stroller toward where Katie and her mom were now seated along with three men wearing dark suits.

Christy realized that she and Todd hadn't dressed the way the rest of the group had. He was wearing a light-blue, long-sleeved shirt, dark navy khakis, and the nicest of the four ties he owned. He looked the same way he did every day when he taught at South Coast Believers Academy and not the way a minister would look at such a formal funeral.

I didn't even think that we should have bought Todd a suit.

Christy spotted Uncle Bob's Mercedes

and waited for them to park so she could walk over to the gravesite with them. Hana called out her own version of a "hi" when she saw the familiar family members coming their way. Christy's dad zeroed in on Hana in the stroller, and she put her arms up, trying to convince him to pick her up.

"You want your Paw Paw, don't you?" Christy's dad undid the straps and lifted Hana in his brawny arms. She gleefully patted her "Paw Paw's" face as he puffed out his cheeks and let her deflate them. It was her favorite game lately, and Christy's dad loved it.

They solemnly made their way to the gravesite. Christy slid in next to Todd in the front row with the stroller beside her and hoped she wouldn't regret leaving Hana with her parents and Bob and Marti who sat in the row behind them. Todd was seated next to Katie, who was next to her mother. Two of Katie's brothers stood to the side, both wearing dark sunglasses, as if they were Secret Service men.

A few more people arrived and sat scattered in the empty chairs. No one spoke. Hana was content to eat a cracker on Paw Paw's lap. Christy glanced back several times and felt as if the other people there kept looking at them, trying to figure out who they were.

Todd stood up and invited the group to join him in a prayer. He thanked God for the life of Katie's father and thanked God for being our heavenly Father. Then he thanked God for the lives of the family and friends who had gathered today. When he said, "amen," several of Katie's relatives echoed, "amen" loudly as if that was their cue in the service.

"I'd like to read to you from the book of Psalms today." Todd opened his Bible. "These words were written thousands of years ago. They have brought comfort and hope to millions of people over the centuries. As we remember the life of Joseph Weldon today, I hope these words will bring light during this dark time."

Christy recognized Psalm 139, one of her favorite chapters in the Bible, as Todd read most of it to the group. He moved on to several other passages that were familiar to her and spoke of the greatness of Almighty God and how all things are in Him and come from Him. The final verse he read was from the first chapter of the book of Job: "The Lord gave, and the Lord has taken away; blessed be the name of the Lord."

Todd closed his Bible and looked up with a somber expression. "All of us are given life by our Maker, and none of us knows when that life will end. As I thought about what to say today, I kept thinking of what happened on Good Friday over two thousand years ago. Christ died. He died for us, to carry the burden of our sin and make it possible for us — all of us — to be made right before Almighty God, the Creator of heaven and earth. Through Christ alone we can receive eternal life."

Christy had slid over to the seat beside Katie and slipped her hand in Katie's, hoping it would be a comfort to her. Katie sat completely still, as did her mother.

Todd's voice had just the right tender tone, and his expression made it clear that he felt every word he was saying. His eyes rested on Katie and her mother. "On the same day that Jesus was crucified, another man died. He is known to us as a 'thief.' The Roman authorities had ruled that he deserved to die, and yet he received new life, eternal life, that day. The way it happened for him can happen for you, today. As the thief hung on a cross next to Jesus, he said eight simple words of faith. 'Remember me when you come into your kingdom.' What Jesus said to that man gives all of us the assurance that when we sincerely call out to God, He accepts us, forgives us, and welcomes us into His kingdom. What Jesus said to the thief was, 'Today you will be with me in paradise.' "

Hana seemed to have noticed that her daddy was only a few feet away, and she began to call out, "Dada! Dada!"

Christy got up and reached for her fussy daughter. She whispered in Hana's ear as they walked back toward the car with Christy's left arm holding Hana on her hip and her right hand pushing the stroller over the grass.

She couldn't hear what Todd was saying, but she could see that he concluded only a few minutes later and returned to the seat next to Katie. Hana was squirming and fussing to get down so Christy let her walk down the road where the cars were parked. She realized Hana had been cooped up for almost three hours. No wonder she wanted to get her wiggles out.

A few minutes later, people started walking toward their cars. Christy corralled Hana but let her keep walking around on the grass. Katie came over to Christy and threw her arms around her in a tight hug.

"Thank you for coming." Katie cried, and Christy held her.

Out of the corner of her eye, Christy was grateful to see that her mom was right there to take Hana's hand and keep walking with her on the grass.

"Katie," Christy said with tenderness. "Oh, Katie." She didn't know what else to say.

Katie pulled back, and Christy took in the distressed expression on her friend's face.

"Are you okay?" Christy whispered.

"I will be."

"What can I do?"

"Nothing. I'm glad you came."

"Of course. We're all here for you, Katie. What can we do? Do you want us to come back to the house with you?"

"No." Katie shook her head. "I don't think you should." She wiped her tears. "You know how I told you that my parents were in the middle of moving when my dad died?"

Christy remembered Katie saying something about them moving to an apartment in a retirement community. "Your mom isn't going through with making the move now, is she?"

"She has to. The house sold. They were on a waiting list for the apartment for nine months, so if she gives it up, who knows when there will be another opening."

"I didn't realize you had all that to deal with, too."

"It'll be okay. It will. This is why I came. To be here for my mom. I got a lot done the last couple of days, but there's lots more to do. I'm going to stay the next few days and help her get everything done."

"Do you need another person to help?" Christy asked. "I can stay. Or I could come back tomorrow if that's better. It's not a problem. My parents can take Hana for me."

Katie mustered one of her eternally optimistic expressions. "You're the best, Chris. You really are. But you know how things can be with my family. Trust me, it will be less stressful if I do this by myself. I'm pretty sure that's the way my mom would prefer it, too. Is that okay?"

"Of course it's okay." Christy tried to offer a reassuring look.

"Good." Katie sniffed and cleared her throat. "So, if we get everything done the way my mom thinks we will, I'll be back to your place on Tuesday night."

"All right."

The two friends lingered a moment, both of them expressing with their misty eyes that they wished things could be different. Christy wished Eli were here. Katie needed him.

"Just promise you'll call me if you want

me to come down to help in any way. It's not a problem. I want to do whatever I can for you."

"I know." Katie rounded her shoulders back and cast a warm glance over at Christy's parents, who were standing by the car, waiting to find out what the plan was. "Please tell your family how much I appreciate them being here. I'll see you in a couple of days." Katie wrapped her arms around Christy in a brief but tight hug and then turned to return to the Cadillac where her brother and mother were waiting.

Christy watched the Cadillac drive away and blinked back tears. She had seen Katie in some difficult situations in the past, but she had never felt so helpless.

"Everything okay?" Todd slid his arm around Christy's shoulders.

"Katie asked that we not go back to her mom's house. She's going to stay with her for a couple of days and help her to settle in her new apartment."

"All right." Todd stroked Christy's long hair and pressed a kiss on the side of her head.

"I told her I'd come down anytime if she needs me."

"Good."

Christy stretched her arm around Todd's

waist and leaned her head on his shoulder as they walked back to Gussie.

"I really wish I could do something," Christy said with a sigh.

"You'll get a chance. When Katie comes home on Tuesday, you'll be able to give her all the encouragement she needs."

It somehow comforted Christy when Todd said the word, "home." Katie was going to face the next few difficult days alone at her mother's "house." But then she would come "home" to Christy and Todd's. Between now and then, Christy knew she was going to be praying for her best friend like never before.

The day felt hazy to Christy even though the sky was a pristine shade of early summer blue. Her extended family decided to stop for lunch in Laguna Beach at one of Marti's favorite restaurants that provided a gorgeous view of the ocean. They all fit around a long table by the window overlooking a rose garden, and beyond the garden was a bench at the end of a cliff that looked out on the Pacific Ocean. The view was spectacular, and the food seemed to lift everyone's spirits. Christy felt quieted inside but couldn't stop thinking about Katie.

Uncle Bob complimented Todd on the way he handled the service. Christy's mom told Todd he said just the right thing, especially at the end. Christy missed that part and decided she would ask him about it later.

"By the way." Christy gave her dad an apologetic smile. "Happy Father's Day. I have a little gift for you but I didn't think to bring it with me."

"Just being together today is the only gift I need."

Christy had a card and gift for Uncle Bob, too. She offered him a silent smile and he grinned back. The topic changed to how things were going at the apartment complex Christy's parents managed in Costa Mesa. Then, as it often did, the focus turned to Marti as she gave a full report of how the renovations were complete at the rental house she and Bob had purchased five months ago. The small bungalow was located on the same street where Bob and Marti lived and was now listed for summer rentals at a high price because of all the upgrades.

"Let us know if you hear of anyone who is looking for a perfect little hideaway to rent for the summer," Marti said. "We're only accepting stays of two weeks or more and no children or pets."

Christy had heard all the details before.

She didn't know anyone who could afford the rates Marti was charging. Still, she nodded and let her thoughts drift to how the remainder of the week would roll out once Katie returned from her mom's. The two of them would have only a few days together. Christy was determined to make them the best couple of days either of them had had in a long time.

THREE

Katie did not return to Todd and Christy's on Tuesday night as she said she would. She stayed at her mother's house until Thursday.

Christy had a few anxious moments as well as calming stretches when she realized that Katie had come all this way to be there for her mom, and that's what she was doing. They texted each other regularly throughout the days, and Christy sensed how frustrated Katie was becoming. Everything was taking longer than expected, and her mom didn't seem to be doing well.

Aunt Marti had checked in with Christy twice to see if Katie had returned to Newport Beach. Marti wanted to treat the two of them to lunch, which was a kind gesture that Christy appreciated.

When she told Marti how difficult things were for Katie and her mom, Marti said, "It's such a pity. Losing a loved one is extremely stressful. Moving is extremely stressful. To combine both of those traumatic events and then turn down well-intentioned help is pitiable. Have you considered going down there anyway and lending a hand?"

"Yes. I've thought of that several times. Katie made it clear that she wants to do this by herself. Her mom is a very private person."

"Oh, I remember well from how she and Katie's father turned down the chance to go to the party after Katie's college graduation. If Robert and I hadn't gone to Katie and Eli's wedding, the dear girl wouldn't have had any parental type of support."

"I know. Katie dearly appreciates you and Uncle Bob and all the ways you've been involved in her life over the years."

"Well, she's family." Marti made her statement firmly and added, "If she comes back to Newport in the next few days, tell her I want to take her to lunch. If not, I will see her Sunday at our monthly family night dinner. She has to be at your house by then because doesn't she fly out on Monday?"

"Yes, that's the plan. I don't think she can extend her trip."

"She might have to," Marti said matter-of-factly. "Plane tickets can be changed."

When Marti ended the call, Christy took

a quiet little internal trip to the land of if-only. If only Katie could change her flight, she could stay another week with Christy.

Wouldn't that be great? For both of us. It's been so long since I've had social time with girlfriends.

Ever since Tracy moved to Glenbrooke and especially since Hana was born, Christy felt as if she hadn't done anything fun with any women except a few short shopping trips with her aunt and her mom. But those trips always turned into a chance for Marti to buy things for Hana, and Christy felt like she was just along for the ride. Every time they tried to go out to lunch afterwards there was nothing leisurely or relaxing about being in charge of a wiggly, tired baby in a restaurant.

Christy hoped and prayed and waited to see what was going to happen.

A text from Katie on Thursday afternoon lifted Christy's hopes. It was short but filled with promise.

LEAVING NOW. SEE YOU IN AN HOUR OR TWO.

Christy went to work freshening up Katie's guest room. She let Todd know that Katie was on her way. He was at work, finishing his last two days of faculty meetings before the end of the school year. He said he would be home around five and would be glad to barbecue for dinner or take over with Hana if Christy and Katie wanted to go out.

Christy dreamed up possibilities for restaurants the two of them could go to. She had so many places she wanted to take Katie to in the area.

Katie arrived on Christy's doorstep with a crumpled bag from a fast-food restaurant. She looked exhausted.

Christy wrapped her arms around her and held her tight. Katie pulled away and handed the garbage bag to Christy. "I love you, too. But I've waited since Mission Viejo to go to the bathroom and if you don't let go of me . . ."

Christy released her with a chuckle and went to the kitchen to throw away the trash. She started the electric teakettle, thinking that a cup of tea would be a good thing. In all the British movies Christy loved to watch, someone was always putting on the kettle when a friend needed comfort.

Katie emerged from the bathroom with a damp washcloth in her hand. She folded it and placed it on the back of her neck. Lowering herself to the nearest stool at the counter, she seemed to be trying hard to force a pleasant expression.

"You okay?"

"I will be. Rough stuff."

"Did you get your mom moved in all the way?"

"No."

Christy waited for an explanation.

"She's mostly moved in. The house is almost empty. All the furniture that wasn't sold is in the apartment. She got really upset with me for trying to throw away some of the stuff that's still at the house." Katie looked up at Christy who was standing across the kitchen island. Katie's eyes were red and puffy.

"She said she wanted to make all the decisions by herself and that I should leave. So I did. It wasn't a great way to say good-bye . . ." Katie shrugged.

The electric kettle sounded a click and a short beep. "Would you like some tea?"

"No."

"Are you hungry?"

"No."

"Sorry it was such a rough time for you, Katie."

In a low voice, as if trying to counsel herself, Katie said, "I don't know why I hoped it would be different."

Christy wished she could say something or do something, but she had run out of ideas.

Katie stood up. "Would you mind if I just went to bed? I'm fried."

"Of course I wouldn't mind." Christy's mothering instincts wanted to suggest a hot bath first or maybe some juice. She wanted to follow Katie into the guest room so she could tuck her in, pray over her, stroke her hair, lay her cool hand on Katie's forehead, and bless her.

Christy did none of those gestures though. She knew her friend well. Since Katie made it clear that she wanted to be alone, Christy honored her request. In that way, maybe Katie was a bit like her mother. But Christy would never tell her that.

The afternoon stretched into the evening. Todd came home, and she explained why she and Hana were staying out on the deck, trying to keep things quiet so Katie could sleep.

"How about if I pick up some fish tacos?" Todd suggested.

"Sure, thanks." Christy knew that Todd's favorite choice for dinner would make his day a little brighter, even though she was at the point that if she never ate another fish taco in her life, she would be just fine.

Hana had been her more usual, happy self the past few days. Both molars were in, and her sleep pattern was back on track. She seemed more interested in some of her tactile toys than in the past so that made it easier to keep her entertained for a longer stretch of time out on the deck. Eventually, though, Christy would have to take her inside and give her a bath before bed. She knew that the water sounds from upstairs could be heard in the guest room. It would have to be what it was.

By the time Christy and Todd were ready to go to bed, Katie still hadn't emerged from her cocoon room. Christy left her a note on the counter and then slipped into bed next to Todd. "Are you asleep?"

"Almost."

"Tomorrow's your last day of school."

"Yeah."

"Are you excited for summer break?"

"Hmmm . . ." His voice trailed off as he was falling asleep.

Christy turned over and listened to the slight whirl of the ceiling fan. She had received several texts from David with open dates for the cabin at Camp Heather Brook and was waiting for the right time to talk about their vacation plans with Todd. She had hoped tonight might be her chance. Clearly, she would have to wait another day.

She and Todd had only two events on the calendar that weekend. One was the weekly

Gathering that Todd had started years ago. The group of high schoolers still met in the garage of one of the students who had graduated and was away at college in Europe. His dad was connected to South Coast Academy where Todd taught, and they liked having the group continue to meet at their home. Christy went occasionally, but soon after Hana was born she had found two moms who were happy to bring snacks each week.

The other event for them that weekend was their traditional family night gathering on Sunday night. About a year ago Christy and Todd had designated the last Sunday of the month as a potluck dinner they would host at their house. Todd's Aunt Linda, who also happened to be the doctor who delivered Hana, had come to every one of the family gatherings and said it was the highlight of her month. Sometimes they played a board game, sometimes they just talked. Todd loved having everyone over and had greatly improved his barbecue skills under Uncle Bob's tutelage.

As Christy drifted off to sleep, she told herself that regardless of what was on the schedule or the fun ideas she had, if Katie needed to sleep straight through the next three days, then that was the best gift

Christy could give her friend.

The next morning after Todd had dashed out the door, Christy wondered if her "best gift" might actually happen. Katie had left a note on the counter saying that she had been awake from midnight till four o'clock and hoped she hadn't woken them up. She wrote that she was going back to bed, and she hoped it was okay if she slept as long as she needed to.

Christy gave up trying to keep Hana quiet during breakfast and went ahead and washed all the dishes she had left in the sink from the day before. When she and Katie were roommates in college, many times Katie managed to sleep through anything. With that in mind, Christy moved through a normal day around the house with her cheerful toddler. Katie didn't stir.

Christy decided to go grocery shopping before Hana's afternoon nap, just so she would have plenty of food for the weekend. She left Katie another note and then tiptoed over to the closed bedroom door, listening, just in case Katie might be awake.

No noise came from the bedroom. It was torture having Katie so close but out of reach. Christy used her set of keys to unlock Clover and was glad to see that the car seat was in the backseat, as usual. It was holding a box. Boxes were on the front seat and on the backseat. Christy checked the trunk, and yes, there were more boxes. Some of them were labeled in Katie's writing. One box had the words "High School" written on the side.

Christy unloaded the boxes from the front and back seats and stacked them in the corner of the garage. She and Hana made a super quick trip to the nearest grocery store. When she returned home and pushed the button to open the garage door, Katie was bending over the boxes. She stood back so Christy could ease the car into the garage and waved.

"Sorry you ended up moving all this junk."

"No problem." Christy removed Hana from her car seat.

Katie came around to the other side and pulled out the two grocery bags. "I can take those. Do you want me to get the boxes out of the trunk, too?"

"Sure."

"Sorry I didn't warn you about all this."

"It's not a problem. Really. Let me put Hana down for her nap, and then I can come back and help you, if you need any help." Over her shoulder Christy added, "It's good to see you up. How are you feeling?"

"Better."

When Christy returned to the garage, she found Katie vigorously sorting through all the boxes, making instant decisions on everything she touched. She had one large garbage bag already filled.

"I didn't want to take the time to sort all this at my mom's. Apparently, she saved everything that was ever mine." Katie looked up with a refreshingly optimistic expression. "It was kind of sweet. I never knew she kept everything."

"That is sweet." Christy tried to figure out the process Katie had in motion. "Are you going to try to ship some of it back to Kenya?"

"Some of it. A lot needs to be thrown away." She held up a crumpled teen magazine. "Not exactly in collector's condition." The magazine went into the black trash bag.

"I'm putting everything that is good enough to be donated into these two boxes." Katie extracted a bright-green knit ski cap that had a big pom-pom on the top. "Like this gem. Future Halloween costume for someone, right?"

"Wait. Did you wear that when we went to Tahoe with the Ski Club from school?"

"Who knows? Hey, look at this. It's our Kelley High yearbook!"

Christy recognized the cover right away. "Our sophomore year."

"That's the year we met. At Janelle's sleep-over."

"How could we forget that night?"

Katie flipped through the pages. "It was the night we TPed Rick Doyle's house."

Christy leaned in. "Where's the mascot picture? We have to find that famous picture of Katie the Kelley High Cougar."

Katie turned right to it because the corner of the page was folded over. "You mean this one?"

"Oh, Katie." They both laughed. The photo took up half the page and showed Katie inside a plush mascot costume out on the football field making a crazy jumping jack leap into the air as she tried to get the students in the stands to cheer. The shot captured Katie's personality during that era of life.

"Look at you."

"I was crazy."

"No, you were fun. And so cute. I never could figure out where you got all that energy," Christy said.

"It was from all the junk food I ate. That's what I lived on."

"At least until you met Michael and turned into the organic earth child who tried to get me to try tofu."

"True." Katie turned a few pages to Christy's sophomore picture. "Christy Miller, look at you!"

"I hated how my hair looked in that picture." Christy examined it more closely. "I look so young."

"You look like Little Miss Heartbreaker, that's what you look like."

"What are you talking about?"

"Let's see, there was Todd, of course, always Todd. But then Rick talked you into trying out for cheerleading because he wanted to make you into his kind of girl and win your heart. But then Doug stepped in when you dumped Rick. And let's not forget Fred from yearbook staff who wanted to take you to the prom. I bet he still hasn't gotten over your rejection."

"Katie." Christy couldn't deny Katie's abbreviated summary of her high school love interests. "That did not all happen our sophomore year."

"I know. I thought I'd speed through the highlights."

Christy felt embarrassed. "You of all people know that I was the most unsure, insecure, inexperienced girl in the whole high school."

"I know." Katie gave her a friendly elbow

54

nudge. "You were as much fun to tease then as you are now. Oh, check this out. Lance! I'd forgotten all about this disaster of my high school career."

Christy recognized the photo of the guy who had taken Katie to the prom their sophomore year.

"Remember how he gave me a corsage that doubled as a head of lettuce and then sent me home in his rented limo so he could keep dancing with all the other girls?"

"I wasn't there to witness the disaster, but I remember the story quite well."

"Good times." Katie bobbed her head. "Yeah, good times."

Christy laughed, and soon both of them were laughing as they turned the pages together. A couple of times they laughed so hard Christy had tears in her eyes. Katie was back to her truest self, and the world seemed like a better place.

They worked together for the next half hour, teasing each other and laughing at some of the items in the boxes, such as a child's pull toy. It was a plastic telephone with a receiver on a frayed string and a smiling face under the circle with holes that were the rotary dial.

"Our children won't even know what this is!" Christy said. "When was the last time you saw a phone like this?"

"I've seen more than you have, I'm sure, because we still have some around at Brockhurst. But you're right. That is a toy from an era gone by."

"Keep it or toss it?" Christy asked.

"Donate it. Somebody might want it for a history lesson or something."

"This is a classic." Christy pulled an old photograph from the bottom of the last box. The girl in the photo was about eight years old. She had an adorable tomboy look to her with messy red hair, her pants rolled up on only one leg, and her arm bent to display a big strawberry burn on her elbow and forearm. "This is you, right?"

Katie grinned. "I remember the day that was taken. I got that beaut of a scrape on my arm in a rollerblading race with two of the neighbor boys. It was worth it, though, because I won."

"Of course you did," Christy said. "It's an adorable picture."

Katie took the photo and stared at it. "I remember a girl on our street, Tammie, got a new camera for Christmas. She took this picture and gave it to me at school. It was a big deal because the only other photos I remember seeing of myself during those years were the ones they took in the cafeteria at school and sold to us like postage stamps by the sheets. Remember those?"

Christy nodded. "My mom always bought the package with the largest portrait size. It was so embarrassing because she framed the really big one every year. At our house in Wisconsin, whenever you walked down the hallway to the bathroom, you were surrounded by portraits of me from every year on the right side of the hall and David's school pictures on the left. Whenever my friends came over, I always hoped they wouldn't say they had to use the bathroom."

Katie's expression turned wistful. "You shouldn't have been embarrassed, Christy."

"I still don't like having my picture up on the wall. When you go to my parents' apartment now, right when you walk in, a huge picture of our whole family on the beach from last Christmas greets you. Hana was only a month old. I look so large. I'm the only one not smiling naturally because I was so busy trying to adjust Hana so you could see her face and her frilly Christmas dress from Aunt Marti." Christy shook her head. "Every time I go over there it brings back all the memories of those jumbo school pictures. You don't even have to go down a dark hallway to see this one."

"Christy." Katie's expression looked serious. "Don't think of those pictures as a negative thing. My mom never bought the jumbo package. She never framed any pictures of anyone in our family. At least none that I can remember."

Christy felt humbled.

"If I wanted the postage-stamp ones, I had to buy them with my allowance. I remember cutting them out and saving them for Valentine's Day. I'd only give them to people I liked. I put them in those tiny envelopes that came with the valentines from the grocery store."

Katie stared at the photo in her hand. It seemed as if she was trying to envision the eight-year-old version of herself doling out the valuable photos to just the right people. If her mom didn't want to keep a picture of her, then who would want one? Christy imagined those photos represented currency to Katie. Friendship currency. If she invested the valued gift of a photo and valentine to a classmate, would that person appreciate what the gesture cost her?

Katie looked up at Christy with tears in her eyes. "I just realized something. My mom always bought the valentines for me every year. She let me pick the ones I wanted. I remember sitting at the kitchen table, writing people's names on the envelopes and deciding who should get one of my pictures."

Christy stood up and grabbed a roll of paper towels from the supply shelf by the kitchen door. She offered the roll to Katie in lieu of tissues. Katie pulled off a towel and held it in her hand, barely moving. Another memory seemed to be coming into focus.

"I remember one year, I think it was fifth grade, my mom saw what I was doing at the kitchen table, and she said that if I had any pictures left over, could I give her one?"

Katie dabbed under her nose with the paper towel. "I gave her one right then and there, and I watched her go over to her purse, take out her wallet . . ." Katie's expression curled inward as she said, "She put my picture in the first slot, right across from her driver's license."

Christy was crying now, too. She reached over and gave Katie's forearm a squeeze. She knew what a gesture like that would have meant to Katie.

"I remember thinking," Katie said with a sniff, "my mother likes me. She put my picture in her wallet, and now whenever she shows her driver's license, she'll be showing that she has a daughter, and she's proud that she has a daughter."

The tenderness in Katie's voice and the poignancy of her memory undid both of the two Forever Friends. They hugged, cried, and hugged again.

Drawing back and straightening her posture, Katie wiped her eyes and looked at Christy with deep creases across her forehead. "I have to go to Escondido. Now. Is it okay if I take Clover?"

"Of course, but why are you going back?"

"I forgot something."

"What?"

"I forgot to tell my mom that I love her. If I don't tell her face-to-face now, before I leave on Monday, I might not have another chance."

FOUR

An hour later both Christy and Katie were seated in Clover, scooting down the 5 freeway with the windows down. Christy was glad that she had asked to come with Katie. Christy was also grateful that her mom was free to come over and take care of Hana after she woke from her nap. Todd had texted back a short, SOUNDS GOOD, when Christy quickly tapped out an explanation of what was going on. Everyone was understanding and supportive, and that gave Christy the freedom to be understanding and supportive of Katie.

I don't tell my family enough how much I appreciate them.

"What you're doing," Christy said as she glanced at Katie. "Going back to tell your mom that you love her, is really noble, Katie. I admire you so much."

"No, no, it's not noble. It's a God-thing. I mean, for me, it has to be a God-thing, or it's not real. I feel like God has given me so much. So much love, hope, and joy. He has filled me to overflowing, really. I have the best life. So, if my mother is unable to give me the kind of nurturing and affirming that I wish I had, then I can give her what she's not been able to give me. I can give away a lot of love. I didn't see that earlier this week when I was with her, but I see it now. I can pour out buckets of love on her, and it won't deplete me because Jesus will just fill me back up."

"But you are kind of depleted right now, Katie."

"I know. But that's because I think I spent the last week giving to my mom out of my own bucket, and that bucket is empty. Maybe I want a do-over now that I feel a little rested. The memory of the valentines showed me that I've painted my mother in my mind as irritating and mean all the time. Maybe I need a different image I can hold on to. I want to acknowledge that she has her own version of what could be considered love."

"You mean, like when she put your picture in her wallet."

"Yes. And probably a hundred other things that she thought were gestures that I should interpret as her caring about me.

But those things weren't the way I would have expressed affection, so I didn't understand. It's like someone talking in a foreign language."

Katie kept her bent arm out the passenger window and fixed her gaze straight ahead. She seemed to be deep in thought. They were almost to San Clemente when she spoke next, still looking straight ahead.

"I don't know, Chris. Maybe I just don't want to be done with my relationship with her. My relationship with my dad is over. There's so much I would have loved to have improved or changed with him. But now it's too late."

"And it's not too late with your mom," Christy suggested.

Katie let out a long sigh. "We'll see."

They were quiet for a few minutes, side by side, friends together on the precarious journey that left their childhood ways far behind them and took them into the place where, as adults, they could choose how they were going to enter the next season in their relationships with their parents.

"You know how my parents, and especially my mom, were so strict in high school about me going to events at church?"

Christy remembered. "I know she wouldn't let you go to Palm Springs with me when Aunt Marti set up that getaway weekend."

"And I had to drop out of being a camp counselor," Katie added.

"That's right. I'd forgotten about that. You were always so mature about accepting their decisions."

Katie let out a funny snort. "I wouldn't call it mature. As a matter of fact, I can't remember anything I did during my teen years that could be considered mature."

"What I mean is, you honored your parents when we were teens, and I always thought that was admirable."

"It's all because of our Peculiar Treasure verse, you know." Katie turned to face Christy. "Do you remember how we used to call each other 'Peculiar Treasures'?"

"Yes, of course. I love our little nickname for each other."

"When you started calling us that in high school, a God-thing happened. I don't know if I ever told you about it."

"Tell me now." Christy was loving all the nostalgic trails they were hiking down.

"I remember going into my room, closing the door, and pulling out my Bible so I could find our Peculiar Treasure verse in Exodus and underline it. I didn't have many verses underlined, and I wanted to be cool like some of the others at church who had passages highlighted in yellow and notes written in the margins. On my hunt for Exodus, I found the Ten Commandments. I'd never read them before, and I never knew that the fifth commandment said to honor your father and mother so it would go well and you would live a long life. Something like that."

Katie adjusted her seat belt and leaned back. "So I underlined that verse, and I told God that whenever my parents said no, I'd honor their decision even if I disagreed with it. That was probably the biggest step-of-faith kind of promise I'd ever made at that point in my life. It was hard because I never really felt like they were thinking about my feelings or my interests. But the thing was, I felt — I mean, really felt — like God was telling me that He knew all about my feelings and everything that was in my heart. He wanted me to trust Him that He would make the important stuff happen in my life and that my parents' restrictions wouldn't keep Him from accomplishing His purposes for me."

Katie paused. "I don't think I'm explaining this very clearly, but it was definitely a God-thing that day. Me and my pen, face-to-face with the fifth commandment. Was I going to abide by it or not? I mean, the other nine commandments about not killing people and stuff weren't exactly issues in my life. Honoring my parents was a huge issue. That day was like I switched my hope from getting what I wanted from my parents, stuff like affirmation and freedom, to telling God that I was agreeing to wait for Him to give me what He wanted for me."

"That's really beautiful, Katie. I've seen how that's all come about in your life in a way that has gone well for you. Very well."

Katie shifted in her seat and adjusted the seat belt again. "The thing is, all the times my parents restricted me from doing stuff in high school, I thought they were being unfair to me. Eli told me one time that he thought that was their way of expressing their concern for me. It was their form of love. They were trying to protect me, and to them, that was good. That was kind. That was love. I just thought it was mean."

"I never thought of it that way." Christy carefully changed lanes.

"Eli has unraveled a lot of my childhood angst for me. I've kept him busy the first few years of our marriage. He sees things differently than most people. I wish he was here." Katie sighed. "I also wish I'd been a nicer person to my mom this week. I don't know why I was so mad and miserable the whole time. It wasn't good."

"It's completely understandable under the difficult circumstances."

"I know. But it was hard for her, too, and I wasn't very patient. If Eli had been there he would have put things into perspective. He has this way of bringing peace into difficult situations."

Turning her gaze out the window, Katie said, "My brothers made me mad, too. They did the bare minimum and only came over one day, on Tuesday. They brought a truck to move all the furniture to the apartment. When they came into Mom's house, she was yelling at me because I'd thrown out a pair of shoes she hadn't worn in fifty years. I yelled back that I was just trying to help."

Katie caught her breath after shouting and added, "So one of my brothers said I should stop trying to be a do-gooder, trying to help people who didn't want help, like all the people in Africa. It was awful. He doesn't know what we do. I wanted to stomp out of there and leave so badly. I called Eli, and he told me to stay. 'Just get the work done,' he said. 'Get your mom in a good place. Calm down. Finish well. Don't get in any more fights with your brothers.' "

Katie rolled up her window and fiddled

with the air-conditioning. "Oh, man, this is rough. Tell me again why I thought it was a good idea to go back there?"

"You wanted to tell your mother that you love her." Christy cautiously added, "Face-to-face."

Katie leaned back staring at the car's ceiling. "Grace on her. Grace on me. Grace on us all."

As the cool breeze from the air conditioner toned down the red in Katie's face, Christy kept driving. And she kept glancing over to make sure Katie was okay.

A few minutes later, Katie let out a long breath and in a more subdued voice said, "Eli's mom taught me something. I just thought of it. Wish I'd remembered it earlier this week."

"What is it?" Christy asked.

"Cheryl once told me, 'Be remembered for what you do, not what was done to you.' "

Christy nodded and repeated the words in her mind.

"People say and do hurtful things all the time. But their actions don't define me. It's up to me to decide what I want to do. How I want to express who I am."

Before Christy could add a comment, Katie said, "You know what I just realized?

The reason I feel like I have this full bucket in my life with plenty of grace to pour out on my mom is because when God gave me Eli, He also gave me one of the very best mothers on the planet. Cheryl has given me so much. She's the caring, listening mom I always wanted."

Katie closed her eyes and leaned back. All the talking and processing seemed to have worn her out. She had a settled smiled on her closed lips, and Christy thought she looked like she was dreaming of Africa.

Christy drove the rest of the way to Escondido, thinking through all the things Katie had been processing. She admired her favorite Peculiar Treasure for her fortitude and was convinced all over again that Katie had married the right man for her. Christy wove through a maze of residential streets, relying on her memory, and pulled up in front of a small, blue house that had a For Sale sign in the yard. A big, red Sold sign now hung from the bottom of the sign.

She turned off the engine. "We're here, Katie."

Katie squinted and tried to wake up. "You remembered how to get here." She hesitated before opening her door.

"You okay?"

"Yeah. I'm good." Katie opened the door.

"Do you want to stay in the car or come in? It's up to you. I won't be in there long."

"I'll come in," Christy said decidedly.

The living room looked odd without any furniture. The carpet was faded so you could see exactly where each piece of furniture had been.

"Mom?" Katie proceeded into the kitchen where they found her mother wiping out the emptied cupboards.

"Katie, what are you doing here?"

"I wanted to say something to you."

Katie's mother looked over Katie's shoulder. "Hello, Christy."

"Hi, Mrs. Weldon. I'm very sorry for your loss." Christy went to her and gave her a precarious side hug. "I didn't get a chance to say anything on Sunday."

"Thank you. I appreciated you and your husband and the rest of your family coming to the service. That was nice of you."

Christy nodded, not sure what else to say.

It turned quiet between the three of them. Christy finally pointed over her shoulder and said, "I think I'll just go in here, in the living room."

Since there was no furniture left, Christy stood near the front door. She didn't think she should go out to the car since she said she would wait in the living room. The voices echoed in the emptied house, and Christy could hear everything. Katie started out by apologizing for not having a better attitude earlier in the week. Then she moved right into telling her mom about finding the photo and remembering the valentines and how much it meant to her when her mother put Katie's photo in her wallet. It seemed to Christy that Katie was rushing through all those details as a way of getting up the nerve to say what she had really come to say.

Katie's voice lowered. "Mom, I know you and Dad didn't plan on having me. You didn't want any more kids. I know that. And I know you didn't really know what to do with me and all my energy. But I want to thank you for hanging in there and providing for me and everything."

"Well, of course we provided for you. We didn't have a lot to give, but we tried."

"I know. And I appreciate all you've done for me over the years." Katie paused before she added, "I just wanted to come back here and look you in the eye and tell you that I love you."

It was quiet for a painfully long minute. Christy bit her lower lip and wished she had stayed in the kitchen or had at least better positioned herself so she could see what was

71

happening right now.

Then Christy heard the quavering voice of Katie's mom. "Well, thank you, Katie. Thank you for saying that. Your father and I, we tried to do the best we could with what we had."

"I know." Katie's voice had lost its confident strength. "And I appreciate it, Mom. I really do." She sounded like her eight-year-old self as she added, "I didn't want to go home without telling you that I love you."

There was another long pause. Christy squeezed her eyes tight and held her breath, waiting for the echo she knew her friend had waited her whole life to hear.

But Katie's mom didn't return the words, "I love you."

Instead, she said, "Are you still planning to go back to Africa on Monday?"

"Yes."

"Are you going back to Christy's now?"

"We can stay for a little while, if you need any more help around here."

"Well, if the two of you want to finish cleaning the kitchen, I can finish the bathroom."

"Okay. We can do that."

Christy returned to the kitchen and saw remnants of tears drying on Katie's cheeks. Her mouth was turned up in a sincere smile.

Katie's mom had left the kitchen.

"You okay?" Christy whispered.

Katie nodded. Christy thought Katie was extremely brave to be so steady after not hearing an "I love you, too" from her mom.

The two of them got on task without talking and made quick work of cleaning out the kitchen cupboards and scouring the sink. Christy had gotten down on her hands and knees with the bucket and a scrub brush, ready to see what could be done to brighten up the original vinyl flooring in the kitchen that was many decades old.

"Don't bother with that," Katie said quickly. "The new owners are renovating. They're knocking out this wall to the living room and pulling out all the flooring. I think they're putting in wood floors."

"What else can we do then?"

Katie's mom entered just then and pulled off the plastic gloves she was wearing and dropped them in the trash bag. "That's it. It wasn't much." Her expression seemed to have softened. "Thank you for your help."

"So, what's next?" Katie asked.

Mrs. Weldon looked timidly at Katie and then at Christy. "Would you like to see my new place, Christy?"

"Yes, I would."

Katie nodded her agreement, and the two

of them got in Clover and followed Katie's mom as she drove slowly across town to the retirement home.

"I'm glad we came," Katie said. "I think it went about the way I thought it would. I'm glad I did it. I'm glad I said the words. I meant them. That was a big moment for me."

Christy reached over and gave Katie's arm a squeeze. She wanted to say something like, "I'm proud of you" or "You did a good job," but none of those lines seemed to fit the depth of what had happened for Katie.

In a small voice, all Christy could come up with was, "I know." She hoped that it was enough for Katie to know that her closest friend was aware that the effort to honor her mother was a lavish gift.

They pulled into the parking lot at La Fontana retirement home and walked behind Katie's mom through the nicely decorated lobby, and up the elevator to her new apartment on the third floor. The room was small, but everything looked nice and organized. Pictures already were hung on the walls. One was of a mountain landscape, and the other was of a bird on a log. Christy couldn't help but think how nice it would be if a framed picture of Katie and Eli were on the bookshelf or the end table by the recliner. Maybe a picture of them would be added some day.

Katie's mom seemed proud of her new nest, and she seemed to appreciate the way Katie talked about the place as they took the grand tour. She told her mom how great it was going to be for her to sleep in her new apartment in her new bed with the new flowery bedding Katie had gotten for her. She described how nice it was going to be for her mom to have breakfast in the residence dining hall and not have to do any cooking. The library off the lobby was filled with books and had tables with puzzles, which Katie's mom loved to work on. She was set. It had taken a lot of heroic effort, but Katie's mom was now right where she wanted to be.

Their good-bye was sweet. Katie's mom gave Christy's hand a squeeze and thanked her for her help. Then, as Christy watched, Katie's mom looked Katie in the eyes, reached for her hand, and in barely a whisper said, "Thank you, Katie."

Christy had hoped the whispered words would have been, "I love you," but Katie seemed to take the "thank you" as if it carried the same meaning.

The mother and daughter exchanged slow smiles, like two shy friends meeting each other for the first time.

"If you need anything over the next two days while I'm still here, call me, okay, Mom?"

"I'll be fine."

"I know you will. You're doing well, Mom. You really are. I'll call you before I leave, and then Eli and I will give you a call in a couple of weeks."

Mrs. Weldon walked with them to the main entrance and waved as they drove away. Neither Christy nor Katie spoke for the first little while. There were so many thoughts and emotions to process. Finally Christy said, "You are amazing, Katie Girl. You know that, don't you?"

Katie didn't reply. The reason was evident when Christy glanced over at her. Katie was fast asleep, her head resting against the closed window. Christy had watched her pour out every last drop of oil from her alabaster heart, and now Christy considered it a privilege to drive her own Miss Daisy back "home" to Todd and Christy's or any other place she wanted to go in the next few days.

FIVE

"Is it really noon?" Katie asked.

"Yes, it is." Todd was cuddled up with Hana on the sofa. "It's a nice, quiet Sunday afternoon."

"Sunday?" Katie paused. "No! It can't be Sunday. There is no way I slept straight through an entire day."

"You're right. It's Saturday. I was just messin' with ya."

"Oh, well, that's the first time that's ever happened," Katie said sarcastically.

Christy heard the conversation as she was coming down the stairs with a storage bin in her arms. "Are you hungry?"

Katie thought a moment. "Yeah, I think I finally am."

"Good. Help yourself to whatever you can find. I have to make a quick delivery of these tablecloths and place mats to a shop on Balboa Island. I'll be back in half an hour."

Hana wiggled down from the couch and

toddled over to Christy. She attached herself to Christy's leg in koala bear fashion and let it be known that her attachment phase was at an all-time high. Apparently she had fussed most of Friday afternoon for Christy's mom when Katie and Christy were in Escondido.

"Hana, Mommy has to go for just a little bit. I'll be back."

Hana whimpered. Christy looked at Todd. "This is a new sound."

"We were watching a documentary on baby monkeys. We were practicing making monkey sounds together."

"Great," Christy said under her breath.

"Sunshine," Todd said in the endearing, preschool teacher voice he always used when he read to Hana or tried to get her to do tricks. "Show Mommy and Aunt Katie what a monkey says."

Hana didn't seem to have figured out yet who Katie was. She gave her a curious glance and then returned to clinging to Christy's leg.

"You remember," Todd said. "Ooh-ooh. Ooh-ooh."

"It's more like this." Katie did her best monkey sound at a shrill, irritating pitch. "And you need to add the motions like this." Katie bent her arms and made a hilarious face as she tried to demonstrate the underarm monkey-scratching trick along with the horrible monkey sounds. "That's what the monkeys outside my bedroom sound like every morning."

Katie had Hana's full attention so she repeated the antics, and Todd chimed in with his mellow monkey sounds and matching armpit scratching.

"I wish I had my phone right now," Christy said.

"You think we'd go viral?" Katie added a funny sort of side-to-side monkey walk.

Todd joined her. Hana clapped her hands and did the sort of sweet belly laugh she did when Todd was tickling her on the rug.

"Better make a run for it," Todd said in between his monkey gyrations. "We're giving you a window here."

Christy slipped out as quickly as she could and made her getaway. She smiled to herself as she drove to Balboa Island. It was good to see that after all Katie had been through, she was bouncing back to her true self.

The other thing that had Christy smiling was that she and Todd had spent a couple of hours at their kitchen island that morning with a calendar and a map on Todd's laptop. They charted out their road trip to Glenbrooke, reserved some campsites, and confirmed the dates with all the friends they hoped to visit. They were still waiting to receive a confirmation from David on the use of the cabin at Camp Heather Brooke. Aside from that, the trip was on for a July 7 departure, and Christy was thrilled. It would be so good to see Doug and Tracy again as well as Sierra and Jordan, and Alissa and Brad. For all the intense emotions that had kicked this summer off, it looked like it was going to turn into one big, happy reunion from here on out.

When Christy returned, she found Katie fresh from the shower wearing jeans and a faded Rancho Corona University hoodie. She was seated on the couch with Hana between her and Todd, and all three of them had bowls of cereal. They were watching the classic animated version of The Jungle Book.

"This is it, Hana," Katie said. "This is where Baloo does his dance."

Hana was more interested in the return of her mommy and dropped her plastic bowl. Her dozen or so remaining Cheerios scattered across the rug.

"Join us," Todd said, unflappable despite the overturned cereal. Hana's bowl didn't have any milk in it, and the tossing of Cheerios had been a frequent event since

80

Hana took joy in feeding herself.

Christy wedged in between Todd and Katie and pulled Hana up on her lap. The three adults sang along as if they were reliving their childhood memories instead of trying to make one for Hana. They all wiggled in their seats along with Baloo and sang out, much to Hana's delight. She looked right, then left, then at the TV, then back at her daddy. When the song ended, Hana clapped and as clear as could be she said, "again." Or at least it sounded like again to Todd and Christy.

"You liked that, huh?" Todd pushed the rewind button and played the song again.

Hana's interest waned this time. She curled up in Christy's lap and tried to burrow in like a baby bird, the way she did when she was tiny.

"Somebody is ready for a n-a-p," Christy said in a low voice. She looped her arms around Hana and got up, carrying her away from the fun center.

Hana popped her head up, recognizing the naptime routine was starting, but she didn't protest. Christy had a feeling Todd had worn her out that morning with a walk on the beach followed by his favorite — the Daddy-Daughter Wrestling Match on the rug. When they had the carpet pulled out and changed to a tile floor, the first thing Christy did was hunt down an oversized shag rug that occupied the space between the couch and the TV console. They bought a smaller coffee table that could be easily moved to the side so that the rug made the perfect wrestling and cuddling spot.

Aunt Marti thought the rug was "atrocious." With her involvement in decorating beach houses over the past few years, she deemed herself a professional and let Christy know that the ivory color of the rug was impractical, the shag was a dust collecting nightmare, and the quality was so poor the rug wouldn't last a year.

Christy told her aunt she was right on all accounts, which pleased Marti immensely. But then Christy had added that for the year the "atrocious" rug did last and collect dust, it would be the place where her little family would make lots of happy memories. Over the last nine months Christy's prediction had come true. Her vacuum had pruned about a fourth of the fluffy threads, but she was confident she could get at least another year out of the big rug before replacing it. Her favorite thing about the rug was that it felt warm and cozy on her bare feet during the winter. Tile floors might be practical for beach homes and easy to keep clean, but they were sure cold.

As the leisurely afternoon unfolded, Todd and Katie settled themselves on the deck and started a long conversation about her parents, her childhood, and the time with her mom yesterday. Christy hadn't told Todd much about their jaunt to Escondido. She excused herself to get some laundry going and to trek upstairs to tidy their bedroom. It was much easier to work on her many projects when she had her sewing machine set up in the downstairs bedroom. With Katie's arrival, Todd had put Christy's sewing machine on an old side table under their bedroom window. It worked for the time being, but she didn't like sleeping in the same room with her unfinished projects. She told Todd it made her feel nervous.

The twenty minutes Christy spent cleaning up, restacking bins, and moving a mound of precut fabric from off her bed was enough to calm the anxiety she had felt when she had returned from Escondido last night. She had four orders that were due before they left for Glenbrooke. But they could all wait until Monday night after Katie left and Todd helped her move the workshop back downstairs. For now, the priority was spending time with Katie.

Christy made some sandwiches and took

them out to Todd and Katie on the deck. Their conversation had moved on to the clean-water ministry, and Katie was giving Todd an overview of what would need to happen if he took a group of students to Africa to help in the villages.

"The biggest thing your students could do is start their own campaign to raise funds for a drilling crew to come in with equipment."

"That's what you did your senior year at Rancho, wasn't it?" Christy asked.

"Well, Eli ran the campaign, but yes. I did a lot to get awareness going on campus. We've had two teams come over so far on short mission trips. We need to connect with student leaders on campus and train them to run the fund-raising campaign. I've developed the whole program, step by step, of what they can do on their own. We just need to connect with key people in each school."

"Do you have a lot of universities that are using the material?" Todd asked.

"Not very many. That's what I'm saying. We don't have the contacts on campus, and that's why Eli and I have been screaming for the past few years that if we could get over here and be on campuses, we're sure we could generate a lot of support. But, as I told you before, the changes that were made a couple of years ago in the ministry's leadership led to a severe cutback in expenses, including Eli's proposal for annual stateside visits to raise funds."

"That doesn't make sense," Christy said.

Katie shrugged. "We have a lot of established pockets of support from Britain and a growing base in western Canada. That's where the mission felt it should focus on volunteers. Several years ago there was some unrest in the area where we work. If you were a foreigner, you were better off with a passport from anywhere other than the U.S."

Todd leaned back in his low beach chair and looked up at Katie, who was perched on "Narangus," the bench seat Todd had made out of his old surfboard when Christy was in college. Katie had brought out a couple of throw pillows Christy had sewn for the living room. They provided needed cushioning, and Katie looked like she had settled onto her perch, which was something Christy had never figured out how to do on the old bench.

Todd folded his hands behind his head. "What would it look like if I organized a group of high school seniors and brought them over for two weeks at the beginning of summer next year?"

Christy watched her husband's eyes as Katie ran through the requirements for such an endeavor. Todd always had held an interest in foreign missions and had spent extended time in Spain when he was twenty. That was eleven years ago, but Christy knew the fervor in him had never waned.

"It could definitely work," Katie concluded. "I have the manual in a file on my phone. I could send it to you. If you pray about it and are sure that is how God is leading you, then, as you said, you should start with seniors you would handpick in the fall. You would be able to go through the necessary training with them during the school year and then come to Kenya next June after they graduate. They have to be eighteen by then, remember."

Katie's invitation seemed to have lit a fire in Todd's belly. He was a "fire in the belly" sort of guy when it came to ministry. This opportunity seemed ideal. He could continue teaching, which was something he liked and, most importantly, which provided the income their family needed, yet focus on a missions trip.

Todd put his arms down and turned to Christy with a questioning look. "What do you think?"

"I think it sounds great."

"I think so, too," Todd said.

Katie looked as if she just caught on that this might really happen. "Does that mean both of you, all three of you, would come stay with us next summer?"

Christy smiled a hope-filled smile. She loved their time at Brockhurst when they were there for Katie's wedding five years ago. She was excited to think about returning. Her first thought, though, was that such a trip with a two-and-a-half-year-old would be nothing like their first visit to Africa.

Christy quickly added, "Even if it doesn't work out for Hana and me, I think it would be amazing, Todd, if you could take a group. I really love the possibility of starting a fund-raising campaign at South Coast Academy. I'd be happy to help with that."

The three friends dreamed some big dreams together and talked through details on the sun-drenched deck. Katie was the one who pulled the curtain on the planning when the sun had hit a position that eliminated all the shady spots on the deck.

"I hope you guys don't mind, but I think I need to lie down. I'm still worn out from the week, and I definitely want to go to church with you in the morning. Would you mind if I took a short nap, and then we can do whatever you want for dinner?"

"Are you up for a sunset picnic on the beach?" Christy asked.

"I'd love it. Let's do it. Wake me by four if I'm not up yet. I still need to sort out the rest of the junk I left in the garage."

"I can haul stuff to the donation center if you want to tell me what's what out there." Todd followed Katie inside and Christy joined them.

They ended up working together in the garage, sorting and tossing, rather than Katie taking a nap. Todd loaded the boxes with the donation items into Gussie while Katie attempted to consolidate the keepers into two boxes.

"I think I need to go through this one more time. If I can get it down to one box, or even better, one suitcase full of stuff, it's going to be a lot less expensive than paying extra for heavy baggage." Katie shoved the boxes to the corner. "I can't do it now, though. My bed is calling."

While Todd was gone and Katie tucked herself away in the guest room for her nap, Christy listened for Hana and busied herself tidying up the house. Tomorrow night was their monthly Family Night, and she was glad that Katie would be there and have a chance to meet Todd's Aunt Linda. The meal plan was simple. At Katie's request, they were having hamburgers on the grill, barbecue potato chips, wedge salad with blue cheese, and hot fudge sundaes with vanilla bean ice cream and Christy's home-made hot fudge.

Christy was checking her pantry and refrigerator to make sure she had everything she needed when she heard Hana cry out for "Mama!" Even though Christy had grown weary of this koala bear stage Hana was in, her heart melted whenever she heard, "Mama."

She scurried upstairs and opened the door to the nursery. "Hello, my little baby. How was your sleep?"

Hana's wispy blonde hair stuck up on one side, and she had her pacifier in her mouth upside down. Christy chuckled. "Rough nap, huh?" As she reached into the crib she caught a whiff of what was sure to be a significant dirty diaper. "Oh, Hana, what did your nana and daddy feed you while I was gone last night?"

The change required a bath and a wash of not only Hana's clothes, but also her crib sheet. By the time Christy finished and had her contented daughter all freshened up, Todd had returned, and Katie was at the kitchen counter talking with him.

"I hope I didn't wake you," Christy said when she and Hana joined them in the kitchen.

"No, I couldn't sleep. But I helped myself to some more cereal." The emptied bowl was on the counter next to a paper bag that seemed to have a quickly expanding grease mark on the side.

"What is going on there?" Christy pointed to the paper bag.

"Dinner," Todd said proudly. "We're having a picnic on the beach, right?"

Christy nodded.

"I remembered how much Katie used to like chimichangas back in the day so I picked up some for dinner. I also got extra chips and salsa."

Katie blinked as if she had forgotten what a chimichanga was. She looked up at Todd slowly and said, "Hey, thanks."

Christy couldn't tell if Katie was grateful or if the cereal bingeing had left little room for the food that Christy thought of as huge, overstuffed burritos.

Hana, who had been staring at Katie, seemed to make some connection as to who this woman was. She stretched out her arms and made a funny "ooooo" sound. Katie looked at her and laughed. "Are you being a monkey? Ooh-ooh!" Katie added the armpit scratching motions.

Hana smiled gleefully and kept going with her own version of what a monkey said.

"What do you think about grabbing a beach blanket and some drinks and moving this band of monkeys down to the sand?" Todd suggested. "It's a great afternoon. We don't have to wait till sunset. I'll bring the chimis."

The merry bunch trotted down to the beach and spread out the big blanket close to the shore. Hana immediately dipped her hands and bare toes in the sand and played with the toys in the sand bucket Christy had brought with them. Katie stretched out on her back and closed her eyes.

"This is pretty great," she said. "Please tell me you guys come out here every day. You live too close to all this beauty to stay cooped up inside."

Christy pulled her knees up and wrapped her arms around her legs. She rested her chin on the top of her knees and said, "It is beautiful."

Undaunted by a thin film of hazy, inversion-layer coastal clouds, the late-afternoon sun was casting a searchlight sort of brightness over the teal-colored ocean. The sand felt warm on Christy's bare feet, and the view to the horizon was broken only by a large barge in the distance, heading south. To the left, the Balboa Pier stretched out into the Pacific like a giant paper clip whose job was to faithfully keep the shore attached to the ocean.

Todd was helping Hana figure out how to get the shovelful of sand into the bucket. He was using his cute preschool teacher's voice again, and it made Christy smile.

"You guys are blessed," Katie said without moving from her settled position. "We all are. So blessed."

They nestled into the warm sand and were lulled by the ancient melody of the steady waves. Christy had a feeling that moments of surrendered serenity like this had been very rare in Katie's life. She caught Todd's eye, and the two of them exchanged looks that were filled with invisible little love notes. He seemed to understand how much this peace-filled time with Christy's closest friend meant to her, as well.

If the only time Christy was able to spend with Katie during this trip was the last two days, she was content knowing that every second had been well spent. Her hopes were high, though, that Sunday, their final day together, would be the best. In Christy's experience, it seemed that their heavenly Father always saved the best for last.

Six

If an ordinary day could feel like a perfect holiday, that's how Sunday felt to Christy.

Church with Katie was great. Christy's parents saved seats for them, and to Christy's surprise, both Uncle Bob and Aunt Marti sat with them as well. The weather was chilly with the June gloom that was typical this time of year, but by mid-afternoon it was nice enough for Christy, Todd, and Katie to bike ride down the cement path that separated the long stretch of sand at Newport Beach from the clustered together beach houses. Todd had Hana in her secure toddler seat on the back of his bike. Hana protested having to wear her pink helmet, but Todd solved the issue by sticking a cracker in her mouth. She didn't even whine the rest of the short ride up and down the sidewalk.

Katie sorted her things and packed them when they returned from the bike ride. She needed to be at the airport by ten thirty the next morning and suggested that she schedule a shuttle so Christy and Todd wouldn't have to make the drive in Monday morning traffic.

"No, we want to take you. I want to have as much time with you as I can," Christy said. "We don't mind. Really. Todd is officially on summer vacation now so this is kind of a treat for him to do something other than go to school."

"Okay, if you're sure then, I'll be ready to leave at eight thirty. Two hours should be plenty of time, don't you think?"

"Yes, I think so."

Katie sat on the edge of the bed in the guest room and ran her hand over the yearbook that rested on top of her clothes. "This was an intense week. It feels like I've been here for a month."

"A lot happened," Christy said.

Katie nodded. "I wish I felt better. I'm hoping I can sleep on the plane. Emotional stuff is really draining, isn't it?"

Christy offered Katie a reassuring smile. "For all you went though, I think you're doing great, Katie. Tell Eli that you need time to rest when you get home. He'll understand."

"I already told him when I called him this

morning. He took me off the conference center kitchen duty schedule for all this week. I'm sure I'll be fine once I rest up."

Christy heard her mom's voice echoing from the entry. "Sounds like Mom and Dad are here a little early for our Family Night Dinner. I'll start the food prep. Do you need anything?"

"Nope." Katie grinned. "Thanks, Chris. Really, thanks for everything."

"Of course." Christy gave Katie a quick hug and headed out to the kitchen just as her parents were coming in the front door. Todd was holding the door open for them and Hana was wiggling and repeating, "Paw Paw, Paw Paw" over and over.

Christy's mom shook her head and caught Christy's eye. Her thick, wavy gray hair fell across her forehead. "She certainly is Grandpa's girl, isn't she? I come in the house, and she barely looks up. Grandpa comes over, and she turns into a Tinker Bell."

Christy laughed. "I feel the same way sometimes. This little girl definitely has all the men in this family well trained."

"Speaking of the men in this family." Christy's mom placed a bag of potato chips on the counter. "We heard from your brother today that you and Todd are planning to go to Glenbrooke."

"Yes, we finally made our plans. I was going to tell you tonight. We're driving up the coast on July 7 and should be back by the 20th. Maybe sooner."

"That's wonderful, Christy. The two of you have wanted to take this trip for several years now, haven't you?"

Christy nodded. "We're really looking forward to it."

Christy's dad stopped his game of blowing raspberry kisses on Hana's bare tummy. He held her in a cradle position in his arms and said to Christy, "Don't worry a bit about Short Stuff here while you're gone. We promise to take good care of her. I'm sure she won't miss you at all."

"Hana's going with us, Dad."

"He's only teasing," Christy's mom said.

"Not entirely. If you take this child away from us for two weeks, she might not know me when she gets back."

"She'll know you, Dad."

Hana was saying her new word that sounded like "again" and was patting her grandpa's face, waiting for his next tickle attack. Christy and her mom exchanged glances and shook their heads. What made Christy the happiest at moments like this was when she had vague memories of her dad being playful like this when she was young. She remembered how he used to call her his little mouse, and how they had a game where she would hide and then try to scurry away to another hiding spot before he could find her.

Her most vivid memories of her dad, though, were the ones impressed on her from her teen years. When she was around eleven and had started to develop into a young woman, her dad had turned into a strict, serious father who was always trying to make sure she didn't turn into one of those rebellious teenagers who did wild things like getting their ears pierced or dyeing their hair or sneaking out of the house at night.

Christy had attempted none of those, and in some ways, her father had gotten his little girl to stay young and innocent.

Dr. Avery arrived just then, and Todd introduced her to Katie as his Aunt Linda, "the woman who brought Hana into the world."

Linda was tall and slender with short bleached-white hair and a healthy, efficient look about her. Her lime green reading glasses were perched on top of her head and the row of silver stud earrings that lined her earlobe seemed especially sparkly.

She greeted Katie warmly. "I'd love to hear about what your life is like in Kenya. Christy and Todd have talked about you and Eli so much, I feel like I'm meeting a new relative."

Linda and Katie struck up a conversation, and Todd got the hamburgers started on the grill. He had put some music on earlier, and now their little dwelling place seemed to pulsate with life and laughter.

After Bob and Marti arrived, Marti hurried over and cornered Christy by the kitchen sink and said, "Your mother said you're going to Glenbrooke."

"Yes. We're leaving on the seventh."

"You're going to see David, correct?"

"Yes."

"Then you'll have to tell me everything. I want to hear all the details." Aunt Marti's expression seemed to be fixed, even though the tone of her voice made it sound as if she was excited. Christy had never known Marti to be excited about anything related to her brother.

"All the details about what?"

"Why, about her, of course."

Christy was lost. "Her, who?"

"His girlfriend!" Marti looked at Christy incredulously. "Didn't he tell you?"

Uncle Bob sidled over to the sink and

scratched the side of his face in a sheepish way. "I'm pretty sure David told me that in confidence, Martha. He didn't refer to Fina as his girlfriend. At least not officially his girlfriend."

"Fina?" Christy repeated. *What sort of name is Fina?*

Marti took the admonition from her husband better than she usually did. She put her perfectly manicured fingers up to her mouth and tapped her lips as if telling them in Morse code not to say another word.

"I'm sure we'll find out what's what once we see him." Christy hoped her diplomatic response would conclude the conversation. She was having a hard time picturing her brother with a serious girlfriend.

True, he was twenty-two and had graduated from Rancho Corona University. And also true, he had had a handful of girls that Christy had seen pictures of on social media from various events at Rancho. She knew David had dated a couple of fellow Rancho Corona girls off and on. But David had never told Christy about any girls he was particularly serious about. The big sister part of her felt a little hurt that she was hearing news like this from Aunt Marti. She dismissed it and decided to hold off on forming any opinions until they went to Glenbrooke.

"On to another topic, then." Marti glanced at Bob. "That is, if I'm able to discuss the deck."

"Of course. Far be it from me to try and stop you from doing anything you've set your mind on." Uncle Bob gave Christy a wink and reached for a potato chip.

Marti rolled her eyes at his comment and plowed ahead. "Your uncle finally secured the permit, and Todd can start working on the deck off your bedroom."

"Wait. What?" Christy looked to Bob for confirmation of this grand announcement. "A deck?"

"Yes, a deck," Marti repeated. "You and Todd told me when you moved in here that you would love to build a deck off the master bedroom. There's room for it, as you know, but I told you when I bought the house that it would take forever to get permission because of the restrictions on external structural changes on all the cottages in this part of Newport Beach."

"Yes," Christy said. "But that was . . . what? Five years ago."

"Yes." Marti's dark eyes carried their familiar twinkle of delight that showed up every time she had an idea she was determined to execute. "Now let me finish because I have good news. The plans have been approved! And as the owner, I would like to invest in this upgrade. It will add value to the house. There's no reason Todd can't help with the labor, the way he worked for me last summer. He can start this week by knocking out the wall where your bedroom window is."

Christy felt a headache coming on. "We need to bring Todd in on this conversation. He's scheduled some time to help out at Zane's with the surfboard benches this week."

"Well, he can cancel those plans and build the deck." Marti's matter-of-fact tone was a familiar one to Christy and one that didn't bode well for Christy if she had any hope of stopping the freight train known as Marti on a Mission.

Christy extracted herself from her aunt's force field and went to work putting out plates, cutlery, and drinks. Too many thoughts were spinning in her brain at the moment. But she had learned something about herself once she became a mother. She had no problem multitasking when it came to hands-on projects. But for mental projects, or "dreaming," as Todd sometimes liked to call it, her brain could only handle a few possibilities at a time.

Thinking about going to Kenya next summer was a dream project that had been spinning in her thoughts since yesterday. Plans for their road trip to Glenbrooke were also spinning through all the stations in her mind as she made mental lists of what to pack in Gussie, how much toddler equipment they needed to take in anticipation of Hana's needs at all the places they'd be staying, along with a dozen other small details like remembering to buy a decent pair of jeans before they left. Her two semi-presentable pairs of jeans were too baggy on her these days now that she'd finally lost most of her baby weight. She wanted to look nice since they were seeing so many of their friends.

With those projects already filling up the whiteboards in her brain, Christy had no space left to think about knocking out their bedroom wall tomorrow and having Todd build a deck before they left on vacation.

Oh, Aunt Marti, sometimes you drive me crazy. Utterly crazy. Completely bonkers!

Christy filled her lungs with the fresh air that was skimming into the kitchen through the open window. She willed herself to calm down and enjoy her family and her last few hours with Katie. Todd had proven more than once that he could handle Aunt Marti's mania. He could decide what to do with her plans.

Everyone had drifted out to the deck where Todd was grilling the burgers. Christy carried the bowl of chips outside and took orders for those who wanted passion fruit iced tea, lemon lime soda, or ice water infused with cucumbers and strawberries, the way they used to serve it at the spa she worked at.

On her second round of carrying out the requested drinks, Christy noticed that Katie was sitting on Narangus with her eyes closed, her arms folded over her middle, and her face toward the waning rays of sunlight that squeezed past their neighbor's house and touched a sliver of the deck.

Soak it up, Katie Girl. I wish your visit had been longer.

Christy went back inside since everyone had a beverage and went to work putting the ingredients in place for the homemade hot fudge so that all she would have to do is warm it up when they were ready for dessert. She hummed along with the song that was rolling into the room on Todd's pride-and-joy speakers he had installed two Christmases ago.

Over the years more than one person had

told Christy they thought she had the gift of hospitality. At moments like this, she believed it. She loved having people over, and she loved serving food that everyone liked. She felt happy when her home was filled with people who were enjoying themselves. The little details about what she served or how it turned out mattered less and less to her. What mattered was that people felt welcomed and loved when they entered her home.

Tonight, that was definitely the vibe she felt.

Katie came inside and asked if Christy needed help. With a quick scan over the counter where all the fixings for the burgers had been spread, Christy said, "Nope, I think we're ready."

Christy scooted out to the deck with a platter for Todd to put the burgers on. Then she went over to the extension cord Todd had fixed so it bent under the deck and connected to a hidden electric outlet. He had managed to make it kid safe but still easy enough for Christy to plug in her beloved café lights that she had convinced him to string across the top of the deck last summer. As soon as the lights came on, everyone produced the usual "ahh" sounds that made Christy smile. It always felt like a party when the lights were on.

"Come on inside to dress up your burger," Christy said. "If anyone wants to eat outside and gets chilly, you know where the blankets are in the chest."

The group gathered around the kitchen island. Hana had attached herself to Uncle Bob now and had curled up in his arms, resting her dandelion head on his shoulder at the curve of his neck. Uncle Bob's expression made it clear that he felt like the happiest man alive.

Christy's heart was full. They all joined hands around the island, as had become their custom, and Todd prayed a blessing over them. It felt to Christy as if her immediate family had changed over the many months of gathering for Family Night. They all felt more like friends than simply blood relatives. She knew that was backwards but that was because, from her high school days on, her closest relationships had been with her friends and not family. Now they felt the same to her.

The music tumbled into a more soothing mix as they all ended up outside, under the lights. Todd pulled the high chair outside, but for some reason Hana was only interested in mooching off of Aunt Linda's plate.

"We have the same food," Linda told her. "See?"

It didn't matter. Hana wanted what Aunt Linda had, and Linda was happy to accommodate her.

Christy noticed that Katie had been pretty quiet. She got up and slid over next to Katie on Narangus. "You doing okay?" Katie had only eaten half of her burger.

"I think my stomach shrunk from barely eating all week. Is that possible?"

"We could ask Linda. She's the doctor."

"It's all really good, Christy. And this place." Katie motioned to the lights with her hand. "Your home, your people . . ." Katie teared up. "They're really wonderful. I know you know that, but you're living a pretty charmed life right now."

"I know," Christy said in a small voice. It was the first time she consciously compared her life to Katie's, and she felt a sense of survivor's guilt. Katie's dad was gone. Christy's dad was three feet away. Katie had to work hard and make all the effort to connect with her family members. Christy's family all lived nearby and gathered like this every month. They were involved in each other's lives. Christy's eyes filled with tears. It wasn't fair.

"I need some water." Katie stood up and

seemed to almost lose her balance. "You want me to bring you anything while I'm up?"

"No, I'm good. Thanks."

Katie took one step toward the sliding door and stopped. As Christy watched, Katie seemed to fall in slow motion, a knee-bent sort of swoon that landed her on her side on the deck before anyone else had noticed.

Katie had collapsed.

SEVEN

Christy immediately dashed to her side. "Katie?" She shook Katie's shoulder. "Katie, are you okay?"

Aunt Linda was beside Christy, gently pushed her back, and leaned in to assess the moment with the methodical skill of a physician. "Katie. Can you look at me, Katie? That's good." Linda's hand pressed against Katie's forehead. "How do you feel?"

"I . . . What . . . Did I fall?"

"It was more of a faint," Linda said. "Do you think you can lift your head?"

Katie bolstered herself up on her elbow. "I just needed a drink of water."

"Katie, we're going to help you up. Todd's here next to me. He and I are going to help you into the house. We're going to take you to your room. You need to lie still for a little while."

Christy and the others stood back as

Linda and Todd helped Katie stand up and walk into the house.

"I feel so stupid," Katie said. "I must have tripped over something."

"It's okay," Linda said calmly. "We'll get you some water. All you have to do is rest for a few minutes."

Christy took that as her cue to follow them and fill a glass of water. First she went ahead of them into the bedroom and moved Katie's suitcase off the bed. She could hear Katie protesting over all the TLC and insisting that she was fine. Christy took the water into the guest room, and Todd stepped out now that Katie was comfortably settled on the bed.

"Take small sips." Linda held the glass for Katie.

Christy wasn't sure if she should stay or let Linda be alone with Katie. She decided to leave them because, knowing Katie, she would be embarrassed and try to come up with jokes if she had a small audience. Christy closed the door behind her and felt her heart still pounding.

Aunt Marti was only a few feet away when Christy exited.

"What happened? I didn't see her fall."

"I don't know exactly."

"Good thing we invited a doctor into the

family," Marti remarked.

Christy's instinct was to correct her aunt and say that they didn't "invite" Linda into their family. Linda was Todd's mom's sister. She was family. Christy let it go and suggested they return to the deck to finish eating. She tried to herd her aunt outside, but Marti insisted on staying in the kitchen so she could "help clean up." Christy didn't argue. She went back outside where the others asked if Katie was all right.

"I think so. I'm glad Linda is here. Katie has been stretched to her limits ever since she arrived. She has to be exhausted physically, mentally, emotionally."

"She might be coming down with something," Todd said. "I've never known her to turn down a chimichanga, but she did last night."

"It's been a long time since she's eaten our kind of food," Bob said. "Remember all the good vegetables and fresh fruit we ate when we were at Brockhurst? Could be she's not used to our cuisine anymore."

The others added their speculations as to what Katie might have eaten while she was at her mother's. Hana was done with the whole adventure of dinner on the deck since Aunt Linda, her supply wagon, had left the scene. Christy's mom was trying to convince

Hana to eat a bite of hamburger bun, but she wasn't interested. She rubbed her eyes and looked around for her mommy. As soon as Hana saw Christy she put up her hands and said, "Mama."

Christy plucked Hana out of the messy high chair. "Time for this little one to get ready for bed. Say good night to everyone, Hana. Do you want to blow kisses?" Christy demonstrated, and Hana followed with her open palm to her open mouth and then flung her drool-soaked paw out to the gang.

"Okay, come on. Let's go upstairs." Christy made it as far as the kitchen. The guest room door opened, and Linda stepped out with a calm expression. "Oh, good. You're right here. Katie wants to see you."

Christy stepped into the room with Hana on her hip. Katie was stretched out on the bed on her back. Her eyes were open wide. She had a stunned look on her face. Christy wasn't sure what it meant and looked to Linda for clues.

The combination of Katie's shocked expression and Linda's knowing smile led Christy to suddenly realize the obvious cause for all Katie's symptoms. "Are you?"

Katie nodded.

"Katie!" Christy's elation exploded. "That's wonderful! Of course! How did we miss all the signs?"

"It was a busy week," Linda said.

"I'm so, so happy for you!" Christy leaned over to give Katie a hug. Hana was still clinging to her, and now she wanted to crawl off of Christy and cuddle up with Katie. They managed a bumped heads sort of group hug, and Christy pulled Hana back with her, much to the protest of her little one.

"This is wonderful, Katie. Really wonderful. Let me get this little screaming mimi off to bed, and I'll be right back."

"Christina?" Marti ushered herself in through the open door and looked irritated that she was out of the loop. "What happened? We heard shouting."

"Katie, do you want to tell her?" Christy wrestled with squirming Hana in her arms.

Katie, who still hadn't said a word, blinked and gave Christy a nod as if she had forgotten how to open her mouth. When no words came forth, Christy took the signal as Katie's handoff of the announcement baton.

"She's going to have a baby."

"Oh!" Marti quickly enfolded herself into the moment, going to Katie's side and taking her hand in hers. "I had a feeling. I really did. But I didn't say anything, of course."

Christy left the room, knowing that Aunt Linda could mitigate anything Marti tried to convince Katie of in her state of shock. After settling Hana in bed, Christy calmed her by putting on some soothing music. It also toned down all the cheers and lively conversation that were going on downstairs and floating up to Hana's room.

Hana was sleepy enough to take her blessing from Christy and cuddle up with her bunny without protest. Christy couldn't stop smiling as she hurried back downstairs. The family gathering had moved to the guest room and everyone was squeezed into the tight quarters.

"That's what I would advise." Linda looked at Christy when she entered. "We're talking about Katie staying here for a bit. I think she needs to delay her flight for at least a week. The stress of such a long flight could be detrimental to the child. Katie needs to rest and get hydrated."

"Of course she should stay," Marti said quickly. "I've offered for her stay with us, if you don't want her here, Christy. She would have her choice of the upstairs guest room or the downstairs one if taking the stairs would be too much for her."

Christy focused in on Katie and gave her a big smile. "You decide what's best for you and that little stowaway you brought with you. You know you can stay here as long as you want."

"I'd like . . ." Katie was holding a half-filled glass of water that seemed to be shaking slightly. "I'd like to call Eli and talk to him about everything."

"Of course," Marti agreed. "He should be here. Tell him to come. We'll cover the airfare, won't we, Robert?"

"Certainly. But we should let Katie and Eli decide what they want to do next, don't you think?"

"We'll give you some privacy," Christy's mom said in a comforting tone. She was the first to try to herd the others out of the guest room. They exited and closed the door behind them. The party returned to the deck where the twinkle lights seemed to have started a dance party on their own. The wind had stirred them up, and they were swaying while a bunch of napkins were doing a tumbleweed-roll dance move across the deck.

The group gathered everything up and moved the party inside, out of the wind. Christy thought it was funny that everyone was congregating in the kitchen instead of the living room. They all were acting as if they were there to help Christy clean up, but she knew they were trying to catch a hint of how Eli reacted to the news. It was sweet and at the same time crowded.

About ten minutes had passed since they had all exited the guest room when Christy took matters into her hands. "I'm going to check on her. You guys can get everything ready for the ice cream sundaes."

Christy tapped on the door before she opened it, slid inside, and closed the door behind her. "Hey, little mama."

Katie was lying on her back, her left arm resting behind her head. "I couldn't get Eli on a call so I texted him. I'm in shock, Christy. I didn't expect this. I don't know what he's going to say."

"He'll be thrilled, Katie. You know he will." Christy stretched out on the bed next to her and looped her arm through Katie's right arm that was resting by her side. "I'm so, so, so happy for you."

"I'm terrified. What have I done to this poor little human? I have nothing to give it right now. I was sick to my stomach a couple of times at my mom's, but I thought it was from the stress and the stuff I was eating. Linda says I'm dehydrated. She wants me to go into her office at eight in the morning and do blood work. If I'm still weak in a couple of days, she says she might put me in the hospital on an IV to replenish my fluids."

"It probably won't come to that. You can get rest and plenty to drink here."

"Christy, I'm a terrible mother." Tears trickled down Katie's cheeks.

"Oh, Katie, no you're not. Your little one is taking everything you've got from you right now. That's why you're low on energy and why your resources are depleted as soon as you take them in. It's all going to your baby. You're taking good care of it naturally, and now that you know, you can start taking the very best care of it."

"What am I going to do about the flight?"

"I'm sure we can call the airline and cancel or reschedule you. We'll figure that out."

"What if I can't stay hydrated and I end up having to go to the hospital?"

"Then you'll get what your body needs, and you'll get strong again. It'll be fine."

"Christy, what if I'm not really pregnant? What if I have a fatal disease or a weird growth or something? Linda didn't do a test. She just went by symptoms."

"Well, it's what she does. She's an OB-GYN who has been diagnosing pregnancies for many years. When you go into her office tomorrow, you'll take all the necessary tests, and you'll know for sure."

Katie still had the deer-in-the-headlights look.

"Take a deep breath." Christy gave Katie's hand a squeeze. "You're going to be fine."

Katie breathed in and out slowly. She put both her hands over her flat stomach. "Hello, little alien."

Christy grinned. "You're both going to be fine. You'll see, all the immediate fears are normal. The most important thing you can do right now is rest."

Katie's phone pinged, and she anxiously reached for it to read the text from Eli. "He's coming." She started to cry again. "Eli is going to come and be with me."

Christy teared up, too. "Good. That's as it should be. Tell Eli you guys can stay here as long you want. If you get tired of us, you heard Aunt Marti. She's ready for you to stay at her house, if you want. Don't worry about anything. We'll figure it out."

"Okay, I'll tell him." Katie's phone pinged again. "Oh, he told me to call him. He said the call should go through now."

Christy leaned over and kissed Katie on the cheek and then left the room as Katie placed the call to Eli.

When Christy entered the kitchen, a choir of eager faces all looked at her. "She's calling Eli right now. He texted her that he's coming."

"That's good," Mom said.

"We'll help with airfare," Bob said.

"And she knows they can stay with us, doesn't she?" Marti added.

"When is Eli coming?" Todd asked.

Christy put her hands up to halt the volley of questions and comments. "I'm sure Katie will fill us in after she talks to him."

Christy appreciated her family. She really did. Even when they all seemed a little too "on point" at times, Christy knew their concerns for Katie were heartfelt and that was pretty wonderful.

The hot fudge sundaes capped off the evening around the kitchen island. Katie ventured out to join them and sat at the counter, relaying the few details she knew about Eli's plans. Her update was cut short when she had no appetite for ice cream and her skin tone turned pale as it had earlier that night.

"Back to bed," Linda said firmly. "And stay there."

The family left earlier than usual so the house would be quiet and restful. Christy promised to send everyone a group text after the appointment in the morning. The hot topic of Marti's plans for the second-story deck was put aside in light of this development. Christy was relieved that no one would be putting a sledgehammer to her bedroom wall in the morning.

Instead of renovations beginning on Monday morning, Christy drove Katie to her appointment and waited while she ran through the tests and had the office exam. Linda's diagnosis was correct. Katie was about four weeks pregnant, and if her last weigh-in at home was right, she had lost about eleven pounds since arriving in California. If she lost any more weight or if she couldn't keep any food down, Linda wanted her in the hospital and on an IV.

"Bedrest," Katie muttered as Christy pulled into the parking lot of a fast-food restaurant. "I've never stayed in bed for days on end my entire life. What are we doing here?"

"I thought you said you wanted a milk shake?"

"That's right. I said that earlier, didn't I? Are they even open yet? Oh, they are. Wow. So much convenience living in California that I forgot about. You can simply drive through and order a milk shake at nine o'clock in the morning. I don't think you can do that anywhere in Nairobi. At least not in any of the places I've been to."

"What flavor?" Christy asked.

"Vanilla. Plain, bland. See if they can make it without any added flavor at all."

Christy asked at the drive-through, and yes, they could make a plain, unflavored milk shake.

"Soft serve ice cream or frozen yogurt?" Christy asked.

"More choices? Oh, man. Yogurt. No, ice cream. I don't care."

Christy ordered both. If one didn't stay down, she'd have the backup in the freezer at home for Katie to try later.

"Oh," Katie added. "And I think I heard the heartbeat."

"You think?"

"Well, all I could hear was this low, swishy noise. I think the machine was transmitting sounds from the fish aquarium in the waiting room."

"Oh, Katie." Christy grinned. "That was your baby's heartbeat. You got to hear your baby's heart beating."

Katie still didn't look convinced that what she had heard in her private exam with Linda was related to any of the precarious health issues that were being monitored in her body.

"Weird." It was the only word Katie seemed to be able to manage. "I still feel like I'm just kind of tired and coming down with a cold or the flu or something. None of this seems real."

"I'll pull out all my pregnancy books, if you want to start looking at them. And I can send you links to some great websites that will help you to envision what's happening inside right now. It's miraculous."

Christy stopped at a red light and glanced over at Katie. It appeared that the thought of more information was freaking her out.

"Or we can wait on all the detailed information. It will get real for you soon enough. For now, the goal is for you to take it easy."

"That I can do. Going back to bed is about all I think I can handle."

The rest of Monday felt like a normal weekday to Christy when she sat down to sew as usual during Hana's naptime. The big difference, though, was that she had her best friend sequestered in her downstairs guest room and she had her husband shuffling around the house trying to stay quiet but at the same time do something. Todd finally decided to go to Zane's to work on surfboard benches even though he said he wouldn't go in until Tuesday. Todd promised to be back when Hana woke up because he was going to take her for another bike ride.

As was often the case, Todd was sucked

into the vortex of Zane's workshop and stayed until after dinner, trying to help one of the guys figure out the wrought-iron base for a new plant stand the company had been commissioned to create for an outdoor shopping plaza.

Katie did as she was told. She slept, and she sipped both her shakes throughout the day, and both of them stayed down. All she wanted for dinner was bananas. Three of them.

"How long were you in this nausea stage?" Katie asked. "I mean, I don't mind a diet of ice cream and bananas, but I'm sure this itty-bitty alien is going to need more than that pretty soon."

"I've kind of forgotten. I think I ate mostly bland food for a couple of months. I know I had an odd craving for barbecue potato chips toward the end, and Uncle Bob made sure I had a good supply."

Katie made a face. "Barbecue potato chips? Really?" She gave a shiver.

"Sorry. Didn't mean to make you even more nauseous."

"Do you have any cereal? I can't believe I'm saying this, but what I really wish I had right now was some ugali. If you have anything like Cream of Rice or Malt-o-Meal, I think I could keep that down."

"I'll see what I have."

"And feel free to add all the butter and brown sugar and milk that you can. I'm goin' for it here! Bring on the calories!"

The next three days Christy enjoyed coming up with ideas of calorie-dense, nutrition-rich foods for her grateful patient. The results were a variety of smoothies and bland vegetable casseroles with cheese. And it was having a good effect on Katie. She was up four pounds and had developed a craving for fettuccini with a mild Alfredo sauce.

Christy also put to use all the oils and herbal teas she had accumulated in her vitamin cupboard. The calming fragrance of lavender lingered in the guest room, and the electric tea kettle was clicked on and off throughout the day.

Katie warmed up to the idea of seeing images of how her baby was developing and pored over every one of Christy's pregnancy books. She became obsessed in true Katie style with details she found on various websites and had started a list of questions to ask Linda on her next visit. Best of all, she slept. A lot.

Christy loved that her little nest had become a haven for Katie.

On Thursday afternoon Todd left for the

airport to pick up Eli. Eli's flight had been delayed a full day in Frankfurt due to a mechanical problem. But all was well, and he arrived at Christy and Todd's house tired but happy to see his wife.

Eli Lorenzo had the stature of an athletic runner and was only a few inches taller than Katie. His face often bore a kindly, curious expression, especially when he was listening. As a missionary kid, he had grown up in Africa, and ever since Christy had first met him, she had the sense that he was from another culture. A culture that used gentleness rather than force to get a point across.

Eli had always impressed Christy as someone who was capable. Whatever was thrown his way, he could reason out a solution and patiently wait for the results. In this situation, with his wife and possibly his unborn child at risk, he was capable of adapting quickly and doing everything necessary to ensure Katie's well-being.

The first week Eli was with them was like summer camp for Todd. When Katie was resting, Todd took Eli surfing. While Christy sewed, Todd and Eli took Hana to the park and then grocery shopping. The two old friends had a barbeque cook-off one night, and Eli joined Todd at the Friday Night Gathering where he spoke to the high school students about what life was like in Africa. According to Todd, the group loved him.

Katie did as she was told and improved each day. Hana was happy and loved the extra attention from not only her daddy, but also from Uncle Eli and Auntie Katie, who had captured Hana's attention and affections with an ongoing puppet show using pen marker faces on the tips of her fingers. The week was ideal.

The days seemed to melt off the calendar once they celebrated the Fourth of July with lots of sparklers on the deck and a big sheet cake Christy had decorated as an American flag. She knew the time had come for her and Todd to make a decision about their vacation, so she bravely brought up the subject when the four of them were seated in the living room, after another pasta-based dinner.

"So, Todd and I had been talking about leaving on our road trip next Friday. But if you guys end up needing to stay longer than what Linda said at your last appointment, we can stay. It's not a problem."

Eli and Katie exchanged glances. "You don't need to stay. We won't know if I'm cleared to travel until my next appointment on Monday. But I feel good. I'm sure Linda is going to give me two thumbs up." Katie added with a mischievous grin, "Are you getting tired of us? Because, you know, Aunt Marti has been pitching for us to stay with them."

"You have definitely not worn out your welcome. You could stay here forever, and we would love it," Christy said. "The thing is, if Linda says more bedrest and you guys stay here, are you okay with us going on our trip?"

"Of course. We said it earlier, you guys can't cancel your vacation again this summer just because we've moved in and taken over your house and your lives." Eli's voice sounded serious.

"Well, you know . . ." Todd glanced at Christy with a questioning look. "The other option is for you guys to come with us."

"Yes!" Christy said eagerly. "Great idea, Todd."

"That is," Todd held up his palm, "only if Aunt Linda considers a long road trip in a renovated VW bus with an nineteen-month-old as therapeutic bedrest."

"I love the idea, too!" Katie looked expectantly at Eli. "I love it a lot. In fact, I love it more than fettuccini, and all of you know how much I love fettuccini these days!"

Eli nodded calmly. He seemed to agree

with the excitement, but at the same time he was considering all that was involved.

Katie's expression mellowed. "Although, I guess I'd feel guilty if we took a vacation on top of a vacation."

"I wouldn't," Eli said plainly. "Coming here for your dad's funeral was not a vacation. If you're okay to travel by car and if you feel up for it, I would rather try a trip up the California coast where there are hospitals every twenty miles along the way than put you on a plane for a twenty-hour flight and take you home where the nearest hospital is fifty miles away on a road filled with potholes."

No one contested Eli's conclusion. It was decided.

"California Surfin' Safari," Todd said with a voice that sounded like a cartoon surfer-dude character.

"Depending on what the doctor says," Eli added.

"She'll say yes." Katie patted her stomach. "I mean, what could be better? I feel relaxed just thinking about it."

Christy knew the trip would be many things. Relaxing was not one of the anticipated aspects she would put at the top of her list.

"You know what I think Linda is going to

say?" Katie's voice sounded confident and eager. "Linda is going to insist on coming with us! I mean, this is a once-in-a-lifetime adventure. Who wouldn't want to drive up the California coast with you guys?"

EIGHT

In spite of Katie's prediction, Linda did not jump at the chance to join the Surfin' Safari. She was stern with Katie at her appointment. Not only did she say that the trip was not a good idea for Katie, but she also told her to take the order of complete bedrest more seriously.

"She said I should plan to lay low for two weeks . . ." Katie gave an exaggerated pout as she and Eli updated Christy and Todd on the office visit.

Katie added, "And she recommended that I not fly until I'm in the second trimester."

"When would that be?" Todd asked.

"August," Katie said solemnly.

Eli nodded. "That's right. August. Probably the second week, just to be safe."

Todd put his hand on Eli's shoulder. "The most important thing right now is protecting the life that's trying to grow inside of Katie."

"Of course," Eli agreed quickly.

"And you know you guys can stay here," Todd added. "Christy and I can help with whatever you need."

Christy secretly loved the thought of them staying on this side of the world until the middle of August. She tried to read Katie's expression. Was she frightened? Relieved in a small way to know that she didn't have to worry about getting on a long flight home yet? Christy knew she had to be disappointed that the road trip was no longer an option.

Christy thought about how much Katie had done over the past week when she was supposed to be on bedrest and not lifting anything. She had walked to the beach twice and carried a load of laundry into the guest room. Christy had protested, but Katie said she felt good and wanted to do a little something. Eli appeared ready to make sure that Katie took it easy, whether she said she felt good or not.

Christy didn't sleep much that night. She kept thinking about Katie and the little life her body was carrying. Linda wouldn't have diagnosed complete bedrest unless she was concerned about the safety of the baby. Christy didn't want to think it, but she couldn't escape the possibility that Katie might be in a more precarious position than she or Eli were letting on. Had Linda told them a miscarriage was a possibility? Christy didn't want to mull over the thought, but it wouldn't leave her. Why else would Linda have been so strict about the bedrest?

In the morning, when Christy lifted Hana out of her crib, she kissed her soft cheeks and held her tight. No life should be taken for granted.

Hana was in a cuddly mood, so after Christy changed her diaper and put her in one of her cute little ruffled outfits from Aunt Marti, Christy brushed Hana's soft white-blonde hair and played a clapping game with her.

Many times during the first year and a half of Hana's life, all Christy could do was make it through to the next day, the next week, the next feeding, or the next changing. That phase was just now beginning to give way to moments like this when Hana was focused on Christy and trying to use her cute squeaky sounds to communicate back.

Christy wished she knew more songs or had more Bible storybooks. Todd had sung to Hana from the day she was born, and one of his most calming songs was simply, "Jesus, Jesus, Oh Jesus. There's just something about that name." At moments like this, Christy wanted to have her own go-to song that would stir in her daughter a sense of comfort when she heard the name "Jesus." So much of Christy's coping with her newborn had been done in silence with lots of smiles and "shh's."

Christy picked up Hana and danced with her around the nursery while singing, *"Jesus loves me, this I know, for the Bible tells me so."* Hana's glee in the moment was adorable. She tilted her head back as Christy twirled around and gave Christy a parent's best reward. Hana laughed.

As soon as Christy came to a spinning halt, Hana patted Christy's face and said, "Gan. Gan."

"Again?" Christy echoed. "Okay. Let's dance our way downstairs. Ready?" Christy stepped into the hallway singing and twirling and then carried Hana down the stairs while singing in a whisper with her lips pressed against the side of Hana's head. At the bottom of the stairs, she put Hana down and quietly said, "Let's not wake Auntie Katie."

They found Eli in the kitchen setting up a serving tray for Katie with a protein drink Linda had suggested, a small bowl of oatmeal with lots of milk, and a glass of orange juice.

"How's she doing?" Christy asked softly.

"I don't think she moved all night." Eli's voice was low. He glanced at the open guest room. "I think she was doing better before. She's frightened to death that if she sneezes she's going to harm the baby."

"You guys know I can hear everything you're saying," Katie called out. Then to add a bit of her humor, Katie gave a big, fake sneeze.

Christy and Eli exchanged grins. They went into the guest room with Hana trotting along behind them. She reached her pudgy little fingers out and opened the dresser drawers that used to contain her toys for when she played while Christy sewed. The drawers now held Eli's and Katie's clothes, and Hana pulled them out one by one.

"Do you mind if she does that?" Christy asked. "I used to keep her toys in that drawer."

Katie stretched her neck to see. "No, of course not. We're in her territory."

Eli left the tray for Katie and said he was going to make some oatmeal for himself. Katie adjusted her position and started to eat. "Eli and I talked about it, and we're going to move over to Bob and Marti's."

Christy thought Katie was joking. But her face made it clear that she was serious.

"Why are you saying that?"

"Because I remember all too well what it was like when Tracy and Doug and little Daniel lived with you, and she had to go on bedrest with the twins during her last trimester."

"That was different."

"Not much."

"Yes, it was. First, I was working full-time, my life was scattered, and I was tired all the time. Todd was working night and day so I had no help around the house. Next, you don't have a rambunctious little boy." Christy paused and smiled. "At least not yet."

Katie's expression softened.

"And third, or maybe it's fourth, but there are some people you are more comfortable sharing space with than other people. It's a personality thing. Some people make great friends but wear you out when you're under the same roof twenty-four/seven. Todd and I don't feel that way about you guys."

"At least not yet." Katie played off of Christy's earlier comment and watched her expression.

"Here's the thing." Christy bent down to

pick up the clothes Hana had left on the floor when she toddled back to the kitchen. "Todd and I will be gone for almost two weeks. I'm really, really bummed that we can't take you with us, but you'll have our home all to yourselves while we're on vacation."

"You mean, you're going to go without us?"

Christy was caught off guard by Katie's question. She thought they had discussed all this.

Katie grinned mischievously. "I'm only kidding! Of course you're going. I'd feel wretched if you guys changed your vacation plans. And feeling wretched is a stressor, and I'm not supposed to add any more of those to my life right now, remember?"

Even though Christy believed that Katie was trying to make a joke, she felt unsettled. It brought up familiar memories of when they were in high school and Christy went on trips when Katie wasn't allowed to.

Eli called from the kitchen, "Is it okay if I give your little ballerina some oatmeal? She's begging for some of mine."

"Sure. Do you mind putting her in the high chair? There's a bib in the third drawer down to the right of the dishwasher. She likes to feed herself if you give her one of the small plastic spoons in the silverware drawer. Be sure to add milk to cool it down."

"Got it."

"Thanks, Eli."

"Just keep in mind that you're dealing with a dad-in-training here."

Christy and Katie smiled. Eli sounded nervous. "You'll do fine," Christy called back.

"You did a great job on the oatmeal," Katie chimed in. "It's just right."

"You sound like Goldilocks." Christy repeated a line she had read to Hana many times. "But Baby Bear's porridge was ju-u-u-ust right. So she ate it all up. Yum."

Katie gave her an odd look.

Christy chuckled. "Be prepared. You'll find yourself quoting fairy tales and cartoons before long, too. I was thinking the other day that somebody should make a trivia game for moms. It could have questions like, complete this sentence: 'You'll have things you'll want to talk about . . .' "

Katie gave Christy an even more peculiar look before taking a stab at finishing the sentence. "So go see a therapist?"

"No." Christy laughed and took on her best game-show host voice. "I'm sorry, the correct answer is, 'I will, too.' "

Katie looked confused.

"It's from basic baby TV shows. You'll see. There are songs, too, that you'll find yourself singing in the shower." To demonstrate, Christy broke into a little ditty about how we all work together to pick up our toys.

Katie shook her head. "I am so not ready to be a mother."

"She's putting the oatmeal in her hair," Eli reported from the kitchen. "What should I do?"

"Coming!" Christy gave Katie a pat on the leg. "You're going to be a wonderful mother. It's nice that God gives us nine months to warm up to the idea before He brings the little blessings into our lives."

Throughout the day Christy kept wishing Katie and Eli could come with them on the trip to Glenbrooke. It would be such a fun memory if all of them could go together. Plus, Christy was going to miss Katie. She had grown used to having her right there for ongoing conversations every day like they used to have when they were college roommates. Going back to texting and trying to find time to do video calls would be hard.

That night when Christy and Todd had gone to bed, she asked if he thought they should postpone the trip or even cancel it.

"I'd hate if Katie had any complications while we were gone, or if, and I don't even want to say the words, she miscarried while we were on vacation."

"Hey, don't go there. Katie's getting good care. She has Eli with her. This is the best place for the two of them to be. They have each other, as it should be. They don't need us hanging around."

Christy partially agreed. Sometimes she felt that Todd didn't understand the intense heart-to-heart bond she had with Katie. She didn't think it was the same between guys.

"Listen." Todd propped himself up on his elbow and kept his voice low. "I know you love Katie. You're kindred hearties or whatever you call yourselves. But we're a family. You and me and Hana. Sometimes we have to put our family in a priority position. Can you see that? How many years have we been trying to go on vacation?"

Christy curled up to Todd and put her arm around his middle. "You're right. I know you're right. I'm going to be thinking about her and praying for her the whole time."

Todd kissed the top of her head. "You would be doing the same thing if you were here. Or if she was back in Kenya. You'd still care about what she's going through as much as you're going to care while you're with your husband and your daughter driving up the coast."

Christy knew how much Todd had been looking forward to this trip. She couldn't do anything for Katie except provide emotional support and maybe make meals and do laundry. They could keep rolling along with their ongoing conversation through texts and calls.

"Okay." Christy tilted her head back and gave Todd a kiss.

"Okay, what?"

"Okay, let's go on vacation and have a good time. Katie and Eli will still be here when we come back, and giving them a quiet haven without a toddler around will make things even more restful for her."

Todd drew Christy close. "Thank you."

"You don't have to thank me." Christy whispered in Todd's ear, "You just have to kiss me. A lot."

Todd didn't have to be asked twice.

The sweetness of their intimate night lingered into the next morning. Christy woke at six thirty, but to her surprise, not because Hana was awake and calling for them. For once, Hana was still sleeping. Christy cuddled up to Todd. In the dim morning light she could see his lips curling up in a grin. Neither of them spoke. They didn't need to. Their closeness was doing all the talking for them. It was the best sort of morning conversation a married couple could have. The joy of their extended moments together felt like a luxury. Todd was usually dressed and ready to leave for work by now, and Christy was usually getting Hana's day going.

In a small way, Christy felt as if they were already on vacation. If this was what it was going to be like not to have to rush to stay on schedule, then she welcomed their overdue retreat.

NINE

The days that led up to Christy and Todd's departure on their road trip were dotted by fun afternoons playing Scrabble with Katie in the guest room and lots of great conversations. Todd and Eli worked on details for taking students to Kenya next summer, and Eli put into motion a plan to do some fundraising and connecting with a number of local schools and churches over the next few weeks.

"Doesn't it feel like God is doing one of His God-things through all this, but we just can't figure out what it is yet?" Katie asked the day before Christy and Todd left for Glenbrooke. "I mean, it's not so great that we have to stay here because of my confinement."

"Confinement?" Christy chuckled at the term Katie chose to use. She had kept to her bed in the mornings, slowly moved to the couch for most of the afternoons to watch TV, and returned to her bed where Eli insisted she eat her dinner each night on a tray.

"Yes, my confinement."

"You've been watching too many Jane Austen movies."

"A person in my condition can never watch too many Jane Austen movies."

"I won't argue with that."

"But I do believe, my dear." Katie took on a funny British accent and straightened her posture in bed. "I shall make good use of your absence by availing myself of the remote control. Not that I haven't found pleasure in watching a singing tiger with Hana for hours on end or reruns of surfing competitions with your charming husband. But I shall catch up on all the delightful series that aired whilst I was sequestered in deepest, darkest Africa."

Katie's accent waned. She cleared her throat and returned to her normal voice. "All entertainment options aside, what I was starting to say is that I think it's a God-thing for us to be here and for Eli to be able to work on fund-raising."

"I agree. You've had a great attitude about it all."

Katie shrugged. "What other time in my life will I get to wear pj's all day, have my meals brought to me in bed and, best of all, sleep as much as I want?"

"True."

"I mean, who wouldn't want to enjoy such a life of leisure?"

"I'm just glad you're doing better." Christy didn't mention an episode of slight spotting Katie had yesterday. Linda hadn't been overly concerned when Katie called her, so Christy took her cue from Aunt Linda and chose to believe it wasn't serious.

"Are you guys still planning to pull out of here around seven tomorrow morning?" Katie asked.

"Yes, that's the plan. We'll try to be quiet, but I have a feeling we won't be very successful."

"Don't worry. I'm sure Eli will be up and out the door by then, now that Todd has turned him into a surfer boy." Katie grinned. "Who would have ever guessed that my 'Goatee Guy' would turn into 'Surfer Boy'?"

Christy hadn't heard Katie call her husband by that college nickname for a long time. When Katie first met Eli at Christy and Todd's wedding, Katie had decided that his most distinctive feature was his goatee, and until she knew his name, she referred to him as "Goatee Guy."

Christy was more concerned at the moment that Eli be "Attentive Guy" while they were gone. "I hope Eli won't be out surfing very long. I hate the thought of you being here alone."

"I'll be fine, Christy, really. Your mom said she was going to stop by tomorrow. Your aunt and uncle have let me know that they are bringing dinner on Tuesday, Friday, and Sunday. It's going to be a regular circus around here."

"I hope everything goes smoothly."

Katie reached for Christy's hand and gave it a squeeze. "It will. Go have a wonderful vacation. Say hi to everybody for us and promise me you won't worry." She waited for Christy's reply with her chin down and her clear green eyes looking brighter and clearer than they had since she had arrived in California. If Katie's shining eyes were any indication of the improvement in her health, she was in good shape.

"I promise," Christy said solemnly. "I won't worry. But I will pray. Lots."

"Good. And I'll be praying for you guys."

Christy found it easier to keep her promise not to worry than she thought it would be. The excitement and last-minute rush took over and she, Todd, and Hana were on the road, heading up the coast an hour into their road trip before she even thought of Katie. Christy prayed for her and for safe travels for them. As she did, she felt her shoulders relax and her eyebrows lift. She hummed along with the mix of songs Todd had put together for their trip. Hana was content in the backseat. Gussie the Bussie was scooting along smoothly after her recent tune-up and oil change. She even had new tires.

Christy had gone over the to-do lists thoroughly the night before and felt confident they had packed everything they needed. She had nothing to worry about.

They were just past Thousand Oaks and heading up the 101 freeway on their way to Santa Barbara when Todd suddenly said, "Oh no."

"What?" Christy scanned the dashboard, expecting a red light to show that something was wrong with Gussie's engine.

"I forgot my phone."

"I saw it on the counter next to your car keys."

"I know. I was charging it. I was going to give it another few minutes while I put Hana in her car seat. Man! I can't believe I forgot it." Todd was changing lanes, preparing to exit at the next off-ramp.

"Are you going to go back?" Christy's

heart sank. They had been on the road for more than two hours. Their plan was to spend the afternoon and night with Sierra and Jordan in Santa Barbara. If they turned around, it would cut out at least five and probably closer to six hours of the time to spend with them. Not to mention the sense of defeat it would give to their adventure.

Todd didn't answer. The first available off-ramp came up, and he kept going. He still hadn't said anything.

"So, we're not going back?"

"You know what? I can live without my phone for a few days. Could you text Eli and ask him to mail it to us at Doug and Tracy's?"

Christy pulled out her phone for the first time since they had left and noticed that she had three missed phone calls and four text messages from Katie. The first text was about Todd's phone. The next was also about Todd's phone. The third text suggested they mail it to Glenbrooke, and the fourth text asked which button to push on the remote control to get the movie menu.

Christy replied in one long text and forwarded Doug and Tracy's address in case Katie and Eli didn't have it. Then she texted Tracy and told her to watch for a box from Eli. She sent another text to Katie reminding her to have Eli include the phone charger.

When Christy finally looked up, they were already in Ventura.

"I think you have the right idea," she told Todd. "I just disappeared for that whole stretch of road. I can't go cold turkey like you, but I'm going to try to stay off my phone as much as I can."

"Good. It might help us both feel like we're really on vacation. Is Hana asleep?"

Christy leaned over through the opening between the front two seats to look at their awfully quiet daughter.

"Yes," Christy said softly. "This is early for her nap. I think the music did it. Let's keep that track of songs handy for when she has her fussy moments."

"Our daughter? Fussy?" Todd said sarcastically, giving Christy a side wink.

"She's gotten a lot better about the whining, have you noticed?"

"Yeah, now that you say that, she isn't doing that really annoying whine anymore. I'm sure the teething had a lot to do with it. Do you think our son will whine like that, too?"

"Our son?"

"Aren't we ready to have another one? We're past due, according to my plan. But since we're on God's plan, I've been asking

Him if He might bless us with a fresh baby."

Christy gazed at her husband's profile as he drove. Never once in her teen years did she dream about a moment like this where Todd would be driving a VW Bus and talking about having a "fresh baby."

Thinking a moment before answering him, Christy remembered how she had been reluctant to start trying almost a year ago when Todd was eager to repeat the adventure. She was too immersed in diapers and too sleep deprived to think about having two under the age of two. Now, things felt different. She found she missed the newborn coos and the motherly bliss of watching her baby sleep in a snug swaddle with a look of serenity.

"I'm going to be thirty-two next year," Todd said. "I don't want to be the oldest dad at our kid's graduation."

Christy countered Todd's reality check with, "I'm going to be twenty-nine next month." Christy let that number sink in. "Wow, you're right. We are getting old."

"Watching Katie and Eli go through everything made me realize how easy you and I had it with Hana."

"Easy?" Christy laughed. "You can say that because you weren't the one throwing up and getting kicked in the gut in the middle of the night. And you didn't have to push that chunky monkey into this world."

"I know." Todd's tone sounded as if he had heard Christy's half-teasing, half-serious birthing lament one too many times. She never wanted to be one of those mothers who shared her labor and delivery stories at dinner with friends or made it sound like she was some sort of saintly martyr for bringing a child into the world. Still, every now and then, she found herself slipping into you-should-appreciate-me-more mode.

"You're right, though. We did have it relatively easy with Hana," Christy conceded. "Who knows if we'll even be able to have another child or if the pregnancy will be normal and fairly easy."

Todd's mouth turned up into a half grin, showing his dimple. He turned to Christy and said, "Only one way to find out."

"Okay." Christy's voice as well as her heart were steady as she said, "Let's start trying and see what happens."

Todd glanced at her again. "Really?"

Christy smiled and nodded. "Yes. I'm ready for a fresh, new baby."

The rest of their jaunt to Santa Barbara along the sunny coastline was sprinkled with lots of dreaming and discussing the details of what it might be like to have another child. Todd brought up the possibility of adopting, as he had on other long car trips. It seemed that when he was behind the wheel, he was more relaxed and eager to process things he had been thinking about on his own for months.

His list of thoughts was long. Becoming foster parents, moving to a bigger house, finding a way to buy a house, trying to have at least one more child but he was open to having four or five total, if Christy wanted that many, too. Todd had been thinking about getting more schooling so he could qualify for a higher pay scale. He liked teaching Bible classes at South Coast Academy and hoped to stay on there a long time. He also shared that he had talked to Doug about doing some recording of their original worship songs while they were in Glenbrooke, and Doug had set up time with a friend there who had an in-home studio.

Gussie slowed as they came to the first stoplight inside the Santa Barbara area. Todd turned off his waterfall of future possibilities, leaving Christy drenched from the downpour. Her mind seemed to be blinking and gasping for air.

My husband is a deep well. He keeps all these things inside and then, whoa, look out!

It's a deluge of ideas.

What Christy had learned over the last few years of their marriage was that even though Todd had lots of ideas, that didn't mean he was ready to put any or all of them into motion. When he shared with her like this, it was as if he was going through a sorting and stacking exercise. Sometimes as he listened to himself talk he'd verbally cross ideas off the list. Christy knew it was best to just listen.

Hana awoke with a wail when the car stopped at the light. The continual motion seemed to have lulled her to sleep and kept her in dreamland for several hours.

"We're almost there, Hana honey." Christy reached back and rubbed Hana's arm. "It's okay. You'll be able to get out in just a few minutes."

Hana didn't seem convinced. She kept crying in a way that always broke Christy's heart. It was a cry for help. It meant she wanted a dry diaper, or a drink of water, or a change of position from the car seat. All of those needs would be met and more in just a few minutes, but of course Hana wanted all of it right now.

The directions to Sierra and Jordan's home were in Christy's phone so she turned on the program and let the phone tell Todd where to go. A few minutes turned into five heading up into the Santa Barbara hillside while Christy tried offering a sippy cup of water, a book, a cracker, anything to calm Hana down.

"I can't hear the directions," Todd said.

Christy turned up the volume on her phone and checked the map so she could tell Todd when to turn right or left or go straight.

"It says we'll be at our destination in two minutes." Then to Hana she repeated, as if it would do any good. "Two minutes, sweetheart. Hang in there. It's not much farther."

Just as they were turning on the last street, Christy remembered the music and turned it back on. Hana instantly quieted. Christy was sure the music deserved the credit, but Todd said she had worn herself out.

They drove through an open gate of an old hillside estate and found the cottage on the left side, as Sierra had described in her last e-mail. The bungalow had a bright primrose-blue front door and looked as if it might have once been the gardener's shed. Around the front of the cottage were a variety of plants all healthy and sprouting from colorful pots. A garden gnome with a red pointed hat stood guard at the start of the short path that led to the front door.

Todd had just turned off the engine when the front door opened and Sierra stepped out, waving with both hands. Her wild, curly blonde hair seemed to be waving, too. Her hair was always the first thing people noticed about free-spirited Sierra. What Christy also noticed was that Sierra was wearing red cowboy boots. Red! As long as Christy had known her, Sierra had worn an old pair of beat-up cowboy boots. She was definitely stepping things up now with the red boots.

"Welcome!" Sierra called out as her boots clicked down the short path to the gravel driveway. "You found us okay. I'm so happy you're here."

Christy was met with a hug and the scent of wild jasmine before she had even gotten out of the car. Sierra trotted around and hugged Todd in front of the bus and said, "Where's that baby?"

"She's not much of a baby anymore."

Hana had kept her cool in the midst of all the action. As soon as the side door was opened and she saw effusive Sierra with her wild hair and big smile, she let out another wail.

"Oh! Are you tired of that car seat?" Sierra said in a soothing voice. "I have toys waiting for you inside. And graham crackers. Does your mommy let you eat graham crackers?"

At the word "crackers" Hana perked up. It gave Todd enough time to reach in and unlatch her from her seat. He carried her toward the cottage as all the way Hana kept saying, "Kaker. Kaker."

Christy had a pretty good idea that Hana needed a big diaper change. She had grabbed the baby bag but wished she had changed Hana in the car. It's never a good idea to walk into a friend's house for the first time and immediately lay your child on the floor to change a dirty diaper.

"I think she needs a freshie," Christy said to Todd right before they stepped inside. "Do you want me to take her?"

"No. I'll get a cracker from Sierra and then take her in another room. Where's the baby bag?"

Christy handed it to him, and Sierra quickly made good on her promise of a graham cracker. They all seemed to work in unison to keep Hana distracted. Sierra pointed out the bathroom, and Todd went in looking like a champ.

Christy took in the charmingly decorated living room. "Sierra, this is adorable. It's like a Hobbit house."

Sierra broke into an expression that was familiar to Christy from when they had first met at a real castle in England. They were both there on a short-term missions trip, and the mission organization had transformed a rambling old manor into a fabulous training and housing center for outreach teams that traveled all over Europe.

"I'm so happy you said that." Sierra didn't have on any makeup. Her skin looked smooth and natural, just like the tone of her voice. "Cozy Hobbit style was exactly what Jordan and I were going for. No one else has ever made the connection. I've heard that it reminds people of a Hansel and Gretel house or the Seven Dwarves' cottage. You're the first person to say that." Sierra hugged Christy again and began the grand tour.

"This is the living room, all four square inches of it." Sierra laughed. "As you see it opens to the miniature kitchen, complete with a motorhome-sized refrigerator and two stove-top burners." Sierra pointed to the right. "Through there is the one and only bedroom, which is actually a nice size. And you already know where the bathroom is. Four hundred and seventy-five feet of comfort and everything we need. The best part, though, is the patio around back. I'll show it to you when Todd's ready."

The bathroom door opened, and Todd

came out with Hana in his arms and a wadded-up diaper in his hand. "Where do you dispose of your toxic waste?"

Sierra laughed. "Outside. Come on. We have to go past the trash and recycle bins to get to the best feature of this house: the patio. Or as Jordan calls it, 'The Fiesta Room.' "

TEN

Sierra led them out the front door and along a path of stepping-stones past three trash bins and a compost pile. The path turned, and they came to a large, hidden patio. Christy stopped the moment it came into view. Once again, everything about the space shouted "Sierra's personality has been here!" Tucked under a circle of tall trees was a large cement pad that was circled by more beautiful plants in colorful pots. Instead of a standard patio table, the area was set up like an outdoor living room with two big sofas and an old trunk for a coffee table. An old surfboard had been converted into a side bar with three bar stools. A wooden pergola covered the entire area. Café lights hung from the beams, and a fragrant honeysuckle plant wound its way up one side on a woven lattice.

"Wow!" Christy said. "This is very you, Sierra. I love this space."

"It's almost as big as the inside of our house so we spend a lot of time out here. You can see why Jordan named it the Fiesta Room."

Hana wiggled out of Todd's arms and headed for a basket of toys in the corner.

"Is it okay if she gets into those?" Todd asked.

"Of course! That's what I have them here for. We have a home group that meets here every week, and I keep toys on hand for the toddlers."

Hana pulled out a squeaky mouse toy and found great delight in toddling up to each of them and showing them how it made noise.

Sierra settled on one of the sofas and patted the dusty but comfy-looking cushion next to her. "Where do we start? You guys go first. Oh, wait! Are you thirsty?" She popped up and went over to a pitcher on the end of the surfboard bar. "I have iced mint and cucumber water. Would you like some?"

"Sure!" Christy responded while Todd nodded.

"Okay, now," Sierra said as soon as she had handed them tall glasses of the flavored water with floating mint leaves. "Tell me everything. How's Katie? How's life as parents? How's the teaching job, Todd?"

Todd leaned back. He looked happy. Christy knew this was a high-value time to him — quality time with good friends. Hana came over and sat on his lap. Todd helped her to take small sips from his glass of water as he talked about his position as the Bible teacher at the private Christian high school.

Sierra's husband arrived home a few minutes later. Christy liked Jordan from the first time she had met him. He had a gentlemanly yet friendly way about him and was the kind of person who courteously paid attention, really listening, when he talked with you. His calm demeanor was the ideal contrast to Sierra's outgoing temperament.

Jordan was wearing a baseball cap and had a small device hung around his neck on a lanyard. Christy recognized it as a light gauge used by photographers, which was Jordan's profession.

Pointing at the gauge, Christy asked, "Were you out on a shoot?"

He nodded. "Senior photo season."

Sierra stood and said, "I have some lunch for us. Just stay here; I'll bring it out. You should hear about some of the projects Jordan has going this summer."

Christy offered to help but Sierra insisted she stay put. Hana had found some books to look at and settled at Christy's feet while Jordan told them about the few shots he had sold lately to a surfing magazine. His main flow of income was coming from creative senior pictures of athletes who wanted him to capture them in their element, whether that was surfing, rock climbing, or midair at the skate park.

"I have done a few weddings," he added. "Only two or three. I'm better at capturing action shots than hours of still, posed pictures. And to be honest, I don't have a lot of patience with nervous brides who try to direct the shot as I'm taking it. Too much drama for me."

Todd grinned. "Then don't try being a high school teacher to a bunch of mostly privileged kids. I know all about the drama."

Sierra appeared with a large tray containing a big, beautiful mixed salad and a basket of sliced rosemary bread she had made from scratch using rosemary from her garden. They dined to the sound of birds chirping high in the trees and listened to Sierra's update on her job in town as a waitress at an Italian restaurant.

"I really love what I do and could keep waitressing the rest of my life." Sierra came around with the pitcher of mint water and refilled all the glasses. "I learned something about myself after we got married." She shot Jordan a cute grin. "Jordan helped me figure out that I'm good at helps but not service."

Todd said he knew exactly what she meant. Christy wasn't sure.

"When I was in Brazil, that was long term," Sierra said. "Well, five years. That's not really long term. But my job description was more along the lines of service. Serving day in and day out. It was all about doing the small steps for a long time and not necessarily seeing results. When I started waitressing I felt like I was coming back to life. I could do what I love to do — helping people — but it was short term each day with small, measurable tasks. Take an order. Serve a meal. Clear a table. And when I went home, I was done for the day. I don't know if that makes sense, but I discovered I'm wired for sprints, not marathons."

"It must have been hard to be in Brazil so long and not have a sense of accomplishment," Christy said.

Hana had gotten antsy after eating some of the bread. Christy pulled out a small container of applesauce she kept on hand for moments like this. She tried to feed it to Hana, but once Hana saw the spoon she wanted to do it herself.

"Yes, it was hard. But the experience was

good for me in a lot of ways. It gave me more discipline than a job or schooling here in the U.S. would have. I don't regret any of it." She gave Jordan another broad grin. "I'm just really thankful to be where I am now, waking up to that face every morning."

Hana had made a grand mess with the applesauce, and Christy had used up all the napkins to clean Hana and everything around her.

"How about if I take her for a walk?" Todd suggested. "Is it okay to walk on the grounds? Or should I head back down the driveway to the gate?"

"We can all go if you want," Jordan said. "The owners aren't here this week so we can give you a tour of the grounds. I take care of the yard and pool. That's how we get free rent."

"You don't pay rent?" Christy hadn't realized they had that bonus. No wonder they could make a living at photography and waitressing and still manage a surfing photo trip to Bali, as they had a few years ago.

"He pays it in sweat," Sierra said. "Don't let him tell you that it's a breeze. They have seven acres here and a huge grassy area that he keeps perfectly manicured like a golf course. It takes him hours each week to keep up with all of it, trust me."

"Come on. I'll show you." Jordan led them on a tour. The pool was located behind the huge craftsman-style manor. It had the look of an old Hollywood movie set with white metal chaise loungers and a tea cart, also of white metal, with big round wheels.

"Why does it seem like a fluffy poodle should be sitting over there on that cushion wearing a bow between its ears?" Christy asked. "And over there, a butler wearing a black suit and bowtie with one arm behind his back and the other supporting a silver tray of doggie treats?" She could imagine an entire scene of a vintage film.

Sierra laughed. "That's exactly what it feels like." She kept laughing. "You have the perfect way of describing things, Christy. I have the same impressions, but I don't know how to express them."

"Here's the yard." Jordan led them out of the pool area and through an opening in a hedge of evenly trimmed privacy shrubs. Before them stretched a level, open space that was, as Sierra had said, a perfectly manicured lawn. It did look like an upscale golf course.

"The family has had two garden parties on the lawn since we've lived here," Sierra said. "They put up big white tents and hire a formal waitstaff. I snuck around by the trees over there and watched the first time. It's like *Downton Abbey* or *The Great Gatsby.* So posh."

Hana had started heading back to the pool so Christy and Todd followed hot on her trail, and Jordan and Sierra were right behind.

"Did you wish they had invited you?" Christy asked.

"No!" Sierra's response was immediate and strong. "I would have had such a hard time being around so much wealth. All those years in the favelas in Brazil are deeply imprinted on my soul. You can be very happy with little. Most of the people in the world have very little. Whenever I see people with a lot of money trying to make themselves happy by spending it, I want to break into a lecture about what that money could have paid for in other parts of the world."

Jordan placed his hand on Sierra's shoulder. His touch had an immediate calming effect. "We don't know if they do a lot of philanthropic work. They could donate 90 percent of their income and live here off 10 percent of it. We don't know."

"You're right. I'm just eager to do more, and I want others to do more, too, you know?"

They meandered their way through the rose garden, fragrant and in full bloom. Then they took a short path through the trees and came upon a wooden gazebo that had a porch swing hanging from the center. Todd put Hana on the cushioned seat and swung her back and forth, much to her delight.

The whole time they talked about service, ministry, and outreach programs, as a result of Sierra's passionate words. Todd told them about Eli raising funds and how Todd would organize a group of students to go to Kenya next summer.

"Could you use a photographer?" Jordan asked. "I'd be happy to volunteer and let them use all the photos for future promotion of the ministry."

Todd's expression lit up. "That would be great. Eli said that one of the things he planned to work on while we were gone was a presentation, but he was limited on the number of good photos they had from the villages. He said that when he's with a team, they're working the whole time and none of them thinks to take photos until the end when the system is working and the clean water is coming through the pipes."

"I would love to go, too," Sierra said. "I'm not sure what I could do, but certainly they could use help with something. Christy, what do you think? Are you going? We should all go!"

Todd had a dreamer's look in his silver-blue eyes. He had scooped up Hana and was carrying her as they returned to Jordan and Sierra's patio, now bathed in late-afternoon amber sunlight. "What do you think, *Kilikina*?"

Christy felt her heart stir at the possibility. Her first thought, though, was Hana. She would be two and a half next summer. The immunizations alone would be rough on her at that age. She would have to take malaria pills, and as they knew from going to Kenya for Eli and Katie's wedding, the trip was very long.

"I'd love to, but . . ." She motioned to Hana.

"What if your parents took her for those two weeks? She loves them. It would be her own little adventure," Sierra suggested.

Wait until you're a mama one day, Sierra. You'll understand how painful it is to think of leaving your children for any length of time.

Christy mulled over all the possibilities as the evening stretched its long, lazy shadows over them and the air cooled to the point that she needed a sweater. The café lights were twinkling above them as they enjoyed

Sierra's vegetable lasagna for dinner and kept returning to the topic of the service project next summer.

Christy felt uneasy. She didn't think she could leave her daughter for two weeks. She just couldn't. At the same time, she didn't see how she could put her child through the rigors of the trip to Africa. If Hana were older, Christy didn't think she would be as concerned.

Christy also felt a growing anxiety about how they were going to work out their sleeping arrangements for the night. Hana had fallen asleep on the couch next to Christy wrapped up in one of Sierra's hand-crocheted blankets. The plan had been for the three of them to sleep in Gussie. Todd had altered the fold-down bed in the back so there was room for the portable travel bed they had brought for Hana. That meant Todd had to hoist the back bench seat out of Gussie and leave it outside whenever they set up the sleeping arrangements.

Christy finally got Todd's attention. "What do you think? Is it time to set up our bed?"

He seemed to think Hana was fine where she was and there was no reason to disturb her. Christy knew that Hana's diaper was probably overly full and that could disturb her little princess in the middle of the night

167

and make it a much bigger hassle to change her. Christy also knew that Hana was more likely to settle back in and go back to sleep if they made the transfer now.

Christy suggested they do everything now. Todd was too comfortable. He thought they should wait until all three of them were ready to turn in. Sierra wanted to keep talking about the trip to Kenya. Jordan was on the topic of the two guys going surfing early in the morning and the different options of where they could go.

The frustration that was building inside Christy made her clench her teeth. No one else seemed to understand what the repercussions would be if they didn't get Hana calmly and securely nestled in for the night. She would be screaming in the middle of the night in Gussie, and Christy would be the one trying to calm her and get her back to sleep. The routine they had at home was the only way Christy had gotten Hana to sleep through the night. A warm bath at six forty-five, five books read to her in soft light, a cuddle in the rocking chair with a song sung in her ear, a kiss, a prayer, a hand on her forehead, and a blessing. And, of course, Hana's favorite stuffed bunny.

When Christy's mind could no longer handle the thought of how her daughter would be acting in the dead of the night, Christy interrupted the conversation everyone else seemed to be enjoying. "Todd, I need you to help me get Hana settled in her bed. We need to do it now."

He looked surprised at his wife's emphasis on the "now." Hana was still sleeping contentedly, but Christy was sure her expression let him know that she was mad.

"Okay," he said slowly.

"Why don't we all call it a night?" Sierra collected the dinner plates. Jordan looked at her the way Todd had looked at Christy, as if there was no reason to spoil such a great evening.

"I hate to be the one to step out," Christy said. "But if I don't get her in a dry diaper and settled in, it won't go well for us in the middle of the night."

Sierra seemed to understand more than the guys did. They all adjusted to Christy's request, and as soon as Christy picked Hana up, she started crying. Christy felt the tension building as she followed Todd around the house and down to Gussie. He had to find a flashlight so he could see to unhitch the bench seat and yank it out of the car. Hana's foldup bed was packed on Gussie's roof with some camping gear that was all tied down. It took another fifteen minutes for Todd to undo everything in the dark while Christy was inside the van struggling to change Hana's diaper, dress her in her jammies, and convince her to stop crying. Nothing seemed to be working.

"Maybe she's thirsty," Todd suggested in a voice that seemed too loud and gruff to Christy. She could tell he wished they had stuck with his plan of doing nothing. What he didn't realize was that they would have to do all this eventually. For Hana's internal clock it was better to attempt it at eight o'clock rather than wait until the adults were done socializing and ready to go to bed at midnight.

Most of all, Christy hated being the one who initiated all the "drama" as Jordan and Todd had referred to it earlier when talking about their high school students. Why couldn't Todd understand how difficult managing an inflexible toddler was? He wasn't the one who had experimented for months before coming up with the best system to insure that Hana slept through the night.

The whole process of readying their bed, finding Hana something to drink, taking turns inside the house so they could use the bathroom and get ready for bed took almost an hour. Hana had cried herself to sleep in her portable bed. She lay on her side with her bunny's ear clasped in her fist.

Christy tried to quietly slip into the bed on her side next to the window so Todd could be closer to the sliding door. The space felt smaller than she remembered from the last time they had gone camping, which was a long time ago. Todd returned from his trip to the house. He got into the bus and closed the sliding door as quietly as possible. Hana stirred but didn't wake up.

Crawling into his side of the bed, Todd mumbled, "Let's not do this again."

Christy didn't know if he meant not sleep in the van again, or if he was realizing why it was important to keep Hana on her usual schedule while they were on vacation. Whatever his meaning, Christy knew she would have to wait until tomorrow to find out. Todd had turned his back to her. He wouldn't argue in their confined quarters. She also knew that if she pressed him to talk to her right now, it might not go well.

For a long while she laid scrunched up on her side listening to the ruffled breathing of her baby girl as it played the flute notes of the night in concert with Todd's long bass notes that seemed to rumble from his chest.

Unsettled emotions always got the best of Christy. She struggled not to let her feelings

171

sound the blaring bassoon notes of aggravation in her head and upset the natural melody of life playing out around her. This was only the first night of their vacation. She knew they would have to make adjustments. She had predicted early on that Gussie would be less than ideal for the three of them even with the alterations Todd worked so hard to make.

She tried to pray. Tried to release the tension. Tried to stop expecting Hana to wake at any moment. Tried to sleep. Tried and tried until at last her body and mind linked arms and took her to the land of Nod.

ELEVEN

Christy was stunned when she awoke. The early morning light was sending a beam through the windshield of Gussie, etching a thread of pure gold between the front seats, across Hana's bed, and onto the clump of covers Todd had tossed off sometime during the night.

She had slept.

Hana had slept and was still sleeping.

Todd was adjusting his sleeping position. His eyes were half opened. He turned his head and tried to focus on Christy's expression. "You okay?" His voice was low but still carried the irritation — or perhaps it was apprehension — she had heard in it last night when he made his "Let's not do this again" statement.

Christy considered her response for only a moment before she nodded and offered him a slight but sincere grin.

"You okay if I go surfing?"

"Of course," Christy whispered.

Todd bent over and kissed her. It had to be one of the worst smelling kisses she had ever had. All that garlic and the Italian spices in Sierra's vegetarian lasagna had not fully vacated Todd's breath. She wondered if he even brushed his teeth last night.

"Later." Todd slowly opened the side door of Gussie and made his exit as quickly, albeit awkwardly, as possible. Not even one inch of extra space existed for them inside Gussie when the bed was down and Hana's bed was set up.

The commotion was enough to cause Hana to stir. Christy tried to lie still, as if turning into a slit-eyed mannequin would enable her to watch her daughter while at the same time convince her that it was still nighty-night time.

Christy's attempt failed. Hana was fully awake. She was hungry and wet and not at all interested in joining Christy in bed to enjoy a morning cuddle. With an awkward reenactment of Todd's exit from the van, Christy shuffled up to the bungalow's front door carrying Hana on one hip and a beach bag full of their clothes, diapers, and snacks on the other arm.

The guys had already gone but apparently Sierra was still asleep because her bedroom door was closed. Christy tried to take care of herself and Hana in the small bathroom quietly, but at this stage of life, quiet was not possible with Hana. The process took almost half an hour. When the two of them emerged, Sierra was in the kitchen, scrambling eggs and warming up some cinnamon rolls. The fragrance that greeted them was wonderful.

"I was so excited to make these cinnamon rolls for you guys. They're the same ones we had at our wedding. Do you remember that I worked at Mama Bear's Cinnamon Rolls when I was in high school? It's her recipe. She doesn't share it with anyone, but she gave it to me."

"I think Todd and I met the couple you worked for when we were at your wedding. Very sweet people."

"Yes, they are." Sierra leaned down and offered Hana a nibble of warm cinnamon roll. "Are you hungry, Sweetie Bean?" Looking up at Christy she asked, "How did she do last night?"

"Great. She slept all the way through." Christy stepped into the kitchen so she could look Sierra in the eyes. "Sorry I made such an issue of getting her to bed last night."

"Don't worry about it. Listen, I grew up

in a family with six kids. I spent five years around kids in Brazil. It takes a lot to fluster me when it comes to kids and their needs." She looked down at Hana, who was jabbering and holding up her hand. "Oh, you liked that, didn't you? I'll let your mommy decide if you need some eggs first before we give you more of the yummy rolls."

The leisure time Christy had that morning with Sierra was like honey. That's the way she described it to Todd when they were back on the road, driving to the site where they had made camping reservations for the night. They had a chance to talk through the tension from the night before and come up with a plan for setting up their bed every night. Christy understood Todd's perspective of relaxing and letting go of the tight schedule. His case in point was that Hana had slept through the night and probably would have been even more willing to get in her bed if Christy had waited until later, after Todd had a chance to convert the inside of the van.

Todd said he understood Christy's concerns about sticking to the routine. She decided not to jackhammer him with reminders of how difficult Hana's first nine months had been when she didn't sleep through the night. They were on vacation.

Christy knew she needed to lighten up. They had many more nights of trying to adapt to new surroundings.

"I think all the change will help Hana become a more flexible child. What if we made that our goal instead of trying to duplicate everything we do with her at home?"

"You're right. I need to calm down about the schedule. I'm sure Hana can tell when I'm anxious even if I don't say anything."

Todd shot her a half grin. "I'm sure you're right."

"Why are you grinning?"

"I'm simply agreeing with you."

Christy examined his profile and felt her expression involuntarily turning into a frown. "You mean about Hana being able to tell when I'm amped up?"

Todd nodded slowly, looking straight ahead. He seemed to be carefully tiptoeing around the edge of this topic.

"You can always tell when I'm anxious or upset, can't you?"

"I think so. Not always."

Christy leaned back and thought about the kind of vibe her husband and daughter picked up from her expressions and actions. She had a feeling she'd be shocked if someone showed her a video of what she

177

looked like when she was in the throes of a tense situation.

"Sometimes you say the most when you say nothing at all, Kilikina."

Christy let Todd's comment settle on her. She didn't want to react positively or negatively to his observation. She just let the thought sit on her lap like a sleeping kitten. She knew that if there was any chance at all that she and Todd could both go to Kenya next summer and take Hana with them, this trip would be great training.

The drive up Highway 1 was gorgeous, and the view occupied their conversation for the first part of the trip. The road followed the California coast, which meant they had the ocean in view much of the way. When they switched to Highway 101, which was farther inland, they stopped to pick up some snacks and cold drinks. The short break gave Hana a chance to get out and wiggle. When they loaded back up, Christy settled in the backseat, which thrilled Hana and gave Christy a chance to read her some books and play finger-puppet games with her until Hana was ready for a nap. Christy crawled back up to the passenger seat as Todd was driving into the Big Sur area.

"Do you want to stop here for a while?" Christy asked. "I heard you talking about surfing at Big Sur."

"I thought about it. But what would you and Hana do?"

"She's sleeping. I brought books to read. We'll be fine. This is supposed to be our great Surfin' Safari adventure, remember? Seems to me you should surf at all the epic places you always talk about and watch on TV."

Todd looked as if she had just given him a whole pumpkin pie and canister of whipped cream and told him he didn't have to share it with anyone. "Are you sure?"

"Yes." She decided to add a small addendum. "And remember, if I see any really extraordinary fabric stores along the way, you said you would be happy to take Hana for a walk so I could shop my little heart out."

"You're right. I did say that." He looked right and left at the surroundings, which were all countryside without a single store or house in sight. "Don't see any fabric stores at the moment," he said slowly.

"Just wait," Christy said. "I'll find one or two before our journey is over."

"I'm sure you will."

They exchanged the sort of look that was the result of being married for so many years. This was how they expressed mutual respect and consideration of each other's interests. It didn't feel like scorekeeping or trying to balance the scales to Christy. This was the friendship part of their relationship that had taken a while for Todd to understand since he was an only child. The give and take they had developed felt good.

Todd drove into a day-use park facility nestled in a grove of spectacular, tall redwoods and pine trees. Christy knew from the research she and Todd had done before the trip that this area of the California coast was much more rugged and cooler than any of the beach-front parks and campgrounds south of Point Conception. Surfers had to walk a significant distance to reach the water here, and wetsuits were the only way to go, even in the summer. The waves could be large and pounding.

As Christy watched Todd head for the walkway and stairs down the steep cliff to the ocean with his orange surfboard under his arm, she felt a little nervous that he was making the trek on his own. The parking area was almost full and that gave her hope that he wouldn't be the only surfer down there in case of any danger.

Christy took the opportunity to check her phone and try sending some catch-up texts and e-mails. The phone service wasn't strong. She was able to read the messages that had come in earlier and type her responses, but nothing seemed to be going out.

The good news was that Katie was fine. Nobody was awaiting an urgent reply from Christy. She was on vacation. She could relax and dive into one of the books she had brought with her. But she only read to page three before Hana woke up. The usual routine ensued. Change of diaper, something to eat, something to drink, a chance to wiggle and squeal. The final need was easily fulfilled because there was plenty of space to walk and interesting things to pick up like feathers, sticks, and lots of pebbles. Fortunately, Hana had gotten past the stage of putting everything she picked up into her mouth. Uncle Bob watched her once when she was still crawling and had said, "I think she's going to be a scientist. Everything she finds goes into the laboratory of her mouth so she can test it."

The air had been chilly when they first arrived and was getting cooler as a layer of fog rolled in. Christy changed Hana into warmer clothes, and the two of them sat in the front passenger seat with Hana on Christy's lap, looking at books. In what seemed like a matter of minutes, the fog had become so thick Christy could barely make out the objects in front of them. It felt spooky, and she locked the doors, leaving her window open just a crack for fresh air. Hana was tired of the books and wanted to move around. Christy let her roam around inside Gussie and kept a lookout for Todd. She couldn't imagine anyone surfing in these conditions.

I hope he's okay. I don't see anyone else coming back to their cars.

As quickly as the cloud had shrouded them, it thinned, and Christy could see a figure coming their direction carrying a surfboard. "Hana, look, I think it's Daddy. Come sit on my lap, and you can see Daddy."

Hana stopped her game of pulling on the seat belt and crawled up on Christy's lap. To Christy's relief, it was Todd. She had felt a tingle up her neck and wasn't sure if the cause was the chilly air or the fear that something might have happened to him.

"How was the surfing?" She tried to sound as cheerful as possible as he stood outside her open window, looking cold and out of breath.

"Rough. I caught one. I can say . . ." He caught his breath. "I can say I rode Big Sur. Give me a minute to rinse off. Could you pull out some warm clothes for me?"

Getting to their clothes was easier said than done, especially with Hana repeatedly calling out, "Dada, Dada, Dada" and trying to find a way out of the van. The distraught baby syndrome continued when Todd returned from the public restrooms and took a while reattaching his surfboard to the van's roof. Hana wanted her daddy. Her daddy wanted to get on the road with the car's heater cranked up as high as it would go. Hana wailed as if the car seat was a prison and her daddy a thousand miles away instead of only a few feet away, talking to her, singing to her, trying everything he could to calm her hysterics.

"Was she like this the whole time?"

"No, she was fine." Christy was trying to set the car stereo to one of the kids' audio books she had bought before the trip. Tracy had sent a list of recommended ones that included different voices for the characters in the short stories and had calming music at the beginning and end. She pushed the button, and the sound of a jazzy clarinet filled the van's overly heated cab.

"Whoa! Not that one."

Hana instantly quieted, listening for more music.

"Okay, maybe this one after all." Christy

turned it back on and set the speakers to play only in the back so she and Todd could talk. Hana reached into her pouch of toys and picked up the squeaky mouse that Sierra had sent with her. Peace prevailed, with only occasional squeaks from Mr. Mouse.

"You're a good mom, Christy." The discomfort lines had dissolved from Todd's forehead. He kept his focus straight ahead on the winding road. The fog was still settled on them like a sheer veil that made it difficult to gauge the distance of oncoming cars.

"I don't think we should do that again," Todd said.

Christy waited, thinking he was about to process last night again.

"I didn't like that I left you and Hana waiting in the parking lot like that. I couldn't even call you to make sure you were okay. I don't want to have separate vacations. We're doing this as a family. If I want to plan some epic surf-the-coast trip, I need to do it with some guys. Not with you and Hana."

His words hit Christy in an odd place. In one way she was grateful that he was thinking of them and not trying to put his interests and comforts before theirs. In another way, she felt like a lug. A weight.

Before they had Hana they had done a surfing weekend campout. It was a great weekend for both of them. Being a mom had limited Christy's life in ways she hadn't fully expected.

"I still wish that we could do everything," Christy said. "We told each other that having a baby wouldn't change us or our lives, but it has. It does. It just does."

"Let's come up with some things we can do together as a family," Todd suggested.

Christy pulled out her phone, and when she had better cell service, she looked up things to do in Monterey, since they would be driving through there on the way to the campground at Sunset State Beach. The Monterey Bay Aquarium came up as the best family-friendly outing.

When she calculated the admission cost for the three of them, she quickly changed her suggestion to enjoying the campsite as a family instead. They were on a tight budget. Plus it seemed best to wait until Hana was older so she could better understand what she was seeing and have the patience to enjoy the experience.

Hana was enjoying her stories and was in a happy mood when they stopped in the charming coastal town of Carmel-by-the-Sea. Aunt Marti had recommended a place to eat. They tracked down the adorable-looking restaurant only to discover it was only open for dinner. So, with Hana in the stroller, they explored on their own, deciding they would find their own favorite restaurant to recommend to Bob and Marti the next time they came here.

Most of the restaurants they strolled past were Italian, and nothing on the posted menus struck their fancy. Christy spotted a small café off the main street, down a flower-lined alleyway. The small tables outside worked great for Hana, who was content to stay in her stroller as long as Todd and Christy kept filling her tray with food. The prices were good. Christy's roast beef sandwich was great, and Todd thought the fish tacos were "decent."

On their walk back to the van, Christy kept slowing down in front of the windows of many intriguing-looking shops. "You know, if you ever take that all-guys surfing trip, I'm going to take an all-girls shopping trip and come back here."

"Did you want to go in one of the shops?" Todd stopped pushing the stroller. "Did we go past a fabric shop and I missed it? We'd better go back."

Christy could hear the teasing tone in his voice. "No, we didn't miss a fabric store.

I'm good. We need to get on the road."

"I hope you'll tell me if there's any place you want to stop." He was serious this time.

Christy looped her arm through his. Her tummy was happy. Her baby girl was happy. Her husband was handsome and happy. This was all she wanted.

On the drive the rest of that day Christy felt the same sort of happiness. The scenery was beautiful. The weather was at its Northern California best. The audio storybooks and the music kept Hana content. She slept all night again in her folding bed. Nothing was amiss with the journey. Except that it felt like it was taking forever to arrive in Oregon.

They had puttered up the long and winding Highway 1 until they got closer to San Francisco and returned to the 101 freeway so they could drive over the Golden Gate Bridge. Christy liked that part of the trip and took pictures of the bay from her open car window. She welcomed the fond memories of when, as a fifteen-year-old, she had flown to San Francisco with Bob and Marti. So many memories.

But after getting through the traffic in the Bay Area, Christy persuaded Todd not to return to Highway 1. She wanted to get to Oregon and see their friends. Her brother had texted twice asking what day they were going to show up, and Christy answered both times that she didn't know. They were on vacation, she reminded him. They were taking their time, and then she added something about how it's not the destination but the journey.

David finally responded with a text that Christy received as they were driving through Santa Rosa.

I HAVE A GIRLFRIEND. I WANT YOU TO GET HERE SO YOU CAN MEET HER BEFORE SHE LEAVES ON TUESDAY.

Christy read the text twice before reading it to Todd. "I guess Aunt Marti was right." Christy felt a lump growing in her throat. "Todd, my brother has a girlfriend." She repeated the sweet and stunning news as if she needed to hear it aloud before she believed it.

Todd turned to Christy and grinned. "And he wants us to meet her. I'm stoked. Are you?"

Christy pulled up a map on her phone and tried to gauge the distance between Santa Rosa and Glenbrooke. They still had a long way to go.

"Todd, we have to get there before Tuesday. Drive faster!"

TWELVE

After they arrived in Glenbrooke Monday evening, Christy concluded that a leisurely summer tootle up the coast was great if you didn't have a toddler, didn't have anywhere to be, and didn't have anyone to see. In this season of life, the need for speed became real for Christy and Todd. However, the need to make more frequent stops to let Hana get her wiggles out was even more real.

David had arranged for them to stay at a cabin at Camp Heather Brook where he was working so that's where they set their course. They found the camp easily and parked in a gravel area. They could hear hundreds of teens cheering in the distance. A friendly looking woman wearing jeans and a polo shirt embroidered with the camp logo walked past them carrying a stack of bath towels.

"Hello." She kept walking. Her medium-length brown hair was pulled back in a ponytail that bobbed as she continued her way.

"Excuse me," Todd called after her. "We need to find one of the guys on staff here. Do you know David Miller?"

The woman's smile broadened. She came trotting back on the gravel. "Are you Todd and Christy?"

"Yes."

"Hi! Welcome." She extended her right hand from under the stack of towels. "I'm Shelly. My husband, Jonathan, and I run the camp. I heard you might be rolling in tonight. These are for your cabin. We're so glad you're here."

"So are we." Christy meant it. She was tired of sitting. Tired of trying to keep Hana entertained. Tired of the endless stream of big freight trucks that zoomed past them on the freeway for the past few hours. The thought of sleeping in a bed that night in their own cabin thrilled her road-weary soul.

Todd took Hana out of her car seat and put her on the ground. She immediately picked up gravel so Christy scooped her up and shook the pebbles from her eager paw, much to Hana's dismay.

"You can drive to the cabin," Shelly said. "That should make it easier to unpack. It's the one on the far right at the end of the road I was starting down. I can ride there with you, if you like."

They all loaded up in the van. Since Hana was already fussing, and Christy knew she would have a meltdown if she was strapped back in her car seat, Christy suggested that Shelly sit in the passenger seat and Christy would hold Hana for the ride down the dirt road to the cabin. It was against all sensibilities not to strap her daughter in. Christy wasn't one to break the rules. Fortunately, the cabin was close, and the road wasn't too rough. Hana barely bumped about at all.

She was happy to get out again and immediately trotted over to the three steps that led up to the small porch. Two rocking chairs crafted out of bent willow branches caught her eye. Hana desperately wanted to climb up in one of the chairs by herself. Shelly opened the unlocked cabin door and welcomed them inside.

Todd stayed behind, monitoring Hana as she tried to hoist herself up. Christy followed Shelly into the tidy log cabin. It was more of a log bedroom. The space was larger than it looked from the outside. In the far right corner was a king-sized bed with a distinctive wooden headboard. To the left was a bunk bed and next to the bunk bed a portable baby bed had been set up. Next to the door were a sofa, lamp, and end table. To the back of the cabin was a door that opened into a small bathroom with a shower. The décor was homey and felt rustic but inviting.

"This is nice," Christy said. "Thank you for letting us stay here."

"It's our pleasure. We have two cabins we reserve for guests like you. This is the larger one. I hope you'll be comfortable here."

"I'm sure we will."

Shelly turned to go. "I don't know if David let you know, but you are welcome to join us in the dining hall for any and all meals. The schedule for this week along with the menu is on the back of the door. Let me know if you need anything."

Another round of cheers from the happy campers rose in the evening air. Shelly nodded to her left. "It's the first night of the tug-of-war competition over in the meadow. We have 350 high schoolers here this week so be warned. The mealtimes and most other times will be pretty rowdy."

Todd spoke up from the front porch. "Good to know. We were worried that our daughter might be the loudest person around."

"Not a chance." Shelly stopped on the porch and Christy followed her. Shelly leaned down to Hana's eye level. "You have some strong competition for those lungs, little one."

Hana fixed her gaze on Shelly as if trying to figure out who she was.

"You are adorable." Shelly looked up at Christy and then at Todd. "I was going to say you got your mommy's eyes, but maybe it's your daddy's eyes."

Hana had taken command of the rocking chair, sitting pretty, smiling like an angel and letting her daddy slowly rock her as she kept staring at Shelly.

"I'll see you guys around. Have a great, restful week." Shelly waved good-bye to Hana.

Christy took over the careful rocking of the little princess while Todd unloaded the van. She pulled her phone out of her back jeans pocket and texted David to let him know they had arrived. He texted back right away.

DON'T GO ANYWHERE. FINA AND I WILL BE RIGHT THERE.

Christy looked up and saw Todd hauling more than he probably should carry in one load. Behind him, across the way, she could see dozens and then hundreds of teenagers pouring into the main part of camp, heading for the large meeting hall. It had been a long time since Christy had been around a swarm of teenagers like that. There was a definite buoyancy in their cheers and energetic movements. Even their clothes seemed colorful and youthful.

Todd put down the gear inside the cabin and joined Christy on the porch, watching the migration.

"Were we ever that young?" Christy asked.

"Long, long ago," Todd said wistfully. "In a universe far, far away."

Christy thought a moment and looked at Todd. "Isn't it galaxy? A galaxy far, far away?"

Todd shrugged. "I was always more of a Trekkie."

Christy laughed. That one was hard to believe. Her husband had always been an individual. A starter, not a joiner. He was never a fan of anything that was especially popular. She held up her hand and tried to get her fingers to line up in a way that would resemble Spock's signature hand greeting. "Live long and prosper."

"What are you doing?" he asked.

Christy grinned with satisfaction. "You just proved my point, you fake Trekkie."

Just then a bellowing voice called out to

them. Christy looked to the right and spotted her brother, her grown-up man-child brother, jogging toward them. David was wearing a cowboy hat, jeans, and a plaid cowboy-style shirt with silver snaps on the pockets. He had a bandana around his neck and a lasso linked to his jeans.

"Well, howdy, partner," Christy called out playfully. She noticed his big, shiny sheriff's badge that looked like it was made out of aluminum foil.

"It's for our skit tonight. Hey, you made it." He gave Christy a big, sweaty hug first and then did a clasped-hands/shoulder-bump sort of hello to Todd. "Hi, Hana." David leaned over. "What do you think of Camp Heather Brook so far?"

"The rocking chair is a big hit," Christy said.

"Listen, I've gotta run over to help start the evening meeting. Are you guys going anywhere tonight?"

Christy and Todd exchanged glances. "No. We just got here."

"Good. I didn't know if you had plans with Doug and Tracy or some of your other friends. Hey, I've gotta' go, but I'll be back in about an hour with Fina."

"Fina?" Christy echoed.

David had already started toward the

meeting hall. "Short for Josephina. You'll love her!" He turned and broke into a run, the loopy lasso flapping against his leg like a broken wing.

"Who was that?" Christy asked.

"Someone from your side of the family," Todd teased. "Not mine."

"What happened to my brainy little brother?"

"Once again, that was long, long ago, in a district far, far away."

"You have your futuristic shows all mixed up, Todd."

"You think I'm mixed up?" Todd had taken on his sly half grin. "I'm not the one galloping around in a cowboy hat wearing a sheriff's badge."

Christy contemplated the blur that had been her brother. "He was so happy."

"Come on, let's settle in so we can put Hana to bed. We can wait out here on the porch for Sheriff MacHappy to come riding back to see us."

The cabin turned out to be ideal for their inquisitive toddler. Hana had plenty of things to touch but nothing was dangerous. Todd unpacked her toys and clothes while Christy checked out the shower. She hadn't given Hana many showers yet, but this little girl definitely needed more than another washcloth wipe down. It took a little coercing and Christy got soaking wet, but she managed to clean up Hana, wash her hair, and even brush her teeth. The bonus was that Todd found a pair of jammies that Hana hadn't worn yet. She was fresh all the way around.

Todd sat on the sofa with her as Christy pulled out some warm clothes for herself. Since she had gotten so wet, she decided to take a quick, hot shower and oh, did that feel good. Christy hadn't planned to wash her hair, but it felt so good to lather up and rinse her long locks in the cascade of hot water.

Such a luxury! We only camped for three nights, but it seems like it was three weeks.

Christy hurried to run her hair dryer while Todd was still reading to Hana and getting her settled in. The disadvantage of this nice cabin was that they didn't have a separate space to put Hana. They wouldn't be able to turn on a light when they were ready for bed later.

"Do you mind taking over here?" Todd copied Christy and ducked into the shower.

Christy read Hana one more story, cuddled her, sang in her ear, and then tucked her into the baby bed with her bunny. Hana didn't stay lying down. She popped up and held on to the corners of the portable crib.

"Mama. Dada."

"I'm right here, Hana. Daddy is right here, too. I know this is a new place for you to sleep, but we will be right here with you all night long. It's time to go to sleep."

Todd came out of the bathroom with his Rancho Corona hoodie over his head. He went to Hana and firmly said, "Lie down, Sunshine. I want to bless you."

Hana immediately lay on her back and looked up at them with her big blue eyes full of cuteness and expectation. She put her pacifier in her mouth and waited for Todd's hand to rest on her forehead. Apparently this was what she was waiting for, her nightly prayer and blessing.

Christy said a prayer in her sweetest mommy voice. Todd spoke his blessing over Hana. "Hana, may the Lord bless you and keep you. May the Lord make His face to shine upon you and give you His peace. And may you always love Jesus first, above all else."

He lifted his hand, and they could see that her eyes were closed. Her little mouth was rhythmically working on her pacifier. Todd motioned for Christy to follow him out to the porch. Taking the rocking chair next to Todd, Christy sat down and remarked at how comfortable the rockers were.

"Hana knows a good thing when she sees it. I think this is going to be her favorite hangout all week." Todd leaned back with his hands folded behind his head. "This is a beautiful conference center."

Christy looked up at the tall pine trees. The sky was tinted a pale shade of peach. Thin clouds clung to the heavens like spun honey dribbled in a long line. The sunset felt different from the hundreds Christy had watched over the years in Newport Beach. Being this far north, the sky stayed light much longer on a summer night. The air carried the scent of cedar and pine instead of seaweed and salt. The clicks and foraging of the scampering nocturnal forest creatures could be heard as the cool night air rustled the branches that bent over their small cabin as if bowed in evening prayers.

Neither of them spoke. The echoes of hundreds of teens laughing in the meeting hall counterbalanced the sounds of the woods in the nicest way. Christy thought about how, at this moment, in a place like this, it was easy to believe that God was in control, keeping all things in balance and pouring out His lavish grace on this earth.

At moments like this Christy had the most difficulty understanding the flip side of life

— death, pain, loneliness, and sorrow.

She thought about Katie and how the last few weeks had been filled with so much focus on the new life she was carrying that they hadn't talked much about her dad's passing. And so much attention had gone to Katie's mother and all that the move entailed.

I wonder if Katie is having a chance to process all this with Eli while they're alone at our house. Maybe this is what the two of them needed in more ways than one.

"What are you thinking?" Todd asked in a low voice.

"About life and death and Katie and her dad." She drew in a deep breath and reached over, then slid her hand into his. "What are you thinking about?"

"Squirrels."

"Squirrels?"

Todd pointed to a big gray squirrel in the tree next to their cabin. The waning light caught the silver highlights in his big, bushy tail, illuminating his outline and making him look more like a noble Narnia creature than an ordinary gray squirrel.

Her husband was not contemplating the deep mysteries of salvation. He did that every day as a Bible teacher. Tonight, here, he was just enjoying the moment and letting his soul be still.

Christy tried to join him. She closed her eyes and opened them again. She filled her lungs with the cool air and released it slowly. She found it difficult to hold on to a single thought and clear her mind of everything else. It seemed as if always and forever there would be a little voice, a little face, an echo of a happy moment with the precious soul God had entrusted to them rising to the forefront of her thoughts. Christy knew she would never be able to remove the essence of Hana from her heart as long as she lived.

Is this how our heavenly Father feels about each of us, His children? Are we ever and always at the forefront of His thoughts?

She knew the answer was yes.

Christy squeezed Todd's hand, trying to connect with him in this moment and somehow merge the unanswerable questions in her soul with the simple wonder of a summer's night at a cabin in the woods with a Narnian squirrel.

Todd responded with three intentional squeezes, their secret code for *I — love — you.* All the places in her heart that had felt desolate a few moments ago when she was thinking about Katie's father seemed to fill with hope. There was so much Christy didn't understand. But she did understand love. Real love. What a gift love had been in her life. The love of her parents, Todd, Katie, her aunt and uncle and, most importantly, the deep love of God. She longed for every human to know that love.

Christy's thoughts were interrupted when Todd gave her hand another squeeze and whispered, "Looks like the sheriff brought his deputy this time."

Christy looked up to see her brother coming toward them with long strides that were matched by the equally long strides of the tall, slender young woman beside him. They stopped at the steps, and Christy and Todd stood to greet them.

A tingling sensation ran up Christy's neck. Was this going to be a significant moment she would remember the rest of her life?

My baby brother is about to introduce me to his girlfriend.

THIRTEEN

David's face was flushed. His smile was still wide, and he was still wearing the large cowboy hat. Christy couldn't believe how different he seemed to her.

"Fina, this is my sister, Christy, and her husband, Todd."

"It's so nice to meet you." Fina stretched out her arm and shook hands with Todd.

Christy took a small step forward and boldly offered Fina a warm hug instead of just a handshake. Fina's expression made it clear that Christy's hug was unexpected. In the yellow glow of the porch light Christy could see that Fina had high cheekbones and dark eyebrows that made her lovely face especially interesting. Her hair was short with lots of feathery flyaway strands. In the dim light, Fina's silhouette reminded Christy of an Italian statue made of marble.

"We would invite you in," Christy said, "but our daughter is sleeping."

"That's fine," Fina said. "We can just sit here on the porch and talk if it won't bother Hana."

Christy was impressed that Fina knew Hana's name and even pronounced it correctly. She and David had spent enough time together for her to know those details. Interesting.

Todd offered Fina his rocking chair while he and David leaned against the wood railing across the front of the porch. "David told us you're leaving tomorrow," Todd said. "I'm glad we had this chance to see you before then."

"Well, actually." Fina looked up at David and then explained how she had thought she was returning to Arizona to teach a volleyball clinic at the college she was attending. "But then I just heard today that they're cutting back on the junior coaches and my position was cut."

"That was a bad call on their part. She's a fantastic coach." David sounded equally vested in Fina's disappointing news. "But now she's staying in Glenbrooke this summer." He looked happy about that.

"My mom owns the Wildflower Café in town. I'm sure you guys will eat there at least a couple of times. I'm going to work at the café and help out here at camp as much as I can. You'll probably see a lot of me this week."

"I hope so." Christy felt warm toward Fina. She wasn't sure yet if she liked her the way she instantly liked some people. Fina seemed a bit skittish, or maybe she was nervous being around David's relatives. Christy tried to remember what that felt like the first time she met Todd's dad, Bryan.

David cleared his throat and removed his big cowboy hat. Christy noticed for the first time that his muddled shade of reddish-brown hair like their dad's was buzzed short. She hadn't seen it that way since he was a little boy. He had a rounded sort of widow's peak on his forehead that was noticeable now that he was nearly bald. He looked so big and so mature standing in front of her.

"We wanted to toss an idea at you guys," David said. "It's not a final plan or anything, but Fina is thinking about changing schools. She's looking into Irvine or possibly Long Beach."

"That's great." Christy turned to Fina and smiled. Fina still looked nervous.

"If she does change schools, I was wondering if you guys might consider letting her stay with you." David's gaze went back and forth from Todd to Christy and back to Todd.

Christy remembered just then how her mom had said that David planned to move in with them in Costa Mesa after camp ended. That's why he wanted to help find a place for Fina. He was serious about this girl and wanted her to move close to where he was going to be in the fall. Christy couldn't tell if Fina was equally excited about the plan.

"Give us a chance to talk about it," Todd said.

"Sure. Of course." Now David was looking nervous.

Christy reached over and rested her hand on Fina's shoulder, hoping to help at least one of them feel more at ease. "We have friends living with us right now, but like Todd said, we'll talk about what might be possible after they leave."

"Are Katie and Eli living with you?" David asked. "I didn't think they were staying there permanently."

"We're not sure how long they're going to stay. It all depends on how Katie is doing."

"Thanks for letting us throw this at you." Fina placed her hand on top of Christy's. The warm gesture spoke volumes to Christy. Fina leaned over and in a low voice, like one friend confiding to another, said, "I was so upset this afternoon when I found out I was cut. David prayed with me and helped me to think through options. That's how we came up with this idea. I hope it didn't come across as too pushy."

Christy's motherly-sisterly instincts warmed toward Fina. "No. It wasn't pushy at all."

Christy looked up at her brother and shot him the most affirming big-sister look she could give him. Whether his obvious affection for Fina lasted a summer or his entire life, Christy loved that he wanted to include Todd and her in the things that mattered most to him.

"Lots to pray about for you guys." Todd shifted his position against the railing. "Why don't we pray about it right now?"

The next few minutes were some of the most tender Christy remembered spending with her brother. David had stepped closer and reached for Christy's hand when Todd suggested that they pray. David and Todd had rested their arms on each other's shoulders in a brotherly way. Todd and Christy both held hands with Fina, completing the circle. Todd prayed for wisdom and direction for David and Fina, and all four of them agreed with a chorus of "amens."

After the prayer, the atmosphere seemed to lighten. Fina shared more about her schooling and future plans. She had just turned twenty and had one more year of college, but her goal was to go right into a master's program. She wanted to be a physical therapist, specifically for athletes.

"Posture is everything," Fina said. "I love it when I can help active people learn ways to balance their bodies."

"I should have you give me advice on my left leg," Christy said. "It's not because I'm an athlete. I think it hurts because I always carry Hana on my left hip. I have these tingling pains down my left leg."

"I can show you some stretches that will help with that."

The four of them talked for another half hour about jobs, futures, and trusting God. Things felt more natural between them by the time David and Fina left.

When they were out of sight Christy asked Todd, "What do you think?"

"She's a God Lover."

"Do you think she's good for David?"

Todd leaned over and kissed Christy on the forehead. "David seems to think so."

"Do you?"

"I'm withholding my opinion. I've been wrong about couples before. Seems best to wait and see how it goes. Take it as it comes."

Todd's "take it as it comes" line turned out to be the unspoken theme for the two of them during their week in Glenbrooke. They arrived without an agenda, but Christy soon wished she had made a few plans ahead of time. She had hoped to see Teri, her friend from cheerleading tryouts in high school. But after making a few calls the next morning, Christy discovered that Teri and her Australian husband, Gordon, were in Escondido that week, visiting Teri's family.

Christy still had plenty of other friends to spend time with, starting with Tracy, who had asked Christy and Hana to meet her that morning at the Wildflower Café. Tracy had sent a long text with a plan for Christy and Todd's first day in Glenbrooke. She and Christy would have breakfast the way they used to at Julie Ann's Café in Newport Beach. Tracy would have the twins with her, but their eldest son, Daniel, would go fishing with Doug and Todd.

Tracy made it sound easy, but it took Christy and Todd longer than expected to get into town. When Christy and Hana entered the charming Wildflower Café, she didn't see Tracy and immediately wished Todd hadn't driven off. She felt self-conscious until she spotted Fina, who was waiting tables.

"Hello! Welcome. Table for two? Or is Todd coming as well?" Fina sounded a lot more confident than she had the night before.

"I'm meeting Tracy here. Do you know her?"

"Yes, everyone knows Doug and Tracy. I haven't seen her yet. You probably beat her here."

"And I thought I was late."

Fina was joined by a woman who resembled her in face and form except for their hair. Fina had her short, caramel-colored, curly wisps pulled back by a wide, green-and-white cloth headband. It gave her a distinct Gypsy look and emphasized her well-formed eyebrows and high cheekbones.

"This is my mom, Genevieve."

Christy shifted Hana in her arms and hoped she was coming across as warm and welcoming as Genevieve and Fina were.

"We hope you can make it for dinner on Thursday," Genevieve said. "We've enjoyed getting to know your brother and would love to spend some time with you."

"I think that will work," Christy said. "We would love to spend time with your family, too. Although I do need to double-check with Todd."

"If another night works better, just let me know." Genevieve was younger and more stylish than Christy's mom. She didn't know how much younger, but Genevieve's skin made her appear youthful, healthy, and full of life.

The conversation between Christy, Fina, and her mom was brief because Hana had wiggled free and wanted to explore the adjoining play area through the Dutch doors where a half dozen other tikes were coloring, climbing into the indoor fort, and working on wooden block puzzles. Christy excused herself, followed Hana, and was greeted by another mom who already knew who Christy was.

"You met my sister, Shelly, last night at Camp Heather Brook. I'm Meredith Wilde. Call me Meri."

"Okay. Hi."

Meri wore a super-cute pair of glasses that had an aqua-blue stripe running across the top of each frame and along the sides. That was about the only distinguishing feature Christy managed to pick up because she was trying to watch Hana's every move. The other kids in the play area appeared to be older; Christy wasn't sure how Hana would do. She hadn't been around a lot of older children yet.

"Tracy told me you were coming. It's great that you could visit."

"We've been looking forward to this for a long time. Well, ever since Doug and Tracy moved here. Glenbrooke is as charming as Tracy told me it was."

"How is Katie doing?" Meri asked. "We've been praying for her at our moms' group."

Christy's introvert tendencies rose to yellow alert. Tracy had mentioned that she had become friends with a lot of women in Glenbrooke over the last few years. Tracy also said that all of them wanted to meet Christy. This sort of attention wasn't something she was used to.

"Katie's doing well. I had a text from her this morning."

"That's good to hear." Meri smiled at Hana, who was pulling soft toys out of a basket. "Your daughter is beautiful."

"Thank you."

"Have you ever considered having her do modeling?"

Christy was taken aback, and her expression must have showed it.

"Kids modeling, I mean. My husband has a friend at an agency, and he is always looking for children to do photo shoots for catalogs and ads for baby food and diapers."

Christy made the connection of who Meri was. Her husband was an actor named Jacob Wilde. He starred in a movie that was very popular a few years ago. Tracy had talked about Meri and Jake quite a bit. The connection helped Christy feel more at ease.

Before Christy could reply about the modeling, the door of the café opened and Tracy entered carrying Annie, her two-and-a-half-year-old daughter while Annie's twin brother, Sammie, charged ahead to the play area.

Social media had kept Christy up-to-date on how the twins looked from the photos Tracy posted regularly. But it had been some time since Christy had seen a picture of Tracy, and she was surprised at how much Tracy had changed since the last time Christy saw her when the twins were born. Tracy was willowy thin and had grown her blonde hair so it was past her shoulders. It somehow managed to stay perfectly straight without any flyaway renegades. Tracy's distinctive heart-shaped face hadn't changed except for a sprouting of more laugh lines around her eyes.

The two old friends hugged, smiled, and then hugged again.

"I've looked forward to this day for so long." Tracy looked at Meri and asked if they had met yet.

Both Christy and Meri said, "Yes" in unison, and then all three of them laughed.

"It's so good to have you guys here at last. I hope you're ready for breakfast because we sure are, aren't we, Annie?" Tracy had put her daughter down when she hugged Christy, but Annie clung to her leg and kept looking up at Christy.

"This is your Aunt Christy. You don't remember her, but she used to hold you and sing to you for hours when you were a tiny baby."

Hana's distinctive wail permeated the air. Christy dashed over to her and found Sammie with a toy shovel in his hand. Sammie looking guilty.

"I sawwie," he said over and over. "I sawwie."

Christy scooped up Hana and scanned her for obvious lumps or bruises but couldn't find any. Perhaps Sammie had taken the shovel away from her, and that was enough to cause the outrage.

"Let's gather the kids at a table and order some breakfast," Tracy suggested.

The breakfast ordeal, as Christy later described it to Todd, took almost two hours. Hana and Annie were willing to settle in the wooden high chairs, but Sammie wanted to sit by his mom. For most of the meal he sat on his mom or crawled under the table or treated the two spoons he had commandeered as drumsticks and banged them on anything Tracy would let him pound on.

"Having a conversation was impossible," Christy said. "Neither of us was able to complete a sentence. We kept laughing, which was good. And we reminded each other how it used to be when we had our long heart-to-heart conversations without a single interruption over tea and muffins at Julie Ann's Café on Balboa Peninsula. I miss those days."

Todd reached over and gave Christy's hand a squeeze. They were seated in the willow rockers once again while Hana was inside the cabin, supposedly napping. She seemed too wired from the stimulating morning, though, and instead of crashing, she was crying out for "Mama" and then going quiet for a few minutes before letting out another squeak or two.

"Do you think she'll settle down?" Todd asked.

"I think so. She needs a nap badly because, as you and I know so well, she didn't sleep much last night." Christy changed the subject and asked how the fishing trip had been with Doug.

"We didn't catch anything. But we were only there about forty-five minutes. Danny wasn't very interested in standing around holding a stick and looking at the water. He's a rowdy kid."

"He always was the most energetic person in the room when they had lived with us."

Christy shaded her eyes with her bent arm and watched the truck that was heading for their cabin. It looked like a forest service truck. A dark-haired man wearing a uniform got out of the cab and strode up to their cabin.

"Todd?"

"Yes?"

Christy pointed to the closed cabin door and whispered, "Baby sleeping."

The man lowered his voice. "Doug told me yesterday you might need to borrow a fishing rod."

"No, he found one for me. We went out this morning."

"Catch anything?"

"No."

"Well, I have plenty, if you want to borrow one and give it another try. The name's Kyle, by the way." He extended his hand to Todd across the porch railing and gave Christy a nod.

"My wife, Jessica, said she hoped to meet

216

both of you while you're here." Kyle was looking at Christy but seemed to be embarrassed. "Sorry, Doug told me your name, but I forgot it."

"Christy."

"That's right. Christy. Good to meet you guys. I'll be around, so hopefully we'll have a chance to spend some time together while you're here." He pulled a pair of sunglasses from his shirt pocket and put them on. "In case Doug and Tracy didn't tell you, we're in the big Victorian house up on the hill. You're welcome to stop by any time if you're over that way."

"Thanks," Christy kept her voice low. She hadn't heard any squawks from Hana in the last few minutes and hoped she could keep it that way.

As Kyle drove away, Christy noticed the wording on the side of the truck, "Glenbrooke Fire Department."

"Have you seen their house yet?" Todd asked. "We went by it on the way to the fishing spot. You would love it. Big house with a wraparound porch, lots of old trees. It's nice."

"I can't believe I'm saying this, but we're going to need a schedule if we try to fit in visits with all these people."

"They're all friendly, aren't they? It's not

like this where we live. I can see why Doug and Tracy feel so content here."

Christy didn't want to say it aloud, but she wasn't excited about a string of dinner dates with so many new people. This wasn't how she anticipated their vacation would be. She found herself missing the quiet hum of Gussie's tires on the long stretch of freeway that had brought them to this charming town, one thousand miles from home. She realized she should have been more appreciative of the solitude of the campsites where they had stayed and the hours of Hana's sedating audio stories and lullaby music.

Todd, however, was the most relaxed she had seen him in a long time. If this was his idea of a great vacation, Christy only hoped she could keep up with him. Something told her, though, that she was going to enjoy the long ride home more than the free-flowing, four-day journey they had taken to get here.

FOURTEEN

On Wednesday night Fina volunteered to babysit Hana at the cabin, which basically meant making herself comfortable on the porch while Hana slept. David promised to join her once he finished his evening camp duties, so it turned into a win-win evening for all of them.

Christy and Todd drove the short distance to Doug and Tracy's and found that all three of their kids had been put to bed early. That meant the four adults enjoyed the luxury of a long conversation without interruption. Doug met them at the door with his trademark big, burly Doug-hug. Tracy had straightened up the living room, lit several apple-scented candles, and made a carrot cake, remembering how much Christy liked the one Tracy had baked for Christy's birthday three years ago.

"First things first." Doug showed them a stack of old photos he had unearthed recently. They were from the missions trip they went on to England with Christy and Tracy. Sierra was in one of the pictures that had been taken by the huge fireplace.

"Look how young we were!" Christy held the photo and stared at it as if trying to pull up more memories of that roller-coaster time in her life.

"Can you believe that was ten years ago?" Tracy said.

"Ten? Really? How is that possible?"

"We got old," Doug suggested.

"You know, everyone keeps telling me that the years when our children are little go the fastest," Tracy said. "But I don't know. Those years of school, falling in love, and getting married went very fast."

"Can you scan these and send them to me?" Christy asked Doug. "I don't think I have any pictures from that trip."

"Sure. I'm still going through a few boxes of old stuff. If I find any more, I'll send those to you, too."

"Thanks. I always wanted to make an album with the best photos from each year, starting with when we moved to California, but I never got around to doing it. This might motivate me to start."

"I know what you mean," Tracy said. "I have so many unfinished projects." She shook her head. "I feel like I'm about five years behind on everything."

Doug leaned his head toward Todd. "What do you think? How far behind are you on your arts and crafts projects?"

Todd grinned. He glanced at Christy as if trying to decide if he wanted to get into a teasing match with Doug. The two of them had been at it as long as she could remember, starting with when they had co-conspired to toss her into the ocean as a big tease when she was only fifteen.

With a fake serious look on his face, Todd said, "My knitting is way behind schedule. That baby blanket for Hana is still sitting in a box in the closet only half done."

For some reason, Tracy took Todd's comment seriously. "You took up knitting? When?"

Christy shook her head, trying to clue Tracy in on the ruse.

Doug plowed into the moment, as he usually did, with a comment about his latest macramé wall-hanging project.

"Wait till you see it, Todd. It's awesome."

"How do you even know what macramé is?" Tracy asked.

"Hey, I subscribe to Bitsy."

"Bitsy?" Tracy and Christy asked in unison.

"Yeah, you know, that place where all the mothers of the western world have created home businesses and sell their crafts."

"It's not called 'Bitsy.' " Tracy shook her head. "And you don't subscribe to it. Can we change the subject?"

"Sure." Doug took on a sincere expression and dove into the topic of Todd and him recording some of their original worship songs. Doug had arranged for them to go to the local in-home studio tomorrow morning at eight o'clock.

Tracy shifted her position in the big chair by the fireplace and tucked her legs under her. When Christy and Todd arrived and were given the tour of the darling, spacious two-story house, Tracy had pointed to this chair by the fire and said, "That's my snuggle chair. You know, like the one you have in the corner of your bedroom. You told me every woman needed a snuggle chair so when we bought this house, I bought this chair. And you were right. I needed my own place, and this is it."

Now that Christy was looking at Tracy enfolded by the cocoa-brown leather chair with the high back, she knew she would carry this image of her friend for a long time. This was the Glenbrooke version of Tracy, and Christy had to admit, it fit. Doug and Tracy fit here, in this place, with these people, and especially in this house with the wood floors and built-in curio nooks in the hallway and the living room. Tracy's favorite room, she had told Christy, was the separate formal dining room. Tracy already had sweet memories of Thanksgiving dinners and Easter brunches around the table with her little family and her parents, who had moved to Glenbrooke several months before Doug and Tracy followed.

As the evening drew to a close, Todd and Doug confirmed their plans for the sound studio.

"Do you want to come over here while they're recording?" Tracy asked Christy. "I don't know if I mentioned this earlier, but I'm hosting the moms' group at ten o'clock, and I know they would all love to have you join us."

Christy had promised her brother that she and Hana would join him at the lake on the campgrounds tomorrow morning because he was overseeing the midweek water events between the camp teams.

Tracy insisted, absolutely insisted, that Christy leave camp as soon as David's event was over and come to her house to join the other moms for lunch. "Wouldn't you rather eat with us than brave the dining hall with all those lake-soaked, smelly teenagers?"

"Okay, I'll come for lunch."

The next morning Christy awoke in their comfortable bed when she heard Hana calling for her from across the cabin. Hana was standing up in her portable crib, holding her bunny under her arm. The morning sun warmed the room and was bright enough for Christy to shuffle her way over to Hana without bumping into anything. This was an improvement. The other two mornings Hana had sounded her "Mama-Mama" alarm before the sunlight had given her enough reason to even believe it was morning yet.

Christy toted her favorite snuggle bug over to the bed and tucked her under the covers with Todd. Hana tapped on Todd's chest. "Dada. Dada. Dada."

He opened one eye and looked over at their bright-eyed alarm clock. "Morning, Hana," he mumbled.

Christy burrowed under the covers and wished a simple wish — that Hana would close her eyes and all three of them would sleep another twenty minutes. That's all. Just another twenty minutes. Christy was certain it would change her life. She would be able to open her eyes all the way if she had another twenty minutes of sleep. She would be able to form a full sentence and even whisper an intentional morning prayer.

She would also be rested enough to decide what to wear to Tracy's lunch group.

Christy knew that fretting about what to wear was an inconsequential thing. But since she still felt insecure about being tossed into Tracy's new mixed salad of delightful women, it would help if she at least felt good about what she was wearing. The clothes she had packed for this trip were all the things she wouldn't mind ruining since they had, after all, planned on camping and staying in a log cabin.

Hana rested her head on Todd's chest. He had his arm around her and was humming one of the worship songs he and Doug would record that morning. Hana seemed to have just discovered the rolling, rumbling music she could hear when she pressed her ear on Todd's skin. The revelation delighted her and kept both of them engaged while Christy slowly woke up all the way.

She decided on wearing the one dress she had brought with her. It was an old summer dress she had purchased at least a year before Hana was born. Tracy would probably remember it. Christy told herself it didn't matter. The summer dress was better than her baggy jeans or raggedy shorts.

While she dressed, Christy chided herself for not going shopping before their vacation. She had intended to at least buy new jeans, but with Katie's crisis, Christy never went shopping.

She realized she was running out of clean clothes for Hana and wondered if Tracy would let her run a load or two when she went over for lunch. She was pretty sure her friend wouldn't mind so she loaded up Gussie with dirty clothes from all three of them and then carried Hana across camp to the lake.

The sight of 350 hollering teenagers circling a lake caused Hana to grab hold of Christy's long, nutmeg hair and bury her face in Christy's shoulder. "It's okay, Hana. We're going to find your Uncle David."

As Christy threaded her way behind the lineup of students, she thought about how it sounded when she said, "Uncle David." She wondered if one day "Uncle David" would be to Hana the same sort of wonderful uncle that Uncle Bob had been to Christy. She hoped so.

"Christy! Over here!" Fina's voice found its way to Christy over the roar.

That girl can yell! I wonder what she was like as a baby.

Christy and Hana joined Fina in the

enclosed area by the dock. It was roped off and seemed to be set up for the official judges who, at the moment, were watching four teams in a canoe race as they drew near to the finish line at the dock.

"David is down there." Fina pointed to the guy in the white-and-blue jersey with the Dodgers baseball cap. He was blowing the whistle he wore on a camp-style lanyard around his neck and waving his arms like crazy.

I still can't believe that's my brother. How come every time I look at him I keep being surprised? You are such a cool guy now. Look at you. Mom and Dad would be so proud.

Christy made a mental note to call her mom later that day and give her a newsy update. She also suddenly understood why David had been so persistent about Christy and Todd coming to visit him at Camp Heather Brook and making the effort to watch him execute his role. He wanted his family to be proud of him. Christy got that. How else would his parents know the value of what he was doing unless Christy went home with a glowing report?

As Christy switched Hana from side to side, she watched the paddlers come closer and closer to the dock. The race was going to end with a tight finish.

Christy thought back on when she was David's age. During that season she longed for affirmation from their parents more than at any other time during her growing-up years. Their mom and dad were practical Midwestern farmers. They were hard-working, sensible people who held tight to family values, honesty, modesty, and integrity. Christy would have loved to have someone come see her work hard during the time she served at the orphanage in Basel, and then that person would return to the States and give her parents a glowing report. She didn't think they ever fully understood what she was doing at the orphanage.

She realized that David might feel the same way. He graduated from college and then went to work at a camp for very little money. Knowing his parents appreciated his contribution to the camp would mean a lot.

The front paddler in the winning canoe grabbed the red flag on the dock, and a group of students all wearing red T-shirts erupted in a tumultuous cheer.

Hana leaned in to Christy, holding on tighter than ever. Christy pressed her lips to Hana's ear and whispered, "It's okay. They are just being happy."

Hana peeked out over Christy's shoulder

and watched the red team, which was located about thirty yards down the shore from where Christy stood. Hana leaned back in Christy's arms and clapped.

Fina laughed and clapped along with Hana. "Yay, the red team won!"

Christy was comforted to see how Hana was adjusting to so much noise and commotion. David looked proud when he saw Christy and waved to her from the dock.

"Could you let David know that I need to go?" Christy told Fina. "Tell him I think he did a great job."

"Okay, I'll tell him. We'll see you tonight, won't we? Dinner with my family?"

"Yes! Can't wait."

"Great. Perfect. I don't know if David told you, but we decided to eat at the Wildflower since there will be so many of us. I hope you don't mind."

"Of course not. See you then."

Christy wondered, as she drove to Tracy's, exactly how many people would be there. What did Fina mean by "so many of us"? Could it be that her parents' home was too small to accommodate all of them around a table? It didn't matter. They would have a chance to get to know Fina and her family a little better at the café. Once again, Christy was sure she would have a positive and encouraging report to deliver to her parents when they returned home.

Christy remembered the way to Tracy's house. It seemed easy to find things in Glenbrooke. She also took a long look at the Victorian house on the hillside that Todd had seen on the way to the fishing spot. Christy couldn't remember the name of the couple who lived there, but she was sure they had a story about how they came to live in such a grand home. It seemed even larger than the estate house where Sierra and Jordan lived. That made Christy wonder what sort of meadows, pools, or garden houses hid behind the beautiful house.

Hana had just fallen asleep in her car seat when Christy turned down Tracy and Doug's street. She hated to wake her up. She also hated to cancel on Tracy after promising she would be at the moms' luncheon.

The best option seemed to be to keep driving around and let Hana sleep at least for a little bit before pulling her out of her car seat and taking her inside the house that was sure to be bubbling over with children. Christy steered Gussie down the next street and puttered around the neighborhood.

She spotted a woman hanging laundry on a clothesline and was reminded once again of how Glenbrooke was nothing like New-port Beach. She passed a house that had an American flag displayed from a flagpole in the front yard. Two houses over she saw some children taking turns pushing each other in a big, black tire swing hung from an obliging branch of the largest tree she had seen yet in this older neighborhood. Christy didn't know if it was an elm, oak, maple, or some other variety, but the glori-ous tree was made complete by the tire swing.

If Christy wasn't driving, she would be taking photos with her phone, capturing the sweet summer moments dancing all around her. She thought of the expensive camera Uncle Bob had given her when she was in high school and how much she enjoyed tak-ing photos back then, learning how to adjust the lens and set the aperture.

Maybe I'll pull out my camera and start tak-ing pictures again. Too bad I didn't think to bring it on this trip.

She smiled at the thought. If she told Doug, he might tease her again about unfinished arts and crafts projects. It struck her that some interests, talents, and maybe even dreams were planted in them for life. They didn't go away.

Seeing the snapshots Doug had found

made Christy want to create the photo books even more. Maybe it was too ambitious to try to go back ten or fifteen years and capture all those evaporating memories. The more realistic option would be to start with Hana's life. It would be easy to collect those photos from the past two years, starting with a few of the side shots she took of her growing belly in the bathroom mirror. She liked the plan and determined she would dive in when she returned home. It wouldn't take too long.

Christy had forgotten so many details from her teen years that Doug and Tracy had brought up last night. Apparently Tracy had selected to burn green-apple-scented candles in memory of when Christy had come back to Bob and Marti's after having her hair cut. Doug had been there and leaned in to smell her hair, saying that it smelled like green apples. She never would have connected the vague memory to why Tracy was grinning when she revealed the fragrance of her candles.

Christy motored around another ten minutes before she noticed in the rearview mirror that Hana was stirring. Turning back toward Tracy's, Christy drew in a breath of courage. She had already met Shelly and her sister, Meri. Both of them were nice.

She had met a woman named Leah yesterday afternoon at the camp.

"It's going to be fine," Christy coached herself as she and Hana tapped on Tracy's front door. "Just be brave."

FIFTEEN

"So?" Todd asked. "How did it go at Tracy's for the lunch party?" He and Christy were driving back into Glenbrooke that evening to have dinner at the Wildflower Café with Fina and her family.

Christy hadn't said much about being with the Glenbrooke women at Tracy's that afternoon. From the moment Todd had arrived back at the cabin with Doug almost an hour ago, the two guys had talked nonstop about how great the recording went and how they wanted to fit in another couple of hours the next day. Todd had sounded so happy. She loved seeing him this energized and doing what he was created to do. He and Doug had always made a great duo. Christy enjoyed seeing that the bond between them had continued and that they were still both stoked to play guitars together.

She also hadn't said anything because she

was still processing it all.

"It was actually kind of extraordinary," Christy answered.

"In what way?"

"Seeing how close the women were to each other and how easily they welcomed me. That doesn't always happen."

Christy thought another moment and added, "And, to be honest, it was also intimidating and chaotic with so many kids all over the place. I think the noise and activity frightened Hana. She wanted to be on my lap most of the time, but toward the end she warmed up to Annie. I was glad to see the two of them connect in their own little ways."

"Why did you say it was intimidating?"

Christy tried to think of how to explain to Todd how insecure she could feel sometimes in new situations. She always felt more comfortable when she was with only one close friend, having a conversation the way she and Tracy had been so involved in each other's lives several years ago. It struck her at the luncheon that Tracy had moved on. She was sharing the personal details about her life with a cluster of women who seemed to know Tracy better now than Christy did. Texts and a few phones calls every so often had kept Christy and Tracy connected. But their friendship now seemed connected by a long tether and no longer drawn close and tight with heartstrings, the way it used to be.

"I don't know how to explain it," Christy told Todd. The intricacy of what she felt was complex. All friendships go through different seasons. Some women you feel close to even if you haven't seen each other for years. That's how it felt with Katie. Always. The two of them could easily pick up where they had left off and nothing had changed.

Tracy had changed.

Her life had changed significantly since she left Newport Beach, and now, in every way, Tracy seemed like a Glenbrooke Girl, as if she had lived there her whole life. She was thriving in the small-town atmosphere and raising her children in a spacious sixty-year-old house rather than the tiny bungalow in Newport Beach she had lived in. She fit in effortlessly with the other moms as they discussed toddler temper tantrums and sampled a new recipe for a kale, carrot, and quinoa smoothie. The climate even suited Tracy's complexion.

Christy realized that what she felt was loss. She didn't have anything like Tracy did in terms of a moms' support group. And ever since Tracy had moved, Christy didn't even have a friend to meet with at Julie Ann's Café. For the past two years, her life was all about work, family, and adjusting to a baby as well as all the overlapping circles of Todd's life and ministry. While she had been coping, Tracy had been rooting herself into a tight circle of brand-new Forever Friends.

The comparison brought twinges of jealousy. She felt hurt and left out but knew she wouldn't be able to explain the sensation to Todd in a way he would understand. Fortunately they had arrived at the Wildflower Café so she simply got out of the car rather than answer Todd's question about why the afternoon had felt intimidating.

Hana had taken a long nap that afternoon after the stimulating social time at Tracy's. Christy was grateful that her toddler was well rested because she was in one of her cute little girl moods with lots of smiles and eager responses to games of peek-a-boo across the table with Fina's youngest sister, Mallory.

Their group of eight adults and one high chair all fit at a grand round table in the far corner of the café. Genevieve had gone to extra effort by setting the table with a beautiful woven tablecloth she said was from Switzerland and colorful dishes that were different from the café's everyday dishes. A sprig of fresh rosemary was tucked into the folded napkins at each place, and a lovely garland of ivy circled the center of the table. Inside the circle was a round platter overflowing with fresh fruit, bite-sized chunks of cheese, small crescent-shaped cookies, and squares of dark chocolate. Christy felt like she was back at the orphanage in Basel for one of the celebration dinners.

"I love that your mom incorporated her European roots into our dinner tonight." Christy was seated next to Fina, and the two of them had been the only ones at the table to immediately liberate their rosemary sprigs and rub the spindly needles to release the fragrance.

"David told me you lived in Basel for a while. I've only been to Switzerland three times. The last time was six years ago. I would love to go back." Fina wore a black sleeveless top and a short necklace with a pale gem that caught the amber light and sent airy sparkles around the table.

As the evening conversation continued around the table, Christy watched her brother. He interacted effortlessly with Fina and her family. They liked him. He clearly had won them over.

Fina's dad, Steven, captured everyone's

attention when he told about the first time he had met David at the camp six weeks ago. David had just arrived but was helping all the new female counselors to carry their luggage to their cabins.

"At first I thought, 'What a gentleman'. Then I realized he was using the moment to check out all the girl counselors before the other guys had a chance." Steven tapped his forefinger to his temple. "Clever guy."

David turned red. He protested Steven's memory with his hand up and a lot of quick explaining. "The other guys put me up to it. They told me that all of us had been assigned tasks and my name was on the list for carrying the girl counselors' luggage."

"There was no list." Fina grinned at David. "He was just the most gullible new guy."

Steven leaned back in his chair, arms casually folded across his chest, looking as if he liked the idea of his eldest daughter falling for the most gullible guy at camp.

David shot a glance at Fina that carried an unmistakable message. He looked like the guy who was falling hard and falling fast.

In all the ways that Christy had felt left out of Tracy's new life, she felt encircled into her brother's new life. If she and Todd had made the trek to Glenbrooke for no other reason than to be included around the table that night and to drink in the transformation of her baby brother, the experience was well worth the journey.

Glenbrooke had another treasure that made the trip worth it. The blessing came the next morning when Christy and Todd showed up on the doorstep of a darling house nestled in a glen of cedar trees. A huge grassy area sprawled along the side of the house all the way to a creek that ran along the back edge. When Todd turned off Gussie's engine and they got out, they spotted two young girls playing on the swing set on the lawn.

Todd waved to them, and both girls scurried into the house through the back door, giggling and chattering as they fled. He knocked on the front door using the ornate brass door knocker.

Christy felt nervous again, but it wasn't an insecure nervousness like at Tracy's yesterday. This time her heart fluttered from an excited nervousness. They had been in Glenbrooke for four days, but this was the first time to see their friends Brad and Alissa.

The door opened with a whoosh and in one swift motion, Alissa was out the front door, hugged Todd and kissed him on the cheek and then kissed Christy on the cheek, hugging her so tightly it took her breath away. Hana was clinging to Christy's leg. She let out a confused cry and raised her arms to be picked up.

"Look at you!" Alissa held Christy at arm's length. "You've hardly changed at all. Christy, you look so good. You have always been such a natural beauty. I love that you kept your hair long. You have such gorgeous hair."

"Thanks." Christy felt as if she were having a flashback to when she was fifteen and had first met Alissa on the beach. Back then Alissa had the long, blonde hair and was garnering all the compliments on her looks. Christy was in the shadows, feeling stunned and thrilled that such a beach beauty, almost three years older than Christy, would hang out with her.

The last decade and a half showed on Alissa, making her look older than Christy expected. Her radiant blonde hair was now cut short to chin length and was colored a subtle shade of strawberry blonde. Her skin was no longer bronzed to a tawny glow and shimmering with coconut-scented sunscreen. She looked fair and rosy-cheeked, as if she came from a Scandinavian heritage. Alissa's clear eyes were accented by very little makeup, and noticeable laugh lines appeared to be permanently creased at the corners of her eyes.

It now made sense to Christy why Todd had said he didn't immediately recognize Alissa when he saw her two years ago. She was still lovely, but she no longer possessed the striking, attention-getting appearance she had as a teenager.

"Come in!" Alissa led the way, calling out, "Beth! Ami! Come meet our friends."

The two little girls peered at them over the top of the sofa. Like shy bunnies, they ducked back into their burrow, pulling a throw blanket over their heads.

Alissa turned her focus to Hana, who was now in Christy's arms. She lowered her voice and leaned in. "Hi, Hana. How are you? I have two girls who are excited to play with you today."

Hana curled up and tucked her chin, nestling herself against Christy's shoulder. She had reverted to this bashful routine a lot over the past few days of meeting so many new people. She turned her head just enough, though, to keep an eye on the two little grinning faces that kept popping up from the couch.

"Your girls are adorable," Christy said. "Which one is Beth and which one is Ami?"

"Beth?" Alissa called.

The older girl with large, dark, expressive eyes and incredibly long eyelashes popped her head up and then retreated with a squeak. Ami, the younger sister, followed Beth's antics. Both of them were dark-haired darlings and resembled each other in many ways.

Christy had heard some of the story about how these two sisters from Romania were adopted when they were preschool age. Todd had visited Alissa and her husband, Brad, two and a half years ago when he helped Doug and Tracy make their big move to Glenbrooke. Todd hadn't met the girls then because, although the adoption had been finalized, Brad and Alissa were waiting for final clearance before they could fly to Europe to pick up the girls.

"How about something to drink?" Alissa offered. "Are you guys hungry?"

"Nothing for me, thanks. We had breakfast at camp," Christy said.

"You braved the dining hall?" Alissa asked. "I'm impressed. Don't they have a big high school group in this week?"

"Yes. It was pretty noisy," Todd said. "But the food wasn't bad."

They easily fell into a smooth conversation about Camp Heather Brook, what it was like staying there, how much Christy's brother was enjoying being on staff this summer, and how Brad was on the camp's board of directors and had helped Jonathan and Shelly to upgrade the camp's technology.

"That's Brad's thing," Alissa said. "They call him McGyver here in Glenbrooke because he can fix any computer or rewire any sound system. It's turned into a full-time job. Everybody needs tech help at some point."

They had settled themselves in the living room, and the girls had congregated on a rug in the center of the room where they were showing Hana their toys and trying to give her whatever she wanted. It was touching to see how sharing both of the older girls were.

"Speaking of sound systems." Todd glanced at Christy. "Doug set up some recording time for us this morning. I know we had planned to hang out all day, but would you mind if I left Christy and Hana here for a couple of hours?"

"Of course not. Like I said earlier, Brad had a call this morning that took him out to Edgefield. He should be back by mid-afternoon."

Todd stood and gave Christy a look as if trying to make sure she was okay with his departure.

"Have fun," Christy said.

He leaned over and kissed her on the cheek. "Love you," he whispered.

Christy didn't mind having this luxurious stretch of time to spend with Alissa. They had a lot of life stories to catch up on. Christy was encouraged to see how easily the two of them shared back and forth, despite the many years since they had been together on the beach. Alissa's girls kept Hana happily entertained, which made it easier for the moms to continue their conversation.

One of the lengthier topics was Shawna, the daughter Alissa had given up for adoption more than thirteen years ago. Shawna had spent a weekend with Christy and Todd two years ago, when she was almost twelve, and they had kept in close contact ever since. Shawna had also come to visit Brad and Alissa a handful of times. Christy asked Alissa how those visits were for her.

"Exceptional, I think. I don't know how open adoption visits go for most people, but Shawna's parents are extraordinary. They are intelligent, thoughtful, and very respectful of God. We all get along well."

Then Christy asked a question she had been curious about for years. "How difficult was it to give Shawna over to the Lanes? I mean, really?"

Alissa's eyes widened, and she blinked as if caught off guard by the forthright question. Her voice lowered, and she leaned in closer on the couch. Christy thought she saw a burst of angst flash across Alissa's face like lightning.

"It was the hardest thing I've ever done." Alissa drew in a deep breath through her pinched nostrils. "It was also the best thing." She glanced at Beth and Ami. "I've experienced adoption from both sides. The process is like peeling back your skin until your heart is exposed. One minute you think you're going to die, and the next, you think you've never been so alive."

Christy tried to imagine such intense emotions. She had felt those highs and lows after giving birth to Hana, but she didn't think she had ever known the same depth of feelings that Alissa had. No wonder her face had taken on the look of a deeper, more rooted sort of beauty. She had lived through a lot in the past decade and a half.

"You are very beautiful, Alissa. Soul-deep beautiful." Christy heard her lips saying the words, even though she had intended to only think them.

Alissa drew back, surprised. "Why do you

say that?"

Christy felt her face flush. "It just came out. I guess it's because of the depth in you. I listen to what you're saying and I think, 'Wow, what a wise and deeply anchored woman.'"

Alissa's expression warmed like a sunrise. "Thank you, Christy." She reached over and covered Christy's hand with hers. "I've always looked up to you and Todd so much. I know we aren't really connected or anything anymore, but the two of you had such an intense and lasting effect on my life. I feel much more connected to both of you than I think you'll ever know."

Christy smiled but didn't know what to say back.

"Stay right there." Alissa stood and went into another room.

Christy looked around at the comfortable living room. The mantel on the fireplace was made from a thick log that had been finished in a way that highlighted every age line, knot, and change in color. It was a magnificent piece of art in its natural way, and it unobtrusively formed the hub of the home.

Just like Alissa.

Christy smiled at the way Hana was so content to be the peanut butter of the Beth and Ami sandwich, as the sisters read books to Hana. Christy pulled her phone from her purse and quietly took a picture.

Alissa returned with an ornate wooden box and placed it on the sofa next to Christy. "A dear elderly couple I know, Chet and Rosie, gave me this box. It's from Italy." She opened it to reveal a small stack of folded letters. Christy recognized the floral border on one of the pieces of stationery when Alissa unfolded it and held it out to Christy.

"This is the letter that convinced me to become a Christian. Do you remember it?"

Christy could see that the handwriting was hers. That is, the handwriting of her teenage self. She remembered writing to Alissa a couple of times, and she knew that Todd had written to her, but at that moment Christy had no idea what she had said in her letter.

"You don't remember this, do you?"

Christy gave a small shrug and looked closely at the words.

"You can read it if you like." Alissa handed over all the letters. "I'm going to put some lunch together for us. Have a little trip down memory lane."

For the next few minutes the past and the present seemed to catch up with each other inside Christy's mind. She read her words, earnest and bold, telling Alissa why Jesus wasn't like anyone else who ever lived. He was the Son of God. He died for us, and God brought Him back to life so that each of us could become one of God's children, adopted into His family.

She read through another letter she had sent Alissa, and Christy's excitement over Alissa becoming a Christian was evident.

Where did all those fired-up feelings go? I still love God, but it's been a long time since I've tried to share these sorts of God stories with anyone.

The sisters had scooted into the kitchen, and Hana had come over to the couch where she climbed up by herself and was rummaging through Christy's purse, taking things out one by one. Christy let her play with her keys and wallet while she read the rest of the letters. Five of the letters were from Todd. His words to Alissa carried the tone of a big brother communicating to a favorite sister. He sounded so caring, so kind. He wrote about the sacred value of life and the eternal results of love. He pleaded with Alissa to not even consider ending the life of her boyfriend's, Shawn's, child. Shawn had died in a surfing accident, but part of him lived on inside of Alissa.

Christy folded up the last letter from Todd

and thought of how different life would be for all of them if they hadn't met that summer at Newport Beach. Her eye fell on a verse Todd had scrawled on the back of one of the five sheets of lined notebook paper he had used to write on.

"I said to the LORD, 'You are my God. My times are in Your hands.' "

God had been so good to all of them. Their times were in His hands. Alissa chose not to remove her unborn baby from her body prematurely. She gave Shawna life. Christy couldn't imagine it being any other way. The world without Shawna would be a lesser place.

Christy felt as if her heart wanted to give way to a river of tears. But the luxury of a good, long cry would have to wait. Alissa had lunch ready.

SIXTEEN

It shouldn't have surprised Christy how deep the conversation went with Alissa after lunch, but it did.

Alissa's girls settled in to watch a princess video, and Hana slept in Alissa's home office. She went down on the folded futon with her bunny and a cuddly blanket without a fuss. It seemed the various beds Hana had been in during this vacation had made her at ease going to sleep when she was tired, no matter where they put her. Todd had said he hoped this trip would make her more adaptable to new situations, and that was definitely happening.

Christy and Alissa sat at the kitchen table gazing out at the gorgeous green view of the backyard and talked about marriage, children, ministry, friends, parents, and finances. Every topic was met with honesty and vulnerability from both of them. When they were teens, Christy had never felt equal to Alissa. They hadn't talked at the heart-level during their brief times together, and the season of letter writing had been limited to a few short months while Alissa was at her grandmother's in Boston, trying to decide what to do when she found out she was pregnant.

This kitchen table conversation felt rich and meaningful to Christy. She realized that she and Alissa were becoming real friends for the first time.

It's strange how I know Tracy so well and we've been so close for all these years, but yesterday at her house, with all her new friends, I felt as if I barely knew who she was anymore. I didn't fit into Tracy's new world. Yet, with Alissa, it's the opposite.

Christy ventured a question as Alissa stood to refill their glasses of pink lemonade. Alissa had half jokingly said, when she poured it from the pitcher at lunch, that their world had shifted to all things pink when they adopted Beth and Ami — even pink lemonade.

"I went to a moms' group at Tracy's yesterday. Do you ever go?"

"Yes, when I can. Thursdays are one of my busier workdays. I can't always get away from my home office to spend the morning with the group. If they met in the afternoon,

I'd be able to go all the time."

"Do you feel part of the group?"

Alissa returned to the table with the lemonade. "Yes, I do. Even if I haven't been there for a while, I feel welcomed back. I've never felt as close to a group of women as I am to the women here in Glenbrooke."

"That's what Tracy said. They all seem like very caring women."

"They are. Nobody in the group is really impressed with themselves or bossy, if that makes sense."

Christy nodded. If Alissa had answered differently and said she felt outside the circle of moms, then Christy might have shared how unsettled she had felt yesterday. She sipped her pink lemonade and wondered if the discomfort was based on the noticeable changes in her relationship with Tracy and had nothing to do with the other moms.

"Are you part of a moms' group in Newport Beach?" Alissa asked.

"No."

"Do you have a close friend you do tag-team mothering with?"

Christy shook her head.

Alissa looked surprised. "Have you been doing everything on your own?"

Christy didn't expect to cry, but the tears

formed and coursed down her face before she could blink them away.

"Oh, Christy." Alissa stood and came to Christy's side of the table. She wrapped both her arms around Christy and planted a kiss on top of her head.

All Christy could think about was the baby shower Aunt Marti had hosted for Christy right before Hana was born. Marti had invited more than fifty women, but only a few of them came. None of them was a friend of Christy's from work or church. The invitations had mostly gone to Marti's social circles in Newport Beach, but even those women hadn't come.

At the time, the low response hadn't bothered Christy too much because she was so focused on being prepared for the delivery. Later, when she attended the baby shower of a woman whom Todd worked with, she realized she didn't have a circle of same-aged friends like the other new mom did. Christy left that baby shower feeling very alone.

"I recognize those tears." Alissa had settled into the chair next to Christy and was gazing at her with a tender expression. "When tears fall that silently and that quickly, they're coming from your heart. It's like you have a soul-wound, and I just punctured it, and it bled tears."

Alissa's description was precisely what Christy was feeling. The surprise was that she hadn't realized she had the wound. But the injury was in the area of her heart that had tried to heal itself after Katie had moved to Africa and then Tracy had moved to Glenbrooke.

"I have my mom nearby." Christy tried to pull herself up so that her spirit and her shoulders wouldn't slouch. "She and I have grown a lot closer since Hana was born. And my Aunt Marti and Uncle Bob are over all the time. And Todd is a really good dad. He does a lot with Hana and around the house."

The lines around Alissa's eyes seemed to bunch up in a bouquet as she gave Christy a big-sister expression of sympathy. "But it's not the same as having a close friend in your everyday life — another woman or a circle of women who are going through the same season. You need to connect with other moms, Christy."

Christy nodded as if she were already formulating a plan on how to make that happen. In truth, she didn't know where to look for other moms or where to find a friend in Newport Beach who would be on the same heart-level as Katie or Tracy, or even as close as she felt to Alissa right then.

"Do you think you and Brad might consider moving to Newport Beach?" Christy wiped away the final tears and pressed her lips up in a smile.

"No, sorry. I would have jumped at the chance when I was single and living in Pasadena. But for Brad, the girls, and me, this is home."

"Just thought I'd ask." Christy kept her wobbly smile in place. She steadied herself and said, "Thanks, Alissa. I didn't expect to leak all over you like that."

Alissa placed her hand on Christy's shoulder. "Don't worry. I understand. I really do. You know what's crazy? For all these years, I pictured you and Todd as having a surplus of friends. When he was here a couple of years ago, he told us about the Friday Night Gathering and about different people who were staying at your house. I thought you guys had the best grasp on fellowship and friendship of anyone I knew."

"We do have a lot of people in our lives. But it's not the same as having a close girlfriend, like you said."

"You'll find someone." Alissa's voice rose with optimism. "I'm sure lots of moms' groups and women's Bible study groups are at your church. All you have to do is show up to one of them, and you'll make friends. I know you will. You're very good at that, Christy."

Christy didn't know if she agreed with Alissa about being good at making friends. Alissa had been the one who initiated their friendship that first summer, long ago. Katie had been the one to pursue Christy after they first met at a sleepover. And Tracy was already friends with Todd so she sort of added on Christy as a friend when Todd started spending more time with her.

My social skills are definitely lacking. I think I got stuck.

"Just show up," Alissa said. "That's been the banner over my life for a couple of years now. That's how we ended up adopting the girls. I just showed up at a meeting at church about supporting different missionaries and international ministries. One of them was an orphanage in Switzerland, and that's how we ended up connecting with them and adopting our girls."

Christy's heart did a little flutter when Alissa mentioned the orphanage in Switzerland. "Was it in Basel?"

"Yes." Alissa said the name of the orphanage in German and repeated it in English.

"Alissa, I worked at that orphanage ten years ago! I know it inside and out. I had no idea your girls had been there."

"Seriously? You worked there? I remember Todd — or maybe it was Tracy — saying something about your spending time in Europe, but I thought you went to school there."

"The program included an accelerated study program because we received credits for the time we spent with the children."

"That is amazing. Absolutely amazing."

Hana let out a wail from the room Alissa used as her office for the travel agency she managed. As soon as Beth heard Hana, she jumped up and looked at Alissa expectantly, waiting for the all-clear sign to go entertain their new little friend some more.

The rest of the afternoon went quickly as the girls played outside and Hana tried to keep up with them. Hana seemed to be growing up fast on this trip. She was attempting new things and forming new words as a result of all the interaction with the children in Glenbrooke. Christy was convinced that she needed to either find a mom's group or start one when she got home.

Hana needed new friends as much as Christy did.

Seventeen

The final hours in Glenbrooke were the most stressful for Todd and Christy. Todd was set on making an early morning departure on Monday; yet since they had spent their last night talking into the wee hours on the porch with David and Fina, they hadn't done any packing.

Todd had set the alarm for 5:00 a.m., and when it chimed, he rolled out of bed and turned on the light, rousing Christy and Hana, who were both unhappy about their sleep being disrupted. Todd and Christy tossed clothes into their luggage and kept Hana busy with anything they could find to give her to eat. Christy carried all that she could out to Gussie and let Todd do the car packing and strapping while she corralled Hana and did her best to tidy up the cabin.

David jogged over to the cabin as they were in the final stages of strapping Hana into her car seat. "Hey! Glad you're still here. I wanted to tell you guys how much I appreciate your coming and meeting Fina and her family."

"We loved being here," Christy said. "I'm so proud of you, David. I know I said it last night, but you're a natural at what you're doing, and I'm really happy that you and Fina found each other."

"I am, too." He grinned.

"We'll let you know about the possibility of Fina staying with us as soon as we figure out what's going on with Eli and Katie," Christy said.

"Great. And we'll keep you guys updated on what Fina hears back from the schools."

With one last hug and a few salty kisses, Christy climbed into Gussie. She waved as the van chugged out of camp just when the new batch of lively campers were heading for the dining hall in a herd, with a few stragglers here and there.

The first hour on the road was calm. The early morning scenic beauty of the tree-lined highway was invigorating. Christy loved the way the light came through the branches and stained the road with lacy shadows.

"This is such a beautiful place," Christy said. "I know I've said it before, but I can see why Doug and Tracy love it here. This area suits them."

"Would you ever want to move here?"

"No."

Todd seemed surprised at how quickly she responded. "I thought you'd like the small town feel with the close community and all the tea cups and stuff."

"Tea cups?"

"Yeah. It seemed like everybody there used tea cups."

Christy tried to remember when they used tea cups in Glenbrooke. Tracy had served them tea the night they sat up talking by the fire and again for the mom's group. Christy's after dinner tea at the Wildflower Café had also been served in a china tea cup.

"I hadn't noticed, but you're right. There were more tea cups in use in Glenbrooke than in Newport Beach."

"You like that sort of thing, right?"

"Yes. But I can use tea cups at home if I want to host a little gathering. It's not the beautiful green scenery or the cute shops on Main Street or the china tea cups that make a place feel like home for me. I mean, I loved it all. But where we live right now feels more like home to me than any other place I've ever been."

Todd grinned. He reached over and gave

her leg a squeeze. "Good."

"Do you feel at home where we live now?"

Todd glanced at her as if the answer should be obvious. He was quiet for a few minutes. When he spoke, his voice was low and he sounded choked up.

"God has been so good to me. So good to us. I wouldn't want to change any of it. I got to marry you, the only girl I ever loved. We get to raise our daughter in the house I grew up in. I get to teach the Bible every day to teens. And I can pretty much go surfing every week. We're blessed, Christy. So blessed."

"We are." She let the sweetness of his words circle her as they drove through another stretch of magnificent countryside leaving behind the lush greens and towering trees of Glenbrooke. Farmland stretched out behind them and the traffic was getting thicker as they came up to a stoplight and a cluster of industrial buildings.

Glenbrooke, you are a wonderful place to visit but home for us will always be Newport Beach.

"You know what I really liked?" Todd asked.

"Recording with Doug?"

"That was awesome, as Doug kept saying while we were in the studio. But what I really liked was the Bongo Fest at Brad and Alissa's the other night."

Christy had missed the Bongo Fest around the outside fire pit in Brad and Alissa's backyard. She was inside giving Hana a bath and trying to get her to go to bed on the futon in Alissa's home office. Hana wouldn't settle down. She wanted to be with Beth and Ami and Beth and Ami wanted her in their room. Christy hauled the futon in between their twin beds and tried to convince them it was bed time.

The giggling girls wanted more stories. They wanted more dolls and stuffed animals in their beds. More drinks of water. More trips to the bathroom. Hana copied everything Beth and Ami did and Christy found it impossible to halt the shenanigans. She called for backup help from Alissa and the guys.

Todd's solution was for them to head back to camp. It was almost ten o'clock and the summer sky was finally growing dark. Todd had commented then that he could have kept going with Brad for another couple hours of bongo madness.

"What exactly did you guys do? What made it so cool?" Christy asked.

"We made up beat poetry in time with the bongos. Kinda' like rapping. But not. You pat the bongos and go with the beat, making up stuff that rhymes." Todd tapped on the steering wheel to demonstrate.

"We're-on-our-way. Goin'-to-LA. Gonna'-be-a-great-day."

Christy laughed. "I guess I'll have to wait and experience the full effect once you get a Bongo Fest going at home."

"Eli's gonna' be good at it. I can tell you that for sure. There's only one small challenge."

"What's that?"

"I don't have any bongo drums."

Christy laughed again. "I can give you and Eli my plastic mixing bowls. If you turn them over they make a really cool sound. Just ask Hana."

Christy glanced at their sleepy little girl in her car seat. She had a firm grip on her sippy cup and a book was flayed open across her chest. She seemed content to watch the world zoom by outside her car window.

Once Todd was on the freeway and cruising along toward the Oregon-California border, Christy gave Katie a call. Katie filled her in on the latest happenings in Katie-style, which meant her words formed one long sentence, and she only took a breath when absolutely necessary.

The good news was that Katie was doing

fine, and according to her own report, she had done a superior job of lounging about for the last week and a half.

"The bad news is," Katie said slowly. "You know those prenatal vitamins you bought me a few weeks ago? The ones in the big bottle?"

"Yes," Christy answered cautiously.

"Turns out, I'm supposed to actually take them and not just look at the pretty bottle on the nightstand." Katie laughed at her own joke.

Christy didn't laugh. "Katie!"

"I know. I'm taking them now. Don't worry. I'm not super depleted in the vitamin department. Just low on iron. The last blood test showed that I'm slightly anemic. Apparently that's fairly normal. Bonus! I get to be in the normal category for once in my life."

Christy still wasn't amused. She suggested that Eli go to the store and buy a plastic pill container that was marked for each day of the week. That way Katie would be sure to know if she had taken her vitamin every day.

"I'll ask Eli to do that. It's a good idea, Christy. The days are all sort of running together. The really good news is that Eli connected with some of the faculty who helped us at Rancho back when he and I worked on the big fund-raiser our senior year. He met with them last week and went through the whole training program. They're ready to roll. He also heard back from three other schools he contacted, and they want him to do the training with them before we return to Kenya."

"That's great."

"I know. This is exactly what Eli and I have wanted to set up with the schools for the last few years."

Christy felt a mother-hen concern peck at her at the thought of Eli spending the day at Rancho Corona University, which was about a two-hour drive from their house with traffic. "Katie, were you alone for a long time when Eli went to Rancho?"

"No. Eli drove me over to Bob and Marti's, and they babysat me all day. I helped your aunt pick out new paint colors for all the bathrooms. That woman loves to redecorate, doesn't she? Oh, by the way, heads-up for you guys. I think she gave up on the plans for an upstairs deck at your place."

"Good. I wasn't excited about dealing with the mess this summer."

"Well, don't get too relaxed because she showed me plans for putting an additional bedroom upstairs instead of a deck."

"What?"

"She said a bedroom would increase the

value more than a deck. And you know what? I just remembered. I wasn't supposed to tell you any of this. Oops."

Christy could tell that Katie's sorry-not-sorry oops was partially sincere. Katie had never been the gossipy type. Christy appreciated the forewarning so they wouldn't be blindsided with construction workers the day they returned from Glenbrooke.

"So, my mom called yesterday." Katie added the significant piece of info at the very end of their conversation. "I had left four messages for her, and she finally called me back."

"And?" Christy waited for more details.

"It was good. Kind of weird, but good."

"What was weird about it?"

"Well, I told her we were going to have a baby, and she asked a lot of questions about where we lived in Kenya and how far we were from the nearest hospital. She's never taken an interest in details like that. I appreciated it, but it felt foreign, if that makes sense."

"It makes a lot of sense. Did she seem happy for you guys? About the baby, I mean? Was she concerned about your health?"

"I don't know. She said something about it being good that we were still young and that I was strong. I told her that Eli and I would go down to Escondido to see her before we flew home. I think she appreciated that."

"I'm sure she did. You're a good daughter, Katie. Coming for your dad's funeral and helping your mom move was a huge undertaking. You did a good job honoring your father and your mother."

Katie let out a low sigh over the phone. "Thanks for saying that. I knew that coming here was the right thing to do. I never guessed when I boarded the plane in Nairobi that I was carrying a little stowaway on board."

Christy was still thinking about Katie and her little "stowaway" when Todd pulled into a campground early in the midafternoon. Christy knew she and Todd had done the right thing coming on this vacation, just as Katie knew she had done the right thing to come back to the States for her father's funeral. What Christy didn't know was how long Katie and Eli would be staying with them. She honestly didn't mind if they stayed forever.

But the inside information on Marti's plans to add a bedroom made Christy think that if Marti got her way, as she usually did, and if Eli and Katie stayed on for an undetermined time, answering Fina's question about if or when she could live with them was going to be difficult. The more Christy thought about the possibility and recognized how great it was that her brother wanted to include her in this part of his life, the more she wanted to make space in their home and in their lives for Fina. She could become one of the new close friends and possibly new family member that Christy had been hoping for.

Todd released Hana from her car seat after he was satisfied that he had settled Gussie into a fairly level part of the campsite. They had been on the road for almost seven hours, and all three of them were ready to stretch their legs. They couldn't have found a more majestic and peaceful campground. Their site felt conveniently protected under the soaring redwoods. Even though plenty of other sites were around them, they couldn't see or hear the other campers.

Christy surveyed their spot. They had a picnic table and an open fire pit and were sequestered in a misty, enchanting world of ancient trees. It felt as if they had driven into a fairytale land and shouldn't be surprised if a talking centaur came clomping through the trees.

"You were right." Christy wrapped her arms around Todd, who was holding Hana, and gave the two of them a hug. "It was worth it to take the longer route and not rush home. This is gorgeous."

Hana wiggled out of their group hug and tried to walk over to the picnic table. The ground was uneven, but she made it to her desired destination, patted her hands on the wooden bench, and turned around to show her parents how pleased she was with herself.

"What do you think? A short hike?" Todd asked.

"Sure. Do you have the trail map, or is it still in the car?"

Todd pulled the park trail map out of Gussie, locked everything up, and the three of them took off into the woods. The air was moist with the scent of moss. The trail led them uphill, and Hana trotted between them, stopping every so often to reach for a twig or pebble along the way. On every side the massive trees reached for the heavens and seemed to form an expansive, stately cathedral with the full branches forming green, ruffled archways and spires that rivaled any manmade place of worship.

Todd was humming as they walked. Christy smiled. Her husband was happy.

Her daughter was happy. They were experiencing the majestic beauty of God's creation together, and she felt like the most blessed woman on earth. The peace that embraced them as they hiked filled Christy with a sense of hope. She felt as if she was living the life she had always dreamed of having with Todd.

Her heart responded to the beauty that surrounded them and the calm that reverberated through her spirit with a quietly whispered, "Thank You, Father. Thank You."

Hana stopped and sat down in the middle of the trail with her legs straight out in front of her. She was done. Todd picked her up and carried her on his shoulders, holding on to her little legs while she patted the top of his head.

They had turned around and were heading back to their campsite when Christy took a misstep on the uneven path and lost her balance. Her right hand broke her fall, and her right hip took the majority of the impact.

"Whoa! Christy, what happened? Are you okay?" Todd put Hana down and stretched out his hand to help Christy stand.

"Yeah." Christy brushed herself off and made a weak joke about being a klutz.

"It looks like you scraped your palm. Are

you bleeding?"

Christy brushed away the dirt and leaves, revealing a raw-looking skid mark on the outside of her palm up to her little finger. A trickle of blood ran down her wrist. "Ouch."

Todd leaned in and examined her hand more closely. "We have a first-aid kit in Gussie, don't we?"

"It should be in the glove compartment. Oh, man, I am going to have a bruise the size of Texas on this hip." She rubbed her side with her uninjured hand and let out an awkward-sounding guffaw. "I sure didn't see that slip-and-slide coming."

Christy couldn't stop feeling embarrassed even though Todd and Hana were the only ones who saw her tumble. It brought back memories of many childhood attempts at anything athletic.

Hana went to Christy and wrapped her arms around Christy's sore leg. "Mama."

"I'm okay, baby. You'd better carry her, Todd."

He snatched Hana up and they made a much slower descent back to the campground. It didn't take Christy long to wash up in the restroom. The icy-cold water from the spigot helped numb her sore palm. She couldn't do much about the bruise on her hip. When she returned to the campsite,

Todd had the first-aid kit out and was ready to take charge.

Christy found it sweet and at the same time kind of funny the way he slathered on the antibacterial ointment and wrapped her entire hand in gauze and covered it with a stretchy wrap. The end result made it appear as if she had done much worse damage than she really had and would be unable to use her paw for a month.

Todd insisted that she let him take care of everything — starting the fire, hauling the backseat out of Gussie, setting up the bed, and putting everything together for dinner. Todd unstrapped a small tent he had packed on top of the van and had toggled to his surfboard at the last minute. This was the first time they had used it, but the tent turned into the perfect play area to keep Hana warmer and away from the fire pit. Christy made herself comfortable in the surprisingly spacious tent and enjoyed cuddling up with Hana while Todd displayed his best Boy Scout skills just outside the screened opening.

As evening descended, Christy and Hana crawled out of the tent and joined Todd by the fire. The scent of the wood smoke rose and mingled with the sounds of the forest, creating what Todd called "evening vespers."

He sang to Christy and Hana in a voice that was low and reverent. It was an old hymn, one that he loved.

Christy hummed along. She remembered singing this when she was a child, but she didn't know all the words the way Todd did. They sat on the bench seat Todd had pulled from Gussie with sandwiched Hana in between them. The air was chilly so Christy pulled up the hood of Hana's sweatshirt, and Todd took a picture.

"Our daughter really is the cutest little blonde, blue-eyed baby I've ever seen," Todd said with a proud grin. "Not that I'm biased or anything."

"Me either. I'm not biased at all. But I think she gets cuter all the time."

Hana wiggled her feet in her little pink tennis shoes and watched with happy fascination as her daddy roasted hot dogs for them on a long stick. She pointed at the fire and said her own version of "don't touch," since both Todd and Christy had repeated that a dozen times each since they had arrived. Hana imitated Christy when she blew on the very small bite of hot dog before giving it to Hana.

Christy was grateful that Hana was content and had adapted so easily. She probably would have been a lot fussier about this setup if they had stayed here earlier in the trip. It seemed that all the people, houses, and sleeping arrangements of the week in Glenbrooke had made Hana a lot more flexible, and Christy was grateful for that alteration in their little girl's personality.

Christy thought everything tasted good. The potato chips, the root beer, and even the slightly burnt hot dogs. Hana didn't eat much, but she settled into her bed inside Gussie without a fuss as soon as the evening sky faded to soft grays. The mist that had encircled them earlier had lifted, and when they looked straight up through the shaft between the enormous redwoods, they could see the stars piercing the night sky one by one.

"How's your hand?" Todd asked.

"Sore. But I'm sure it will be fine. Thanks for taking such good care of me." She held up her wrapped hand and thought it looked like she was wearing an oven mitt.

"I'm afraid I don't have the same soft touch you had when you took care of me after the car accident."

Just the mention of the bad accident Todd had been in her senior year of college caused a shiver to run up her neck. Christy had been terrified that Todd wouldn't recover, but he had. He still had the scars, and he sometimes felt the pinches of the internal scar tissue. But in every way he had been able to get on with his life.

Thoughts of Todd's accident meshed with feelings she still had tucked away regarding Katie's childhood. Christy combined those thoughts with some of the things she and Alissa had talked about. Terrible things happened to good people. Christy knew that. But she wished she understood why.

"Todd?"

"Um-hmm?" He poked the fire with one of his roasting sticks and cuddled up closer to Christy.

"This is going to sound strange, but I've been thinking that my life has been too easy. I mean, Katie had a rough childhood and grew up without any sort of nurturing from her parents. Alissa's dad died, her mom is an alcoholic, and Alissa gave Shawna up for adoption. You were pretty much raised without a mom and were in a serious car accident. Nothing really terrible has ever happened to me."

"Do you want something terrible to happen?"

"No, of course not. But when I look at all that my friends and family have gone through, I feel like it's about my turn to be next."

"It doesn't work like that."

"I know. I guess what I really wish is that terrible things wouldn't happen to people. I wish your mom wouldn't have abandoned you."

"My dad did a good job of raising me."

"I know, but . . ." Christy remembered similar conversations she had had with Todd along these lines in the past. She knew his position. He believed that God was God and He could do whatever He wanted.

Todd chimed in as if he was on track with what Christy was thinking. "First chapter of Job. 'The Lord gave, and the Lord has taken away. Blessed be the name of the Lord.' I have to understand that truth about God and accept it or else He and I will never have an authentic relationship. It will just be me asking God to grant all my wishes and being frustrated when He doesn't."

"I know. I understand that," Christy said. "I think you've always been more comfortable with the theology that God's ways are beyond our understanding."

"And His thoughts are beyond our thoughts. I mean, just look up, Kilikina. He made all those stars. He is beyond. Beyond us. Beyond our understanding. Beyond this tiny little planet Earth. He is Supreme. I trust Him. Even when what He does makes no sense."

Todd started humming softly. It seemed as if he had been composing all day. He did that sometimes when he was working on a new song. Perhaps the recording time with Doug had filled him up with new song ideas.

Christy tilted her head back and counted the stars. She smiled, remembering a time in high school when she and Todd had sat on the roof of his old VW van, Gus, and counted the stars. In their young lives at that time, every star shone for them with the hope that God saw them, He loved them, He had plans for them. Good plans. Now, more than a decade later, they were still counting stars. Still trusting in God's mysterious plans.

Christy dipped her chin and rested her head on Todd's shoulder. He nestled a long, warm-lipped kiss on the top of her head.

"Over the last few years that I've been teaching the Old Testament," he said. "I think I've become more at peace with trusting God even when He seems capricious. History shows that His love for us is never-ending. If I truly call myself a God Lover and want to spend my life seeking Him with my whole heart, then I have to take all of

Him for who He is on His terms, not on my terms. Because then I would be god. I'd be the one deciding what is best."

Christy agreed with what Todd was saying. Deep in her heart, she loved God. It was just that part of her still felt a mothering, nurturing sort of tenderness that wanted everyone to be safe, happy, and kind.

"You know, I was thinking about this when I was with Doug. I don't think I would have grown up with the kind of concern I have for spending time with teens if I'd had all kinds of attention from my parents. I think God used my childhood to shape me."

Christy nodded. Todd's childhood losses and pains had made him a deeply caring man. "I'm not really sure how God has used my early years to shape me, but I agree with what you just said about how yours shaped you."

Todd reached his arm around Christy and drew her close. "I like the way you're shaped," he whispered in her ear.

His breath tickled her neck, and she grinned, scrunching up her shoulder. "You're giving me goose bumps."

"Good." Todd pressed a scruffy-faced kiss into the curve of her neck. "That's my life goal. I hope when we're a hundred, I still give you chicken skin."

She giggled. "When we're a hundred, my skin will permanently look like chicken skin." She playfully tried to push him away. Todd advanced with more kisses, and Christy easily surrendered to his touch and his kisses. An excellent make-out session ensued, leaving them breathless and more deeply in love than ever before.

Some of God's mysterious ways would never be explained. Others were a gift, meant to be explored and enjoyed to the fullest.

EIGHTEEN

The next morning found the now not-so-happy campers taking their time waking up and getting going. Hana was grumpy. Todd was spacey. Christy was achy all down her right side. She checked out her bruise while in the campsite bathroom stall that morning, and it did indeed feel like the size of Texas.

They couldn't decide if they wanted to stick around for half the day and enjoy the beauty of the camping area, or if they wanted to get on the road. Christy finally suggested, after they had eaten some breakfast bars and tangerines, they get going. The map they had been given when they checked in showed lots of places to stop and view some of the exceptional redwoods, and they could take in their beauty farther down the road.

The first two stops were pretty cool. They didn't have to walk far to reach the base of some enormous trees that seemed to pierce the clouds. Todd read all the information on the signs by the trees and seemed to be captivated with the details.

"It's amazing. Think about it." Todd kept talking about the trees even after they were back on the road. "That tree started growing when Christ was walking around the Sea of Galilee on the other side of the earth. It's two thousand years old and it's still alive. I think that's incredible."

Hana had little interest in the giant redwoods or anything else. She fussed, didn't want crackers, and only wanted her sippy cup so she could gnaw on the spout.

"I think she's teething again," Christy said after giving Hana a soft ring from her bag of toys and watching her chomp onto it and then let out a wail.

"I'm convinced that the reason God didn't allow us to remember much until we're three or four," Todd said, "is because we would all be suffering PTSD if we remembered the pain of teething."

Christy tried every gadget and teething remedy she had with them, but nothing comforted their little girl. When they rolled into the first small town after exiting the redwoods, Todd pulled into a convenience store.

"I know you want to always go natural and organic with her." He turned off Gussie's motor. "But I'm going to get her some children's pain reliever. They have to have something that will help her."

Christy didn't argue. She had taken pain relievers that morning for her aches, and like Todd, she had run out of patience with Hana's crying. As they waited, Christy crawled into the back and took Hana out of her car seat. She changed her diaper, smoothed some baby lavender soothing drops on Hana's bare feet, and tried to interest her in a teething cracker.

All Hana wanted to do was hold on to Christy.

That made it doubly difficult to strap her back in her car seat after Todd returned with the liquid drops that he gave to Hana right away.

"Why don't you hold her a little longer?" Todd said. "I want to go over and check out that pawn shop."

Why in the world her husband looked so excited about visiting a pawn shop was beyond Christy. Why a tiny town even had a pawn shop was beyond her. Todd had said earlier, when Hana was throwing all the toys Christy offered her, they should have bought some new toys for the ride home. If he was thinking of purchasing her toys from the pawn shop, Christy was ready to insist he not give them to her until after Christy had a chance to clean them.

As Christy sang to Hana, she finally relaxed in Christy's arms and stopped crying. Todd returned in five minutes. His arms were behind his back, and his smile was from ear to ear.

"You're not going to believe this."

"What did you find?"

Todd held out a small set of dual bongos. "Vintage," was all he said, as if Christy had as much knowledge about instruments as he did.

"Groovy," Christy teased him back.

"And they told me an ice cream shop is at the end of the block. You want an ice cream cone?"

"Sure."

"Do you want to come with me or stay here?"

Hana hadn't popped up and wiggled to go with Todd so Christy told him, "I'll stay."

"What do you want?"

"Surprise me. Just one scoop. No nuts."

Todd put the bongos on the floor of Gussie and took off for the ice cream shop. Hana had fixed her gaze on the bongo drums and slid out of Christy's lap so she could examine them more closely. She tapped her flattened palm on one of the drum heads and then took out her pacifier and tried to use it as a hammer. Christy pulled the pacifier out of her hand and bent over to show Hana how to pat the drums.

When Todd returned, Hana was still patting the drums. He handed Christy a single scoop vanilla ice cream cone and said, "Hey, look at you! We're ready for our first Bongo Fest. You and me, Sunshine. It's gonna be epic."

Christy laughed. Hana was suddenly more interested in the ice cream cone in Christy's hand. She made all the usual "peeze" begging sounds, and Christy seized this as the opportunity to put her back in her car seat. As soon as she was strapped in, Christy shared her cone with Hana. Todd's choice looked like a variation of Rocky Road with way too many nuts, marshmallows, and other dangers for him to share any of his. Todd climbed back in the driver's seat and pointed Gussie south, heading home.

The rest of the day was a vast improvement over the first half. Hana slept almost three hours and didn't even wake when they stopped for gas. When she did wake, her fascination with the bongo drums returned. They fit across the top of her car seat, and she kept the tapping going as Todd grinned and bobbed his head.

"Our daughter is going to be the greatest bongo player the world has ever seen," Todd said, checking her out in his rearview mirror. "She's got crazy rhythm. Do you hear that?"

Christy heard it. She had been hearing it for more than an hour now and was ready for quiet. Peace and quiet.

The quiet didn't come until much later when they finally made it to their campsite near Half Moon Bay. They discovered that they were so far past the check-in time of their reservation that their spot had been given away, and they couldn't stay there for the night as planned.

Undaunted, Todd suggested that they change Hana and find a place to eat dinner. Then he said he would keep on driving so they wouldn't be facing the traffic in the San Francisco area tomorrow morning.

The plan worked. Hana slept. Christy and Todd talked about everything they could think of as they drove until almost midnight. Christy used her phone to make a reservation for them at an economy-priced hotel in Watsonville. They carried Hana into the clean, efficient room, set up her portable bed, and coaxed her back to sleep. It was well past one thirty when Christy thought for sure that all was well, and she and Todd could go to sleep.

However, Todd decided he couldn't sleep unless he unstrapped his surfboard from Gussie's roof and brought it inside their room. Christy held the door open for him as he lugged the big orange board inside and leaned it against the wall.

They had only been asleep for twenty minutes when a loud thump woke all three of them. The surfboard had slid across the wall and fallen down, missing Hana's bed by inches. Hana cried hysterically, the guests in the room next to Christy and Todd pounded on the wall, and Christy told Todd they should just leave.

"We can't leave. I'm too tired to drive any more tonight." He was holding Hana, bouncing her too roughly for her to ever fall sleep.

"Let me hold her," Christy said. As soon as Todd handed her over, Christy realized that Hana's diaper was wet all the way through her pj's. Christy went on the hunt for a dry diaper as Todd crawled back in bed with his bent forearm covering his eyes. The guests in the neighboring room thumped on the wall as Hana kept crying.

This is the worst night of my life!

Christy was so frustrated with the inflexibility she had due to her right hand still being swaddled in Todd's first-aid wrap that she peeled off the wrapping in a series of dramatic tugs and twists. Hana kept crying.

As soon as Christy managed to put a dry diaper on Hana, she stopped crying. Christy realized she didn't have dry pajamas, and all of Hana's clothes were still in Gussie. The way the surfboard had landed in the close quarters, it was blocking the door so it couldn't be opened. Todd had either given in to exhaustion and was asleep, or he was doing an exceptionally good job of looking like he was asleep. She saw no point in trying to wake him up, moving the surfboard, and going outside for Hana's clothes.

Christy's sore hand was open to the air now, and it felt as if a dozen pins and needles had been inserted at all the tender spots. She haphazardly pulled a pillowcase off the extra pillow on their bed and put Hana inside it, feet first. With her hand stinging, Christy laid Hana back in the bed inside her DIY sleeping bag and hoped it would be enough to keep her warm. She tucked Hana's favorite blanket around her, gave her a pacifier, and turned off the light. Thankfully, Hana didn't make a peep. None of them stirred until after nine o'clock.

The general mood in the Spencer clan was not great, but it was much better than it had been in the middle of the night. The rest of the ride home was all about variety. They stopped often for short stretches. They played an assortment of their audiobooks and music. During the last three hours, as they inched along in LA traffic, Christy did something they had promised each other they wouldn't do.

They let Hana watch a kiddie show on Christy's phone.

From the day Hana was born, they had agreed they didn't want to give their daughter too much screen time too early. Hana was curious about their phones but didn't grab for them. However, the time had come. This was the only option for sanity that they could see happening.

Christy strapped herself into the backseat beside Hana and held the phone. The show came on, and suddenly peace was restored.

"We caved." Was the way Christy explained it the next morning when she was talking to Katie about the ride home. Eli and Katie were already asleep when Christy and Todd finally arrived home and unloaded their necessities as quietly as possible. It felt good to be back in their own bed and to sleep until Hana woke up.

"I'm afraid we've created a monster," Christy said. "I found Hana going through my purse this morning. I think she was on the hunt for my phone."

Katie was sitting up in bed. She had color in her face and looked calm. "If that's the worst choice you've made so far as a parent, I think you're going to be all right. Besides, who's to say that wasn't the best way to parent her in that moment?"

"It's just that we made it almost the whole trip using all the non-techie options." Christy tried to suppress a yawn. "Oh, sorry. I'm so tired."

"You need a vacation from your vacation, right?"

"It's not quite that bad. So tell me. What did Linda say at your appointment yesterday?"

"It was all good news, pretty much. She wants me to take it easy over the next week but start doing some minor activities."

"Like walking on the beach?"

"Yes, like walking on the beach. And she wants me to come back next week. I can't believe how much attention she's giving me."

"You're family to us and she's family to us. Of course she's going to take good care of you. I think it's perfect that you guys are here right now."

"Oh, and she ripped into me for not taking any prenatal vitamins earlier. Eli bought me one of those containers you suggested, and I haven't missed a day since."

Christy didn't want to mention that it hadn't even been a full week yet, but a good start at anything should never be viewed in a negative light.

Eli and Todd came into the guest bedroom just then with Hana right behind them. They had been in the kitchen, and Eli apparently heard what they were saying about the prenatal vitamins because he handed Katie a glass of water.

"Take," Eli said. "Now."

"Wow. Overkill, Lorenzo," Katie teased her husband. Turning to Christy she said, "Please tell this dictator to go away and send in my subtle Goatee Guy. I liked the way he fluffed my pillows and brought me milkshakes on demand."

"Your princess days are numbered, *mpenzi wangu.*"

"What did you call her?" Christy asked.

Katie answered. "That's his Swahili way of trying to charm me. He says it means 'sweetheart.' For all I know it could mean 'sassy old goat.' "

Eli seemed to be repressing a grin as he

gave Christy and Todd a look that seemed to say, "Do you see what I've had to put up with while you were gone?"

Katie opened her vitamin container and popped one of the large pills while Hana continued emptying the two bottom dresser drawers of Eli's clothes. She was now putting them back in the drawers in a much less orderly fashion. Christy quickly tried to put things where they belonged, with an apology to Eli.

"Don't worry about it." Eli grinned. *"Hakuna matata."*

"I told Eli you used to have Hana's toys in that drawer."

"You can put her toys back in the drawers if you want," Eli said. "I can put my clothes somewhere else."

"Before you guys start rearranging everything," Todd said. "Eli and I were talking about tonight. He's agreed to speak at the Gathering again, like he did while we were gone. We were thinking we would go surfing tomorrow morning, and then on Thursday we thought we would take Hana for the whole day so you two can go to a spa."

"A spa?" Katie repeated.

Todd and Eli both had the same sort of trying-to-be-a-good-husband-here look on their faces.

"Thursday?" Christy vaguely remembered something was on the calendar for Thursday. She knew that family dinner was the next Sunday, but what was it on Thursday?

"Is that a yes?" Todd asked.

"Well . . ." Christy appreciated the gesture, and Katie seemed to be doing well enough to have a maternity massage at the spa where Christy used to work. But it was expensive, and she knew they had just spent every last penny of their budgeted vacation money. As nice as it was that the guys had come up with this idea for them to have a girls' day out, Christy thought the idea was way too extravagant.

"Kilikina." Todd got her attention and raised his eyebrows. He seemed to think it was funny that she was faltering. "This is what I'm giving you for your birthday. It's a gift."

"My birthday! It's Thursday, isn't it?"

"Twenty-nine is one that should be celebrated with a spa day. At least that's what Marti told me when she texted me last week and suggested it."

"Twenty-nine." Christy repeated the number as if she had just woken from a long sleep and suddenly had been reminded what day and year it was. She slipped her hand in Todd's, pulled it to her lips, and kissed the back of his brawny fist. "Thank you."

"You're welcome."

"I'm telling ya," Katie said. "The service around here just keeps getting better and better. A spa day. Wow! Just one question. What does one do at a spa day?"

Christy grinned. "Just wait, Katie. You'll see. It's going to be wonderful. Super relaxing."

"Well, that's good." Katie's sarcastic tone was at an all-time high. "Because relaxing is what I've been waiting for! I mean, taking it easy is going to be such a nice change-up from what I've been experiencing around here for weeks now."

The realization of the gift Todd had just offered her sunk in, and Christy thanked him again. Then another thought ricocheted through her.

"By any chance does this mean Aunt Marti is coming, too?"

NINETEEN

"I'm sure your aunt would want to go, if you asked her," Todd replied. "But I didn't include her when I made the reservation."

Christy felt relieved. She liked the idea of having a girls' day with only Katie. No toddler calling out "Mama, Mama." No well-meaning aunt pelting her with questions about Fina or any of her headstrong renovation plans. Christy could hardly wait.

Just to be sure, they ran the plan past Linda, and she gave Katie a few guidelines on what she should and shouldn't do at the spa. The pregnancy massage was fine with Linda. She even remarked that if she could get away, she would love to join them.

"I'll just have to wait, and we can celebrate your birthday on Sunday at Family Night Dinner." Linda volunteered to bring cake and ice cream. Marti and Bob were bringing the main course, and Christy's mom was bringing a salad.

The birthday weekend was shaping up to be relaxing for Christy. The downshifting started the moment she and Katie arrived at the White Orchid Spa, located inside one of the more upscale resorts in Newport Beach. What surprised Christy the most was how much of the staff had changed since she worked there. Eva, the spa manager, greeted Christy with a warm, "Happy birthday! And congratulations! We've missed you around here, Christy. It's good to see you."

"It's good to see you, too."

Eva presented Christy and Katie with small gift bags filled with lots of samples of the high-end lotions and body-care products they sold at the spa. She then showed them to the welcome room, the way Christy used to do with the guests. Eva pointed out the lockers with plush robes and slippers, the fresh towels, and where they could find the showers, hot tub, saunas, and lounge area where fresh fruit and herbal teas were awaiting them.

"You have full access to the resort pool area, as you know," Eva said. "If you choose, however, to stay within the spa facilities and enjoy the cabanas by the smaller spa pool, you can order food and drinks poolside. Please don't hesitate to let us know if we can make this day more special for you in any way."

Christy smiled and thanked Eva. It all felt so familiar, down to the welcome instructions Christy had repeated so many times.

Katie looked more than a little out of her element. "So, we're supposed to leave our clothes in here and put on our bathing suits now?"

"We have massages, first. What I always told guests was to undress to their comfort level, put on the robe and slippers, and enjoy the tranquility room. The massage therapists will come for us there."

"We really do peel down then, huh? Okay. First time for everything, I guess."

After donning their robes and slippers, Christy and Katie settled into the overstuffed chairs in the relaxation room and sipped the herbal tea of the day. Christy recognized it as one of the fruity Rooibos blends she had made many times. The tea was her least favorite of all the blends, but a few sips were enough to help her slip into the relaxing, pamper-time mode.

"This angel music makes me feel like I could fall asleep right here," Katie whispered, closing her eyes. "How did you manage to work here and not doze off during your first hour?"

"I was always on my feet and on the go,"

Christy said. "If we had a lull in clients, we always had something to do on the website or calling clients to confirm their reservations."

"And here I thought all you did was make tea and roll up towels."

"I did that, too." Christy leaned her head back. "These chairs are really comfy, aren't they? I don't think I ever sat in one of them."

The door to the relaxation room opened, and a massage therapist that Christy didn't know stepped inside. She was wearing the standard black top and pants. "Christy? Katie? Welcome. This way, please."

They were led into the largest room where couple's massages usually took place. It turned out that Todd booked that room because he thought Christy and Katie would want to be together so they could talk during their hot stone massage. Clearly, Todd didn't understand the serenity and silence part of an hour-long massage.

The other novice part of the plan was that Todd had made the reservation for two pregnancy massages.

"Only one of us has a baby on board," Katie said glibly to the therapist. "Unless there's something you haven't told me yet, Christy."

Christy calmly slid under the sheet on the

massage table in the darkened room and lowered her voice to about the same tone as the soft music. She hoped Katie would take the cue and lower her voice as well.

"I'm not pregnant, but I'm fine with whatever type of relaxing massage you want to give me. Believe me, I'm ready."

The two friends settled in on the massage tables, and the therapists went to work, starting with a diffusion of lavender in the air. Christy felt as if her face was melting into the face cradle in the massage table as she took a deep breath and let it out slowly. The therapist smoothed down the sheet covering Christy's back and applied her warm hands in long, soothing motions. Christy knew this was going to be good.

Katie started giggling. Christy cringed. She tried to ignore the muffled chortles, but when Katie laughed like that, Christy always found it difficult not to join in. Katie's giggles were the kind that came from the compelling urge to laugh aloud, but since the urge was being repressed, the laughter leaked out in a series of quiet, usually tear-soaked, shoulder-shaking sounds that mimicked the squeaks of a small tropical bird.

"Katie," Christy whispered. She felt embarrassed. Here they were at a high-class resort, indulging in expensive massages by expert therapists, and Katie was laughing.

"It tickles," Katie whispered between her pinched giggles. It sounded as if she was making a supreme effort to curb her undignified laughter and take the goal of relaxing more seriously. Either that or the therapist had moved away from the ticklish areas.

The room grew still again, and fairylike strains of harp music circled them. Christy grinned to herself.

Oh, Katie Girl, only you would crack up laughing at your first massage. I have missed your spontaneous personality so much. You really are my favorite Peculiar Treasure.

Christy gave in to the warm sensation of the hot stones as the therapist smoothed out the tightened muscles in Christy's shoulders. She thought of all the times she had ducked into this same room with her phone over the last few years and spent her lunch break on a video catch-up call with Katie. Now here they were, together in the same room, doing life side by side for a brief but wonderful season. Christy felt grateful.

Her thoughts slipped into a calmly woven tapestry of prayers. She asked God to protect and bless Katie and Eli and their little baby. She thanked God for them and for Todd and Hana, Bob, Marti, her parents, her brother, Fina, and then for her friends in Glenbrooke. The exhaling of thankfulness melded with the massage, and when the hour was over, Christy felt like a relaxed noodle.

"So that wasn't as awkward as I thought it was going to be," Katie said once they had changed into their bathing suits and were stretched out under a cabana by the pool.

"Does that mean you enjoyed it?" Christy felt very posh, stretched out on the thickly cushioned chaise lounge in her bathing suit and wearing her sunglasses.

"I did." Katie flopped on her side. "So, what's next?"

"Nothing. Just this. Relaxing."

"Do we get our own private pool boy who brings us tropical drinks with little umbrellas?"

"They don't have pool boys, Katie. But someone will come by and ask if we want anything to eat or drink. The menu is here." Christy handed her a small, padded folder like waiters used in high-end restaurants to present the bill.

"What are you going to have?" Katie skimmed the short list of options.

"It's all really good. Do they still have the spinach wrap with turkey on the menu?"

"Yep. It comes with sweet potato fries and aioli sauce, whatever that is."

"That's what I'm going to have."

"Make it two of those." Katie snapped the menu closed. "And a banana-strawberry smoothie." She stood up and pulled down the back of the bathing suit she had borrowed from Christy. "It's been ages since I've worn a bathing suit. Not exactly in my comfort zone right now. I'm glad we're the only ones out here."

Christy grinned. It was such a perfect California summer day. The air was warm, and this enclosed, private pool area felt like a luxurious sanctuary. She was content to stretch out in the shade of their blue-and-white-striped cabana and doze off now that she was so relaxed. It made sense that Katie was restless and not excited about taking a nap. She had been stretching out and dozing every day for weeks now.

"What do you think?"

Christy opened her eyes and saw Katie standing in front of her, showing off her profile. "Do I have a baby bump yet?"

Christy lowered her sunglasses. Katie was just beginning to show. "I believe you do. Just a tiny baby bump."

"Would you take a picture?" Katie had brought her phone to the pool and left it resting on the table between their two lounge chairs. "This will be the first one. Then I'll take a side shot every month on the twenty-seventh, no matter where I am, until this little charmer makes its grand entrance into the world. I want my child to know what a classy beginning he or she had. Get the pool in the background."

Katie struck a pose and Christy snapped several shots. Christy couldn't stop smiling. This really was the best birthday gift Todd could have given her. Watching Katie be Katie was always a gift that kept on giving whenever Christy returned to their times together in her memory.

In this case, the memories started being relived only a few days later, on Sunday evening when the clan gathered for their monthly dinner at Todd and Christy's. Marti came with an armful of gifts for both Christy and Katie and wanted to hear all about the spa day.

Katie was hilarious, as she described the sensation of exposing her bare back to someone she never had met before and trying to remain quiet as the woman "pummeled" her with "hot lava stones."

Christy laughed, but Aunt Marti looked confused, as if Katie had missed the point entirely. Todd took advantage of the moment, seeing that Marti was off guard, and asked her about the plans for the upstairs addition of a new bedroom.

Marti did a quick visual sweep of all the possible snitches around the counter. Her eyes narrowed when she looked at Katie.

"Sorry!" Katie held up her hands. "I can't be trusted with secret information. Everyone in this room needs to know that. We'll all get along much better if everyone understands that with my brain, the barn door is always open."

"No matter." Marti regained her composure and ran through the details. Plans were awaiting approval, she hoped construction could start as early as mid-August, and wasn't it wonderful that she had come up with this idea?

Eli was the only one who appeared surprised at the Marti tornado that had just circled the conversation and sucked everything up in its vortex. The rest of them had experienced the whirlwind before.

"We have a few pieces to add to your plan," Todd said diplomatically. Christy couldn't help but wonder if he chose to bring all this up in front of everyone so he would have the counsel of the tribe on his side. "We don't know how long Katie and Eli will be here, but the noise and mess could be a problem while she's still on bed-rest."

Christy was surprised that he wasn't protesting the entire plan. She and Todd had only discussed Marti's agenda briefly and only had Katie's comments to go on. Christy resisted the idea of living in a construction zone for any reason when Hana was toddling about and getting into everything. Adding an upstairs bedroom would make Christy's everyday life very difficult.

The others were all looking at Linda for her advice on Katie's term of bedrest. "If things continue the way they have been, I think you'll be fine to travel in August. That is, if the two of you decide that's what you want to do. I am not so secretly wishing along with Christy that you both could stay, and I could be the one to deliver your baby."

It warmed Christy's heart to see how much Linda cared about Katie and Eli.

The two of them exchanged glances, and Katie said, "We need to go home. Eventually. When it's safe. But, yeah, as much as we love it here, we need to go home."

The word "home" settled on Christy, and she understood. Kenya was now the home of Katie's heart. California was where she came from, but this wasn't the place that made her come alive, the way Africa did. The same was true for Eli and always had been.

Marti gave Todd a satisfied look, as if September was still an acceptable start date. Christy expected him now to pose the argument that they should have a say in the mess since they were the ones occupying the space. Instead, Todd brought up the hot topic of David and Fina and how she had asked to live with them.

It was as if Todd had tossed a handful of firecrackers into a fire pit. Family members wanted details about Fina. They all had opinions about what sort of job David should look for, and they wanted to know arrival dates, which Christy and Todd didn't know.

Marti's voice rose above the rest when she said, "She will live with us. There is no need to discuss this any further. Robert, don't you agree?"

Bob seemed to take the temperature in the room to see how Christy's parents felt about all this. "Fina would be welcome, of course. But listen, here's where we have to settle on the plans for the additional bedroom upstairs." He squared his shoulders and raised his voice as if wanting to make sure his declarations were taken seriously.

"Christy and Todd should have the final say on the addition. They should decide when and if the construction takes place."

Marti agreed but added, "We all can see, though, that it's not a matter of 'if,' as you said, Robert. It's simply a matter of 'when.' " Turning to face Christy with a slightly raised eyebrow, Marti reiterated, "The upstairs bedroom will be added. My preference is that it be completed this year. These things should be in place before you actually need them."

Christy wasn't sure if Marti was trying to say that they needed more bedrooms because of all the company they tended to open their home to, or if Marti was, in her own way, hinting that Christy and Todd should have everything in place so they could have another baby.

Either way, Christy knew then and there that she would be living in a world of dust and noise before long. The tribe had spoken.

Later that evening, when Linda lit the candles on Christy's dark chocolate birthday cake, Christy's thoughts flashed back to three years ago when she had stood in almost the same place at the island in her kitchen and Tracy was lighting the candles on the scrumptious carrot cake she had made. As Christy closed her eyes to make a wish on her twenty-sixth birthday, her thoughts centered around the dreamy possibility of returning to Maui that year.

The thought made her laugh now.

But her second wish had come true the next year. Christy had wished for a baby, and now they had Hana.

The lit candles on the chocolate cake were filling the room with smoke. Christy's family sang the "Happy Birthday" song as Hana clapped in her daddy's arms. Christy closed her eyes, ready to make a wish. She didn't wish for another baby or for Katie to stay indefinitely. She knew Katie wanted to go home. Christy didn't wish for Marti to drop the renovation plans. That would never happen.

Drawing in a slow breath, Christy thought about the only thing that was still floating on top of her heart after their trip to Glenbrooke. She wanted to meet another mom, like her, in the same season of life. She needed a new Peculiar Treasure or two in her life. Not someone who would replace Katie, but someone who would be a nearby heart-to-heart friend the way Tracy had been.

Christy opened her eyes, blew out all the candles, and watched the wavy lines of smoke curve their way upward. She loved the whimsy that such moments brought into her life with wishes and sweet celebrations. What mattered most deeply to her, though, was the prayer that was forming in her heart as she cut into the scrumptious-looking cake and extracted the first piece.

It's not just a wish, Father God. It's really a prayer. A prayer from my heart. In Your way and in Your time, please bless me with a new friend.

TWENTY

The next week and a half was just about perfect.

Katie felt great. Her skin glowed, her face filled out again, and dark shadows no longer haunted her eyes. She and Eli returned from their doctor's visit on the Monday after Family Night Dinner and were ecstatic about having heard their baby's heartbeat together for the first time.

Christy remembered that moment with Todd and how it all finally felt real. A tiny person was inside her, growing and developing. Hana became real to them and was no longer a list of symptoms manifesting themselves in Christy.

The mystery and miracle of life became the theme around Todd and Christy's home. Katie was ready for all the books Christy had on pregnancy, and Eli was ready to download the app Todd had told him about. They were so cute, sharing every slice of information with each other, as if they were study buddies and both wanted very badly to receive an A+ on the upcoming test of childbirth.

Eli had managed to set up four fund-raiser training meetings with universities in the area, and Todd had gone to three of the meetings with him. That left Christy, Katie, and Hana to enjoy some free-spirited times together in between Christy's sewing sessions.

When the two couples were together, they shared some great dinners. They walked on the beach at night with Hana swinging between them. They sat around the fire pit on the deck and talked about the deeper issues of life, marriage, and raising children. Todd even managed to convince Eli to attempt a Bongo Fest one night.

In many ways, that week and a half, as well as most of that summer, seemed like a rite-of-passage season to Christy. She and her closest friends were growing up. Their lives were changing. But God in His tender mercy had allowed them the chance to go through those changes together, on the same side of the planet, under the same roof, around the same fire, with the same heart. The experiences were extraordinary for all of them, and they spoke of it with hushed reverence, as if by openly recognizing the shimmering bits of glory being sprinkled on their lives, the glow would fade.

Christy knew this would be a golden chapter in the book of her days. Even if the memories faded for the others, she would always remember the way her heart was at peace and the depth of joy she felt. She wrote in her journal that the days were like one long, happiness-filled farewell party as the four of them said good-bye to what had passed.

Later in the week, Christy wrote in her journal that she saw the four of them being side by side in two outrigger canoes. They were paddling in tandem through an azure, sun-kissed sea. All the while they knew they were lining up their individual vessels in such a way that when the right swell came, it would propel them in opposite directions.

Until then, they would splash about as if it were the last day of summer vacation before school started and they had been given permission to stay up all night.

The dreaded announcement that the party was coming to an end came from Eli's lips on the second Tuesday morning in August. Katie couldn't even look at Christy when Eli asked if they could all sit down in the living room.

"We booked our flight," Eli said with steady, even words. "We leave on Friday."

"This Friday?" Christy felt needles in her lips as she formed the words.

Eli nodded slowly. "Linda gave us the okay yesterday. When I checked flights, I found it was a lot less expensive if we left this week instead of next week for some reason."

"I'll take you to the airport." Todd's voice sounded gruff, but Christy knew he was holding back his emotions, too, and that always made his throat tighten up.

"We just called Katie's mom and told her we would go down to Escondido to see her today."

"Today?" Christy didn't mean to keep repeating Eli's words, but she felt like she was scrambling for ways to grab on to more pieces of Eli and Katie. More of their precious final days. "Would you like to have a special dinner here with my family or anyone? I'd be happy to put something together."

Katie looked at Christy for the first time. Her green eyes were awash in tears. "No." Katie's voice was small. "I think a dinner would turn into a sappy thing. It's going to be hard enough as it is. We don't need to multiply it."

Hana, who had been looking at books on

Christy's lap in the side chair, wiggled down and went over to Katie. She tried to pull herself up onto the couch. Katie picked her up and put her on the sofa next to her. Hana gazed up at Katie's face, quietly resting beside her.

"See what I mean?" Katie opened her arm and moved Hana close beside her.

"We love you guys." Christy felt an immense fondness for her empathetic little girl right now. "Obviously, none of us wants you to leave, including Hana."

"We'll do whatever we can to help, though," Todd added. "Whatever you need, just let us know."

"Right now what we need is to get out the door. We told Katie's mom we would be there in time to have lunch with her in the dining room at eleven thirty."

Eli and Katie rolled out half an hour later, taking Clover for one last trip to Escondido. Christy felt sick to her stomach. She hadn't eaten much for breakfast and didn't think she could keep anything down. Her emotions were more intense than she thought they would be. She had known this was coming. It was for the best. But it still made her feel wrung out.

"Can you be on full Daddy duty with Hana for a while?" Christy felt that if she

314

didn't go back to bed now and sleep off this severe dip, she wouldn't be much good for the rest of the day.

"Sure. I was planning to go over to your parents' place. Your dad asked if I could help him with a couple of repair projects. I'm sure your mom won't mind having Hana."

"Could you check with her first?"

"Okay. Are you just tired?"

"I'm heart-sick and tired, and my stomach hurts."

"Do you want me to bring back anything for you?"

"No. Well, maybe some sparkling water. I don't think we have any."

"Text me if you want anything else." Todd leaned over to Hana, who was seated on the kitchen floor, pounding on the underside of a plastic food container with a plastic soup ladle. "You're ready for Bongo Fest, aren't you?"

Christy grinned. When Todd had attempted to reenact the Glenbrooke Bongo Fest last week with Eli, Hana had already gone to bed. Their session didn't last long since Eli didn't have a bongo set to echo back when Todd pounded on his vintage set.

Leaving the kitchen as it was in a morning mess and carrying up the laundry from the dryer, Christy returned to her haven and crawled back into her unmade bed.

I loved our golden summer with Eli and Katie. God, bless them. Please protect them and their little one.

Christy curled up and pulled the sheet up to her chin. She heard Todd leaving with Hana a short time later and allowed herself the chance to cry. Her head pounded. Sleep came in snatches. She was uncomfortable in every way. No position felt good. She was too hot, and then she was too cold. Christy finally gave up. She slid her feet into her fuzzy slippers and padded downstairs to the empty kitchen.

Christy opened the refrigerator door and stared at the items on the shelves for a long while before she decided nothing sounded good. She did the same with the pantry, holding onto the cupboard knobs as if the doors would snap shut if she let go. The only thing that appealed to her was graham crackers. Ever since they had visited Sierra, Christy kept a box of graham crackers on hand for Hana. She pulled one out and nibbled on it, immediately deciding it was too dry, and she needed some milk.

The only milk she could find was a box of soy milk at the back of the fridge. It was left over from when Katie first arrived and had been putting together concoctions in the blender. Christy smashed several graham crackers into the glass of soy milk, and since the result wasn't very tasty, she added a banana and mashed it all up in the glass.

Three bites into her graham goulash, Christy was convinced her combo was not a winner. It was too bad, because she had used the last banana and now nothing was in the house that appealed to her. She tried another two bites of goulash and poured the rest down the sink.

She was about to head upstairs to brush her teeth to rid herself of the disagreeable soy taste in her mouth, when the doorbell rang. Christy looked through the peephole and saw Aunt Marti standing on the doorstep with a brawny-looking man in a polo shirt.

"Christina, why don't you answer your phone?" Marti scolded the instant Christy opened the door. "I called and texted you twice. This is Dennis. He is overseeing the renovation, and if you don't mind, we need to come in and get a few measurements."

Christy had thought her aunt couldn't possibly find a new way to throw her off guard, and yet she had.

Christy sheepishly let them in, folding her

arms in front of her because she had taken off her bra when she went back to bed and was lounging around in a cotton T-shirt and her most ragged pair of summer shorts.

"Nice to meet you." Dennis extended his hand to shake with Christy. "We won't be here long. Sorry to disrupt your day."

"It's okay." Christy stood back and let Marti lead the way upstairs.

She followed close behind and was aware of the mess all of them would see as soon as they looked in the master bedroom. The mound of clean laundry had been tossed on her snuggle chair. Christy had made a rule never to put clothes on her snuggle chair because she wanted it to always be open and ready for her to retreat to it whenever she needed to fall into its comforting hug. This morning, though, she had broken her rule, and on top of the haphazard laundry was the bra she had flung off before trying to get comfy for a nap.

Christy knew she had violated the little manners details that her aunt had drilled into her when she was a teenager and had left her clothes scattered around the guest room. Marti's words haunted her this morning: *"A lady never allows her private undergarments to be seen by anyone but her husband. That includes a strap peeking out where it should not be peeking out or even when air drying your finery."*

Marti's decade-and-a-half-old admonition rested on Christy now as she watched Marti and Dennis enter her disastrously cluttered bedroom. Dennis pulled out a fancy-looking tape measure, and after stepping around the boxes of sewing supplies, he measured the window where Christy's sewing machine was set up. Everything in the already small master bedroom had felt even smaller when Eli and Katie moved in. For the first time, Christy found herself warming to the idea of an additional bedroom. Maybe she would turn it into an upstairs workroom, and that way the guest room would always be ready.

Or maybe it would be a bigger room for Hana, and I could turn the nursery back into my workroom.

She liked that possibility a lot. Christy stood back as Dennis recorded information on his iPad. She did her best not to make eye contact with Aunt Marti. She just wanted everyone to leave so she could try to nap again before Todd and Hana returned.

"Okay if I have a look at the end of the hall?" Dennis was already out the bedroom door. "Is that a closet?"

"Yes, it's a small storage closet." Christy's

319

stomach grumbled loudly, and she folded her arms in front of herself again. Her goulash was not adapting to its unhappy environment.

"Looks like you would have more space through here," Dennis said. "You would lose the closet and the bedroom window, but the angle is a better angle for the room because of the amount of square footage you're allowed on the permit."

"Then by all means, go through the closet," Marti said.

"Wait. Did you say we would lose the window?" Christy asked.

"Yes."

"Could you add a new window somewhere?"

Dennis and Marti both looked at her as if she had asked for the moon.

"Not if you want the full square footage allowed for in the permit."

Christy curled back inward, her arms folded across her grumbling stomach. "I really love having a window there. For the fresh air." Christy felt like she needed a breath of fresh air at that moment.

Marti frowned. "Are you all right, dear? You look terribly pale."

"I think I had some bad soy milk." Christy barely finished her sentence when she realized the inevitability of her banana goulash making a return appearance. She ran to the master bathroom, nearly stumbling over a box in her haste. She didn't even take time to close the bathroom door. She barely made it to the bowl.

Christy hadn't thought she could appear any grosser or disheveled to her aunt and the contractor than she had in their ten minutes together. But she had managed to do just that. As soon as she rinsed out her mouth and washed her face, Christy heard her aunt call out from downstairs.

"I'll call you later, dear! Please do take care of yourself."

Christy felt relieved when she heard the front door close behind them. She took a long, slow drink of cool water and returned to bed. Feeling better, she checked her phone that she had left on the nightstand. Yes, Marti had called twice and texted twice. David had sent a long text, too, saying that he and Fina would be done at Camp Heather Brook in three weeks but were sticking around in Glenbrooke for the Labor Day festivities. They would fly into the Orange County airport on September 6.

Pulling the covers back over her, Christy forced herself not to think about what her house and life would look like by September 6 with the renovation underway, and Fina possibly living with them.

In the same way that she had seen a spark of promise and benefit in adding the additional bedroom, Christy also saw a glint of logic and relief when she thought about agreeing that it would be best for Fina to move in with Bob and Marti. She had told Todd earlier that she didn't want to do that to Fina, but maybe the poor young woman should be tossed into the deep end of the Miller family so she could decide if she wanted to swim the distance with David's clan.

The good thing was that they still had a few weeks before anything had to be decided. For now, all Christy wanted to do was sleep. When she woke an hour and a half later, she took a long shower and texted Todd to see how Hana was doing at her parents' apartment. All was well. Hana was napping, and Todd was going to help on a few more projects before coming home.

The house was so quiet, Christy barely knew what to do. She could watch a movie if she wanted or fold her laundry and sit in her snuggle chair, enjoying her bedroom window while it lasted, and read a book. The one thing she didn't want to do was eat anything. Her stomach was still yelling at her for the not-so-joy ride she had sent it on earlier.

Sadly, her stomach continued to yell at her off and on for most of the day. By the time Todd and Hana had returned that afternoon, Christy had almost convinced herself she was coming down with a bug. It wasn't just the bad soy milk. She felt drained and depressed because, if she was in the first stages of some flu virus, she didn't want to accidently share it with Katie and Eli and have them getting sick on their long flight home.

She told Todd that evening, "When Eli and Katie get back, just tell them I'm going to lie low tonight, and I'll see how I'm doing in the morning."

"Sounds wise. Can I get you anything?"

Christy adjusted her position in bed. "No. You better throw out the soy milk, though, so no one else drinks it."

"You don't want anything to eat?"

Christy shook her head.

Todd gave Christy a curious look. She recognized it as the "counselor" look and prepared herself for a bit of his unasked-for advice.

"I know you're really bummed about Katie and Eli leaving. I am, too. But it's what's best for them."

"I know. It is. I agree." Christy felt irritated at what she thought he was insinuating. "If you think that's why I'm not feeling well, it's not that. I really did get sick on the soy milk. Or from a flu bug. It's not because I'm depressed about Katie."

Todd's expression turned more sympathetic, and that bugged Christy even more.

"I know you, Kilikina. You have a tender heart, and when you're sad, it affects your whole body."

Christy did not appreciate Todd's speculation.

My husband should realize how much I hate throwing up. I would never bring that on knowingly. It was the soy milk. He's being so insensitive!

The burst of angry emotions made her face feel hot. She held her tongue behind her pursed lips, and Todd seemed to realize he should leave her alone before anything regrettable happened.

Christy read and fell asleep without hearing Katie and Eli return. She woke at 5:00 a.m., after having slept for almost ten hours. She was starving. Tiptoeing downstairs, Christy tried to be as quiet as possible as she went on a scavenger hunt once again through the larder. Todd had apparently done some grocery shopping because she found plenty of milk, fruit, cereal, and eggs. After making herself some scrambled eggs and a cup of hot tea, she settled herself in the living room with a throw blanket over her legs while she ate. Her stomach felt calmed, and she decided she wasn't coming down with the flu after all. That was encouraging.

Someone was up and moving around in the kitchen. Christy hoped her predawn cooking session hadn't awakened Eli or Katie. The lamp next to Christy in the living room was turned to the lowest level. She stretched and could see Katie shuffling through the kitchen and coming toward her.

"Hey. Morning, early bird. Are you okay?" Katie asked. "Todd said you thought you might be getting sick."

"I feel fine now. I had some soy milk, and I think it was past its expiration date. How did everything go at your mom's?"

Katie sat on the couch and tucked her legs under her. "Really good, I think. I mean, considering that it was my mom and all that she's gone through. She warmed up to Eli, and that made me really happy. He even invited her to come to Kenya to see us after the baby is born."

Christy was surprised. "What did she say?"

"She didn't say much, but her expression said plenty. She wouldn't make a journey like that. She just couldn't. As far as I know, she's never been outside of California. My parents lived a very contained life, and now that my mom has her little apartment and a dining room where she can get all her meals, she's content to stay right where she is."

In the dim light, Katie looked pretty. Her red hair was fluffed out on one side in true Katie bedhead fashion, but her expression was soft and reflective, and her face was still sporting its newly acquired baby glow.

"You look good," Christy said.

"I feel good. Physically and emotionally. This time with my mom healed some old stuff in me. I wish I'd had that with my dad, too." She sighed. "I wrote him a letter last year. Did I tell you that? I wrote it to both my parents and just laid it out. I told them they needed Jesus. My dad didn't take it well. Yesterday my mom said that she kept the letter and she wanted to believe in God."

Christy's eyes opened wide. "Katie, are you saying your mom became a Christian?"

"I don't know."

"Well, what did you say after she said she wanted to believe in God?"

"I didn't say anything. Eli did, though. He

has a really good way of explaining why everyone needs a Savior and how Christ is the only way for us to be made right with God. He does it in such a sincere and non-offensive way. After he said all his perfect, son-of-a-missionary stuff, he asked my mom if she would like for him to pray with her."

"And?"

"She said no."

Christy leaned back. "What do you think of all that?"

"I don't know. Eli thinks she's so inward that she wants whatever is between her and God to stay that way. He said that maybe she already did make her peace with God last year when she read my letter, and that's why she told us that she wanted to believe in God."

Katie readjusted her position and pulled one of the large throw blankets over herself on the sofa. "It's a mysterious thing, isn't it, the way God draws any of us to Himself and how we respond? In high school, I thought if you wanted to become a Christian you had to repeat the exact words of the speaker at camp when he gave the invitation. After meeting believers at Brockhurst who are from so many different countries and hearing so many different stories, I think it's all about the heart. It's not the words you say. It's that heart-level surrender moment. It's repentance in its purest form. You were going one way, you stop, turn around in a moment of surrender, and then you go the other way. God's way."

Christy nodded. She agreed that turning your life over to the Lord was a beautiful and mysterious thing. No two stories of how it happened in the lives of her friends were the same.

"I really hope your mom turned to God, or will turn to God. He can be such a source of peace and strength for her now that your dad is gone."

"I know. I've been praying for my mom for many years," Katie said. "I'm going to keep praying for her. And for Aunt Marti, too."

Christy felt a twinge of conviction. For some stretches of time, she prayed for her aunt consistently and felt a genuine burden for her. Then during other spans in their relationship, like now, Christy tried to think about her aunt as little as possible. These were the spans when Marti's quirks and demands were like the continuous sound of bubble-wrap popping. Not Christy's favorite sound in the world.

"I need to pray for Marti, too. She was here yesterday with the contractor. I didn't know they were coming over. He wants to knock out the hall closet upstairs and push the bedroom out that way. It means we'll lose our bedroom window." Christy made an exaggerated pout. "I love that little bedroom window."

"You'll probably love your extra bedroom even more, once it's done."

"That's the key. Once it's done."

"Are you going to put Hana in the new room?"

"Possibly. I like the idea of setting up my sewing station in the nursery. I love that little room. That way our guest room will be available, especially if Fina moves in with us."

"You've been very patient with us," Katie said. "I know it's not been convenient having everything packed into your bedroom the way it is now."

"It's been fine. I have no complaints. Really. What about you guys and housing? What are you going to do when the baby comes? Your place is tiny."

"We have enough space. I thought it through during my confinement. We just have to move a few things around. When the baby is walking we'll probably move into one of the larger units at the conference center. It'll be fine."

"You're going to be such a good mother, Katie."

"I don't know about that. I worry sometimes that since I didn't get nurtured much that I won't know how to give that kind of motherly attention to our child."

"Oh, you will. You and I both have everything we need, even if it came from an assortment of other women and not our moms. You have Eli's mom right there, and she's such a lovely woman."

"She's a saint," Katie agreed. "I'm so glad we live in a community with Eli's parents. His mom is everything to me when it comes to a role model. They are so excited for us. They can't wait for us to come home."

As soon as Katie said the word "home," Christy felt the sweet melancholy overtake her once again. Katie's home was on the other side of the world, and she would be returning there in two days.

Christy fought back the tears that wanted to start an avalanche. Folding her arms across her clenched stomach, she admitted that Todd was at least somewhat correct. Her emotions were dictating a whole lot of action in her gut.

TWENTY-ONE

Once Bob and Marti found out about Eli and Katie's imminent departure, they insisted on hosting a good-bye dinner at their house on Wednesday night. It turned out to be a good plan, and Katie was especially glad they did it. Linda wasn't able to come. She was doing what she did best — welcoming a new little life into the world.

Hana was happy to wander through Uncle Bob's kitchen where he had prepared a cupboard just for her, filled with plastic bowls, cups, spoons, and a few toys.

They ate around the table on the patio, which had always provided the most romantic views of the sunsets at Newport Beach. That night was no exception. In fact, the clouds seemed to curl themselves into scallops and turn the sky into a stunning pink and frilly Valentine of a good-bye meant especially for Eli and Katie.

Aunt Marti seemed nicer than she had

been for a while. Or maybe it was just that Christy had returned to a more grace-filled place with her aunt after seeing how kind Katie had been to her mom and the fruit that came from the gift of grace.

Marti's change began when they arrived. She pulled Christy aside and said, "I owe you an apology. I was insensitive to barge in on you the other day with Dennis. It's your home. I promise to be more respectful as the renovation begins."

"Thank you." Christy gave her aunt a hug, and Marti received it in her usual slightly stiff way.

Marti had an expression of kindness for Katie, too. As they were all leaving, Marti slid an envelope into Katie's hand and made gestures that Christy thought were saying that Katie could not refuse what she was giving her. It was a gift, and not one that could be returned.

The envelope contained two checks. Katie pulled them from the envelope once they were back at Todd and Christy's. "I don't know why your aunt and uncle did this." Katie looked at the two different checks and showed them to Eli. "This one is supposed to cover our flight home, but we didn't spend that much. This one is a donation to the fund-raiser Todd is going to head up.

It's too much."

"No it's not," Eli said.

Katie looked at him with surprise.

"This isn't about plane tickets or clean water," Eli explained. "It's one of the only ways Marti can show people that she cares about them. She loves you, Katie. That's a big deal. This gift is her way of telling you how much."

Katie teared up.

"Eli, thank you for saying that." Christy felt everything inside her resonating with his comment. He saw Aunt Marti and her actions so clearly.

"I've felt that way with Marti and her sometimes extravagant use of money, but I don't think I've ever been able to define it as one of the only ways she's able to show her love for other people." Christy gave Katie's shoulder a squeeze. "Eli's right. She loves you very much, Katie. Just take it and be thankful."

Katie nodded, keeping her head down. "Okay."

Christy had no idea how much money her uncle and aunt had, but since they didn't have children of their own to invest in, it filled an innate need in them to give to Christy and Todd. Lately, they had been generous with David, too, and had paid for the plane fares for David and Fina to come in September.

"Take it and be thankful," Todd added. "Isn't that what you just said, Christy?"

She nodded.

Katie handed the checks to Eli and suggested that he go to the bank first thing in the morning and have the money transferred to their international account.

In true Katie fashion, she tried to redirect the emotional moment to something more light-hearted. "The last thing I want to do is be responsible for any more bits of paper. I hit my limit on sorting and saving papers when I was at my mom's. My suitcases are not going to shut, I can tell you that right now. Even with my newly expanded backside sitting on top of them, they are not going to hold all the junk I'm taking back to Kenya."

By the next afternoon Katie's prediction proved to be true. She and Eli had three suitcases packed, but none of them would zip closed. Katie and Christy stood in the guest room evaluating the abundance.

"This is evidence right here that I've turned into a materialistic American. When I left Nairobi in June, all I had was this one small, battered suitcase. All Eli brought was one that fit in the overhead of the plane.

Look at this! What an indictment this is."

"Katie, it's not all for you. My mom and Aunt Marti loaded you up with gifts for the baby."

"I know. And I want to keep all of them along with the books you gave me and my heavy yearbooks. Plus the books Todd gave Eli, and the bag of chocolate bars and the new can opener Eli's mom asked us to bring. I guess you're right. It's not all my stuff."

"We have plenty of duffle bags and a big suitcase you're welcome to have. You could transfer the stuff from your beat-up medium-sized suitcase and take our big one." Christy lifted the top of Katie's mangled old suitcase. "Besides, I'm not sure this one would make it home anyway. Not without a lot of duct tape."

"Okay." Katie put her hands on her hips and let her belly stick out as she surveyed the situation. "I'll take your big suitcase but then that means you have to come with Todd next summer to get it back." Katie grinned at Christy, pleased with her solution.

Christy, however, was focused on Katie's protruding tummy and let out an "Eeee!"

"What?" Katie looked around as if Christy had spotted a spider.

"You have a baby bump! Katie, look." Christy pulled her into the guest bathroom and made her stand to the side and smooth her top over her middle. "That's legitimate."

Katie turned right and left. "It is, isn't it?"

"Definitely." She beamed at Katie in the mirror. "The next time I see you, that little bump will be a baby in your arms."

Katie seemed to latch on to the phrase, "next time I see you" more than the part about the "baby in your arms."

"Does that mean you really are going to come with Todd next summer?"

"I want to. I'm not sure how it will all work out. I saw how flexible Hana could be when we went to Glenbrooke. I don't know. Maybe she'll stay here. Maybe she'll come with us. We'll see. But I very much want to come."

Katie threw her arms around Christy and hugged her. "Good," she said in Christy's ear. "Because I very much want you to come."

Both of them got teary again. The "waterworks" as Katie started calling it, had been nonstop since Eli announced that they had booked their flight home. Christy pulled herself together and went to the garage to find the larger suitcase. As soon as she stepped out the kitchen door, she let the tears cascade unhindered down her face. She thought it was better to cry alone than to let Katie or anyone else see her. The truth was, she was tired of crying. She was so tired.

This was so hard. Harder than she thought it would be.

They were down to hours now. One last sunset walk on the beach that evening, one last marshmallow roast around the fire pit, and at Todd's insistence, another Bongo Fest. He had even found a bongo set at a local music store and brought it home that morning in preparation for their final night together.

The Bongo Fest turned out, by far, to be the best way they could have spent their last evening together around the fire pit on their deck. Eli got into it big time. The way he and Todd played off each other with their rhythms and the way they made up beatnik-type poetry to punctuate the flow was a thing of wonder to behold.

Katie took a turn and got into a grove that was funny to watch. She had a way of using her neck to keep pace that made her look like a coo-coo bird popping in and out of a Swiss wall clock. Eli looked at her with affection, and Katie kept all of them laughing with her uneven, nonsensical prose. The rounds of laughter were a welcome relief to all the flashflood crying Christy and Katie had experienced. The laughter also wore them out so that they all found it relatively easy to head to bed at a reasonable hour and not at 2:00 a.m., the way they had the night before.

Christy woke up just before five o'clock Friday morning. She sat up in bed and squinted, trying to see around their darkened bedroom. Did a noise awaken her? Was it Hana? Were Eli and Katie already up?

She heard nothing and tried to calm her racing heart and go back to sleep. Her stomach was in knots, and she was certain she had clenched her teeth all night. She tossed back the covers and lay on her back, staring upward, barely making out the edges of the ceiling fan in the dark. For nearly half an hour she felt suspended between past and present, present and future. She tried thinking happy thoughts about how great it would be to have an additional bedroom. She thought about Fina, and what it would be like to have her and David included now in their Family Night Dinners. She thought about what color she would paint Hana's nursery, if she turned it back into a workroom. All efforts were made for her mind to release its grip on the reality that this was the day Katie was stepping out of her everyday life.

At 6:00 a.m., Todd's alarm went off. He rolled out of bed, and Christy did the same. She pulled on some clothes, padded downstairs, and tried to quietly start making breakfast. It turned out she didn't need to keep quiet. Eli and Katie were up, and behind their closed door they were carrying out a rather long argument in low voices. The disagreement seemed to be over the luggage. Katie apparently was removing items left and right, and Eli was insisting that she take everything with them and pay for the added weight.

"I don't want to have to pay to take this stuff with us," Katie protested.

"Well, I do. It's not that big of a deal. We'll pay for the extra weight."

"It's going to be a lot. Hundreds of dollars. For what? Junk. That's all it is."

"Then we'll pay hundreds of dollars. I want to take with us everything that we packed and had ready to go last night. You will regret it if we leave anything here."

"No I won't."

"Katie, put that back in the suitcase."

"No. I don't want it."

"I do."

"Elijah James Lorenzo!" Katie's voice was

fully elevated now. "Why are you being so stubborn!"

"Because I'm right."

Christy had rarely heard the two of them argue, and when they had it was never like this. She felt like she should go back upstairs and let them work things out. Too late. Katie swung open the bedroom door, stomped into the kitchen, and stopped when she spotted Christy. Katie's lower jaw was set. Her eyes were splotchy and red. She stared at Christy, and Christy stared back with her lips curled in and pressed together. Neither of them spoke.

As if on cue, Hana let out her morning call from upstairs. Christy lowered her head and responded like a downstairs maid whose role in life was to serve the whims and wishes of those in the upper stratosphere. In a way, Christy liked that she had heard the fight. She had her share of irrational fights with Todd, especially when she was pregnant. She understood exactly how Katie was feeling right now. She also sided with Eli and his logic about how Katie would miss anything she left out of the suitcase.

The argument and the return of Christy with Hana to the kitchen alongside Todd's morning energy all led to an awkward twenty minutes with Katie and Eli. From all appearances, Eli had won this time, and Katie was silent about everything. She went through the motions of making a cup of herbal tea without looking at Christy. Katie skirted Hana's arms-up request for Katie to pick her up. She stayed in the downstairs bedroom until Eli and Todd had carried the closed-up suitcases out to Clover and loaded everything into the backseat and the trunk.

The four of them had agreed that only Todd would take them to the airport. Christy regretted that decision now, but something in her rumbling gut told her to let it be.

Don't try to rescue or intervene.

This was going to be difficult no matter what. That's what they had agreed on. Katie had specified that she didn't want to prolong the discomfort by having to wave good-bye to them from an airport security line. She wanted to say good-bye at Christy and Todd's home.

And that's what Katie did.

Her hug lasted a long time. Christy couldn't stop crying. Katie's whole body shook.

"Next summer," Katie finally managed to say.

"Next summer," Christy repeated in barely a whisper. She pulled away first and pressed a salty kiss against Katie's smooth cheek. "Love you, my Forever Friend."

"Love you, my Peculiar Treasure."

They drew back and looked each other in the eyes. Christy was certain she looked as much of a blubbering mess as Katie did. They held hands, each forcing a smile and blinking back tears. Then Katie let go. She turned slowly, gave Hana a hug in Todd's arms, and then gave Todd a cheek-to-cheek hug. He was crying unashamedly. So was Eli.

Hana seemed to be confused by all the tears and reached out for "Mama." Christy took her and held her close. "Say bye-bye, Hana. Bye-bye, Auntie Katie. Bye-bye, Uncle Eli."

Hana fell into her adorable blowing kisses routine, sending out more and more to Eli and Katie on the palm of her hand. Her sweetness brought brave smiles to all the faces. Eli led the way to the garage, and Christy followed, watching them settle into Clover, back down the driveway, and head down the street. From the open back window Katie's outstretched palm shimmied and then moved out of view when Todd turned the corner.

Christy stood where she was, blinking, breathing. Hana leaned in and kissed Christy on the cheek with one of her open-mouthed fish kisses. She kissed Christy a second time and then pulled back. Hana stuck out her tongue and with her little fingers she pulled at her lips and tongue the way she did whenever she tried a new food she didn't like.

"Did you get too many of my salty kisses, baby girl?" Christy wiped her face with the back of her free hand. "Come on, let's get you some breakfast."

A young woman who appeared to be about the same age as Christy was walking toward them. She was tall with dark hair twisted in a messy bun on top of her head and wearing sunglasses. She was also obviously pregnant.

"Morning." She stopped and smiled at Hana, leaning in to be at Hana's eye level. "How are you this beautiful morning?"

Hana curled into Christy's neck in her shy pose. Christy was aware that she was pretty much a sobbing, red-eyed mess and wasn't eager to enter into any kind of conversation, but she knew it would be rude to turn on her heel and go back inside. People in their neighborhood didn't always stop to initiate conversation. Most of the houses on their block were used as vacation rentals, and only a few people lived in the neighboring beach houses year round.

"How old is she?"

Christy had to think a minute. She couldn't count the months in her head. For a moment she wasn't sure what month they were in. The easiest reply came out in a choked voice because her throat was tight from all the crying. "She'll be two in November."

"I'm due in three weeks." The woman smoothed her hand over the bubble under her stretchy workout clothes.

"Congratulations." Christy was struggling to sound gracious at the moment. "I hope everything goes well."

"Thanks."

Pointing toward the open garage, Christy said, "Sorry, but I need to get back inside and make her some breakfast."

The woman waved at Hana. "Hope you have a good day."

"Thanks. You too." Christy felt funny pressing the garage door button, as if she was trying to shut out the friendly woman. If she weren't such an emotional wreck, she would have welcomed the chance to visit the way the neighbors seemed to do in Glenbrooke. She put Hana in her high chair and offered a peeled and broken-up banana.

"The Lord gave and the Lord has taken away. Blessed be the name of the Lord."

The verse that randomly popped into Christy's thoughts was the one Todd had quoted at Katie's dad's funeral. He mentioned it again when they were camping. She thought about how she had wished for a mom-friend when she blew out her birthday candles.

It can't be that easy. Katie leaves, a new friend appears in my driveway? No.

She shook her head. Her emotions were all over the place. She decided, though, that if she happened to see the woman again, she would make more of an effort to engage. Even if the woman was only here for a week, renting one of the neighborhood cottages for summer vacation, it would still be nice to have a conversation about babies and motherhood.

Christy helped herself to a slice of Hana's banana and leaned against the counter, chewing it slowly before swallowing it as a test to see if her rumbling stomach took the bait and liked it.

Why couldn't I figure out how old Hana is? What day is this, anyhow?

Christy went to the calendar on the wall and checked. August 11. Friday. Todd had penciled in Tuesday, August 22 as the day he was going back on campus for staff meetings. She had crossed off the date when the upstairs renovations were supposed to start because Marti had let them know that everything was delayed due to the need to resubmit the plans.

Christy flipped the calendar back to June, remembering the circled day when Katie first arrived. She scanned the month of July with all of Katie's doctor appointments, the long line through all the days they had been on vacation, and then she turned back to August.

Christy froze. She scanned the calendar again, starting with June, then July, then back to August.

"Oh!"

Her hand rose and covered her mouth. She felt her heart do a flip.

Of course. Of course! How did I miss all the obvious clues?

Christy pressed both hands over her stomach and smiled. Her throat tightened, and she knew she was going to cry again. She had a secret. A sweet, sweet secret.

She knew that something this wonderful wouldn't be a secret for long.

TWENTY-TWO

Christy wanted to deliver the news to Todd in a memorable way and considered what she could do. Most likely he would be hungry when he returned from LAX so a nice, private lunch for just the two of them would be fun. It was a treat they hadn't been able to enjoy together for many months between houseguests and vacation travels.

Checking the freezer, she found she had baby back ribs. Perfect! They came from the grocery store already seasoned and pre-cooked. All she had to do was warm them up. She had baby carrots. Again, perfect. The "baby" theme made her laugh aloud. She didn't have any baby fingerling potatoes or Baby Ruth candy bars, but she did have leftover coleslaw. Coleslaw had a baby connection for Todd and her from their first camping trip in Gussie. Todd had declared at the outdoor picnic table, while they ate their coleslaw, that he thought they should name their first son Cole Bryan. Every time they had coleslaw, Todd would always wink at her, letting her know he hadn't forgotten.

Hana contentedly pushed her little plastic shopping cart around the house and found stray toys to put inside it. Uncle Bob had gotten the cart for her a week ago, and it remained her favorite toy. Christy decided her lunch plans with Todd would be even more special if she could send Hana over to her mom and dad's. She made the call and was grateful when her mom said she would come to pick Hana up since she was out running errands.

When Christy's mom arrived, she opened her arms, and Hana trotted over to Grandma with a big smile and a string of words that didn't sound like anything familiar. Mom scooped her up and held her close.

"Do you want to come over and play at my house for a while?"

Hana dipped her chin and blinked her long eyelashes at Grandma.

"Just call when you want her back," Christy's mom said. "We're going to have a fun day, aren't we, Hana?"

When Christy had asked her mom about taking Hana, she said that Eli and Katie had left, and she needed some time to regroup.

It was true, but she also wasn't sure if she wanted to say anything more. Now that her mom was here, Christy felt compelled to let her mom in on the secret. She sidled up to her mom and gave her a hug, looping Hana into the hug as well.

"Mom, can I tell you a secret?"

"I know what you're going to say."

Christy pulled back, stunned. "You do?"

Her mom nodded. Her cheeks looked rosy, and her eyes were smiling. "You were saying at Family Dinner Night that you had been especially tired and thought it was because of staying up so late with Katie and Eli every night. I looked at you and I thought, that's not why she's tired."

"You honestly knew just by looking at me?"

Her mom smiled softly and nodded again. "Congratulations, sweetheart."

"Thanks, Mom. I can't believe you knew." Christy felt a quiet elation that her mother knew her well enough to pick up on the clues. "I guess you were the first one to know, then, because I didn't know until this morning. Todd doesn't know. That's why I wanted to make a special lunch for him."

"I'm very happy for you." She gave Hana a jostle. "Are you ready to go?"

Hana wiggled down and pushed her shopping cart to the door.

"Do you mind taking the cart with you? It's her favorite toy right now."

"Sure. Come on, you can push the cart out to the car."

Christy grinned at the sight of the two of them putting the shopping cart into the car and Hana into the car seat. She waved and went back to work, preparing everything "Pinterest Perfect," as Tracy used to say.

Todd returned road weary from all the traffic to and from LAX. He tossed his car keys on the counter and noticed the small kitchen nook table set with placemats, Christy's best dishes, and a lit candle in the center.

"Are you having a special guest over for lunch?" he asked.

"You could say that, yes." Christy turned off the oven that had been set on warm and used mitts to pull out the baby back ribs.

"Who's coming?"

"You. You're my special guest. My mom took Hana for the day so it's just us."

Todd raised his eyebrows. "What's going on?"

Christy grinned. She put the ribs on a platter and carried them over to the table. "Well, we're having baby back ribs, baby carrots, and . . ." she put the platter on the table and watched to see if he was catching on yet, "Coleslaw."

Todd studied Christy's face. His gaze slid down to her midriff, and a slow smile pulled up the corner of his mouth, revealing his dimple. Looking her in the eye, he asked, "Really?"

Christy nodded.

"You took a test and everything?"

She nodded again. "I had one that I got for Katie months ago when she wanted to double check but she never used it."

Todd wrapped his arms around her and kissed her so suddenly, their teeth tapped. They pulled back, laughing, and then tried it again, more in sync, as the kissing experts they had become over the years.

For the next few weeks, Christy, Todd, and her mom all kept the secret to themselves. Christy wanted to wait until she had seen Aunt Linda and had all the tests so the announcement would feel more official.

Christy wanted to tell Katie on a video call. She had to wait longer than she had hoped for that to happen, but with the time change as well as the amount of time it took for Katie and Eli to settle in once they returned to Brockhurst, almost three weeks passed before they found a time that worked.

As soon as Christy saw Katie's face come up on the screen, she smiled.

"Rafiki!" Katie spouted the Swahili word for "friend" and quickly turned the camera so it caught a way-too-close-up shot of her middle. "Wait." The image shifted and then steadied. Katie stepped away and stood to the side, smoothing her shirt so she could show Christy her baby bump.

"Significant pooch now, huh?" Katie patted her slight bulge. "This kid likes food. Lots and lots of food. I send him regular supplies every couple of hours. I've gained so much weight. It's great. Ha! When did I ever think it would be great to gain weight?"

Katie slid to the side, out of the view of the camera for a moment and then re-appeared with something blue on her hand. She flapped it like a puppet. "Isn't it cute? Eli's mom has been knitting baby caps like crazy. She's having so much fun being a grandma already. Everything has been great. Just great." Katie leaned in toward the camera. "What about you? How's everything and everybody there?"

"Well," Christy stepped away from the laptop on the counter. She stood to the side and smoothed her new, flowy sundress over her not-yet-showing stomach. "Could you ask Eli's mom to knit one more cap and send it our way? I'm going to be right behind you, little mama."

"Christy!" Katie's squeal blasted through the laptop speaker. "Are you kidding me?! When did you find out? I can't believe it!"

Christy told her the whole story and included the part about her mom already having an inkling.

"I am so happy for you!" Katie's expression suddenly turned serious. "Wait. When is your due date?"

"The end of April."

Katie counted on her fingers. "That means he'll be two months old when you come to Kenya with Todd."

Christy's expression sobered. "I won't be able to come, Katie. Not this time. Maybe in a year or two."

"That's like an eternity," Katie said sadly.

"I know. But it's a different season for us. You know. You're experiencing it now, too. It's baby season, and that's what needs to be my top priority right now. Todd and I talked about it a lot, and I still want him to go. I have plenty of support and help here."

"Wow, I mean, I'm super happy for you, but I was really excited about us spending all the time together next summer and for our little monkey to get to know his Auntie Christy right away."

"I know. Me, too." Christy felt the familiar melancholy that had surfaced over the past few months in the wake of all the hellos and good-byes. She thought again of the verse in Job about the Lord giving and taking away. The key to being at peace on the teeter-totter of life seemed to be the next part of the verse. *"Blessed be the name of the Lord."*

Christy had been journaling that week about being thankful in every circumstance. She told Katie about what she'd written the other day.

"I have to consider all of this as part of the blessing during this time in our lives. It's a chance for me to be grateful for what God is giving us and not get hung up on what He is taking away."

"Wise, as ever." Katie sighed. "I know you're right but I guess I want it all. I want this season of becoming parents and taking on new responsibilities. At the same time, I still want to be young and free and able for us to do all the 'us' things we did when I was there this summer."

"Those months were a gift for both of us," Christy said. "I think we sort of realized it at the time, don't you? It was an unexpected blessing at just the right time."

"It definitely was."

They talked only another five minutes before Katie had to go. "We need to set up a regular time each week," Katie suggested. "Or at least every other week. I don't want to lose touch."

"Me either."

"Okay, well, let me know what days and times work best for you, and we'll set it up."

Christy sat staring at the screen on her laptop after the call ended. She understood now why she had been such an emotional wreck when Katie left and why both of them had cried so much. For her, it was more than being pregnant and not realizing it yet. The bigger view was that they both knew, even if neither of them expressed it during their last week together, that they had been given a sliver of time to do life together the way they had always dreamed of and talked about when they were roommates in college. But only for a season. A sweet, unspoiled, sun-drenched summer. A season that would never come again, at least not in the same way.

Later that night, Katie sent a text with a suggested schedule for their weekly calls. The time and day for the next week worked for Christy. Christy said yes to Katie's suggestion and put the dates in her phone, even though she knew they had never been able to stick to a schedule. Weeks would slip by, and then one of them would reach the point that she couldn't bear to go another day without hearing the other's familiar voice, and she would set up the call.

They always would pick up right where they had left off. And they would always laugh. Laughing with Katie was one of Christy's favorite characteristics of their friendship. They had experienced lots of tears over the years, but their laughter had been double.

That's how the next week was when they connected for their call. Katie had hilarious stories about trying to learn how to knit and demonstrated the beginnings of an uneven, spider-web-looking baby blanket.

Christy let Katie know that she would have to reschedule their next call that Katie had set for September 6. "David and Fina arrive that day, and just to keep things interesting, I found out from Marti that the renovation plans have been approved. Dennis and his crew will arrive on our doorstep at eight o'clock that morning."

"That means Fina is staying at Bob and Marti's, I take it," Katie said.

"Yes, it's all been arranged. Todd and I are moving downstairs to your room."

"My room. Oh, I miss my room." Katie

gave an exaggerated sigh. "Will Hana stay upstairs?"

"No, she's moving in with us. We'll see how it goes. They're saying it should only take three weeks, but we'll see."

"I hope you don't get squeezed to the last drop the way I was. At least you're healthier than I was during my first trimester."

What Christy didn't say was that the weeks between Eli and Katie's departure and David and Fina's arrival had been an oasis time for Christy. She found plenty of time to rest and was so grateful that the new plan's approval process delayed the start date. Christy made good use of the quiet and sent Hana to her mom's more than once so Christy could sleep. Morning sickness hit her several times pretty hard, and she spent half the day trying to regain her equilibrium. But the pregnancy wasn't the same as it had been with Hana. Todd had returned to school, and she used the time organizing her house and trying to keep up with her sewing orders.

"What about your work space?" Katie asked. "Did you have to set up a sweat shop in the garage?"

"Not quite that bad. Todd set up the sewing machine in the living room near the sliding doors overlooking the deck. All the boxes and bins are lining the living room walls. It's not ideal, but I did sort through a lot of stuff, and I've kept only what I need inside the house. The rest is stacked up in the garage."

"Are the orders for all the pillow covers and aprons as regular as they were during the summer?"

"Yes. It's been consistent. Not too much. I've kept up with the work, but I don't know if I will after the baby comes. We'll see."

Their call ended when Hana took a tumble while trying to move one of the tall stools at the kitchen counter. She cried her new frustrated cry that came out whenever she didn't get her way. Christy was beginning to anticipate the "terrible twos" stage she had heard about.

Hana's attempts at independence increased at an unexpected rate over the next week. One morning Christy took her eyes off her for only a moment, but when Christy turned around, Hana had crawled up on top of a chair at the breakfast nook and then boosted herself up on the table. She was standing on the kitchen table, looking proud of herself.

Christy had forgotten about that shocking moment that had sent terror to her mother's heart until the first Family Night they had at the end of September. Dinner was at Bob and Marti's since Todd and Christy's house was a construction nightmare of dust, noise, and men tromping in and out. Christy and Hana spent most of their days at her mom and dad's apartment and other days at Bob and Marti's. The mess was wearing on Christy.

The clan was all out on the patio around the new, larger, glass-top patio table Marti had ordered. They had finished dinner, and Hana was sitting on Fina's lap when she wiggled her way to a standing position and stepped up onto the table before Fina realized what she was doing.

"Hana!" Todd rose and lunged for her, as did nearly everyone else around the table. Marti simply let out a shriek. Todd grabbed his adventurous daughter right before she put her foot into the large wooden salad bowl. "Sunshine, what are you doing?"

Hana arched her back and let out a wail. It was the I-want-what-I-want-when-I-want-it cry that Todd hadn't yet experienced. Christy had told him about it and all Hana's daredevil antics. But this was the first time he had heard the piercing decibel of her wail.

"Hana." His voice was firm. Todd pushed his chair back and said, "Excuse us" to the rest of the family. He carried her into the house, corralling her, as she attempted to squirm out of his arms. The wail did not let up.

Christy felt embarrassed. She was glad Todd had taken Hana inside, but she was nervous about what he was going to do next. They had been working together off and on for a few weeks on different disciplinary approaches because Christy said she could tell the difference now. Their darling baby girl had a streak of defiance. Hana continually tested her boundaries, and Christy continually told others the cause was their chaotic lives with all the construction.

Excusing herself, Christy went inside and found Todd in the kitchen with Hana sitting on his lap, doing her endearing little trembling breath-cry that came out whenever she was on the downside of an outburst. Todd had both arms around her, holding her securely. He was talking to her calmly.

When I try that, she screams. Todd has a way with her that I would give anything to duplicate when I'm home with her alone all day. Why does she adore him so much and listen to him but push me to my limits? Am I a pushover, and she knows it?

Since Todd had the situation well in hand,

and especially since Hana hadn't seen Christy and cried out to be released from the daddy prison, Christy returned to the patio. Everyone around the table was laughing. Christy looked at the faces one by one, as if asking one of them to let her in on the joke. She hoped they weren't laughing at her.

Her glance rested on David's face, and he was grinning with satisfaction. "So, everyone turned on their flashlights, and three squirrels popped out of his sleeping bag and ran across the rafters of the cabin."

"Did the squirrels stay in there all night?" Christy's mom asked.

"No, they managed to usher them outside."

Uncle Bob chuckled. "I bet that kid will never steal another candy bar again. At least not one with nuts in it."

Christy settled back in her chair. They were laughing at another one of David's camp stories; they weren't laughing at her or making jokes about Hana's behavior. She relaxed and tried to tell herself that she wasn't a terrible mother. Parenting was challenging. All the time. She had the privilege of parenting alongside Todd, but she still often felt terribly inadequate for the task.

Resting her open palms on her stomach, Christy thought, *If you are a boy, I don't know what I'm going to do. Everyone told me girls were easier. If you have double the curiosity of Hana, I am in so much trouble. Please be a girl. Please.*

TWENTY-THREE

Christy's wish that she was having another girl seemed to change daily as she slid into her second trimester. The week before Thanksgiving, Christy's mom asked her if she had an inkling or a preference over having a boy or a girl.

With a tender pat on her now slightly-rounded belly, Christy said, "No, I don't have any idea. Sometimes I'm sure it's a boy, and other times I think it has to be a girl because the stages feel so similar to when I was carrying Hana. I'm not set on one or the other."

Christy and her mom were both wearing aprons Christy had made and were ready to start decorating the two dozen cupcakes Christy had baked that morning for Hana's birthday party. As Christy lined up a bunch of small containers of sprinkles and candy toppings on her kitchen counter, Hana was in her high chair having a snack and watching the interesting activity.

"Did you have a feeling you were having a boy when you were pregnant with David?" Christy asked.

"No, I don't think so."

"Did you and Dad wait eight years on purpose before you had a second child?"

"No. Not much of anything was on purpose for us." Christy's mom chuckled. She had such a calm way about her and took her time to do things. Sometimes it irritated Christy because she was used to operating at a higher speed because of keeping up with Hana. Her mom had always been slow and steady, though, and Christy knew that her more cautious approach to life had influenced Christy, especially when it came to decision-making.

"Your dad used to say that we were just happy to take what the Good Lord gave us. Boy or girl, it didn't matter. I don't think things were as intentional and calculated as they are for your generation. We worked hard on that farm. For us it wasn't a matter of trying to have another child or planning anything about it. We just lived our lives, and in the end, it took longer for us the second time around. You're blessed that it hasn't been a problem for you."

Christy felt warmed by the way her mom

was working beside her in her kitchen and sharing a few snippets of her life. Because Christy's mom was a private person, Christy knew this was about as personal and as confidential as the conversation on the topic of intimacy would go with her. It was enough, though, to make Christy feel that she and her mom were connected in a stronger and sweeter way than ever before.

Christy had also enjoyed spending extended time with Fina and felt a bond growing with her. Fina had no trouble making herself at home in Bob and Marti's upstairs guest room. She was rarely home, though, because she was carrying a full load of classes at Long Beach State and spending as much time as she could with David. He had landed a job coaching sports for an after-school program and faithfully helped Todd each week at the Friday Night Gathering. Christy couldn't be happier for David and Fina. All the rest of the family was eager to see how their relationship developed.

A knock sounded at the front door. At least, Christy thought someone was knocking. Even though the construction of the upstairs added bedroom had been completed two weeks ago, at times Christy still thought she could hear phantom hammers pounding. She wiped her hands on her apron and went to the door to check if someone was really there.

On the doorstep stood a tall, young woman with a baby wrapped up in her arms. Her dark hair was pulled back in a ponytail, and her dark eyes looked at Christy shyly. "Hi. I don't know if you remember me. I sort of met you a few months ago. I'm Jenn."

When Christy heard her voice, she recognized her as the pregnant woman who had stopped to say hello the morning Katie had left and Christy was standing in the driveway, still blinking away the tears.

"Yes. Hi!" Christy peered at the bundle in Jenn's arms. "Oh, your baby is here. Did you have a boy or a girl?"

"A girl. Eden Grace." Jenn pulled back the soft baby blanket so Christy could see her face.

"She's beautiful. Congratulations."

"Thanks." Jenn was holding a card in her right hand and extended the card to Christy. The envelope was pale yellow with a darling border of bright-orange watercolor poppies. The poppies immediately reminded Christy of Katie. California poppies were Katie's favorite flowers.

"I won't keep you," Jenn said. "I just wanted to invite you to a small gathering at my house. It's the first Saturday of December. The details are on the invitation. I hope you can come."

"Thank you." Christy took the invitation from Jenn and immediately felt suspicious. She had a pretty good idea that Jenn was selling something. Why else would she make the effort to reach out?

Christy had been invited to plenty of home parties from women connected to the school where Todd taught. So many women were starting home businesses selling cosmetics, cookware, or essential oils. Christy had to stop going to the parties because their budget was tight, and last spring she had bought way more good stuff than they could afford.

Jenn may have sensed Christy's polite hesitation because she said, "I should probably explain that it's just a little tea party. A Christmas tea party. It's my attempt to meet new people, that's all. My husband, Joel, and I moved into the little blue cottage at the end of this street about four months ago. I was so busy having a baby that I haven't connected with many of our neighbors." She looked sincere and a little shy. "To be honest, I'm kind of on the hunt for some mom-friends, now that I'm new to all this."

Christy felt like wrapping her arms around

Jenn and giving her a big hug. She also felt terrible that she hadn't been the one to make the effort to reach out after they had met. She didn't have any emotional reserves left in her the day that Jenn strolled by when Christy was standing in her driveway. But Christy had seen her walk by twice since then. Both times Christy was inside, looking out the sliding doors. She concluded that Jenn hadn't just been in the area on vacation, but she didn't realize that Jenn lived on the same street.

"I'd love to come. Thank you so much. I wish I'd reached out to you. It's been crazy around here the last few months."

"I saw all the construction going on."

"We added an upstairs bedroom. Or, well, our landlord did. Would you like to see it?"

They were still standing at the front door, and Eden began to fuss. "I'd love to, but could I do it another time?"

"Of course. Thanks so much for the invitation. I look forward to coming."

"Good." Jenn hesitated before turning to go with her baby in her arms. "I'm really embarrassed to say this, but I don't know your name. That's why I didn't write anything on the front of the invitation. Sorry."

"Oh. No, I'm sorry I didn't tell you. I'm Christy."

Baby Eden was crying now. She sounded like a baby kitten, the way Hana sounded when she was a newborn. Jenn adjusted the blanket, pulling her little one closer. "I should go. I'll see you at the party. The address and my phone number are in the invitation."

"Thanks, Jenn."

"Bye." Jenn's steps were light but quick as she headed down the street to her little blue cottage. Christy watched her go and felt a sense of hope welling in her. A new friend. Another mom. Right at the end of her street.

As Christy closed the front door, she wished again that she had been the one to make at least a small effort to connect with Jenn earlier. The past months had been filled to the brim — including random bouts of morning sickness and three weeks of construction that turned into seven weeks when the workers discovered the house's foundation needed to be reinforced. She and Todd had moved into Bob and Marti's downstairs guest room for a week and a half, and she and Hana had spent most of their days over at her mom and dad's, trying to keep up with her sewing orders.

It was all a blur now that the room was finished and the house had been thoroughly cleaned last week by a professional cleaning service. The new room was wonderful, much better than they had thought it would be. They decided to use it for Christy's sewing room, and Todd had set up her sewing machine under the window. She loved sitting by that open window as she worked and caught the ancient tumbling sound of the waves.

They kept Hana in her room for now. The space was familiar, and it seemed to be comforting to her once she was back in her own crib after that stay at Bob and Marti's.

"Who was at the door?" Christy's mom asked.

"A neighbor. Jenn. She has a newborn baby girl." Christy slid onto one of the stools at the kitchen island and opened the invitation. The simple card with the party details had been handwritten in a lovely, artful way. Christy wondered if Jenn had done them. If so, she was gifted artistically.

Tucking the invitation into her apron's pocket, Christy smiled contentedly at her mom. Something new was stirring inside Christy. She always had believed that women had the ability to bring life, hope, and healing to other women in the simplest ways. For her, that thrill rose in her when she felt included, wanted, invited. Having an invitation to a tea party tucked in her apron's pocket was an invigorating sensation.

"What do you think?" her mom asked. "Do these need more sprinkles?"

Hana let out a squeak and a jabber from her high chair.

"Apparently the birthday girl thinks they do. Do you want more sprinkles, Hana?"

Hana put up her arms toward Christy and gave a fussy sort of cry.

"I think she's ready for a diaper change," Christy's mom said. "I didn't check."

"Do you want a freshie?" Christy went over to the high chair and lifted up her heavy two-year-old. She agreed with her mom's conclusion right away. "Let's take you upstairs. It's time to put you in your new party dress that your Auntie Marti gave you."

Christy climbed up the stairs with Hana riding on her hip and thought about how, now that they were settled back home, potty training needed to start in earnest. The last three months had flown by. This new baby would be here before they knew it, and Christy didn't want to have two in diapers at the same time.

Hana wanted down as soon as they entered her room. She pulled her stuffed bunny rabbit out of the crib by grabbing its long ear and tugging it through the bars until it popped out. She held on to it and jabbered away as Christy changed her diaper and dressed her in her frilly party dress. Even though the dress was over-the-top and frilly, and not something Christy would ever buy for her daughter, Aunt Marti would be pleased to see it on Hana for her birthday party. Christy added a bowed cloth headband that she had made for Hana.

As usual, Hana pulled off the headband as quickly as Christy put it on and threw it on the ground.

"Okay. No headband. I know. But they do look awfully cute on you." Christy glanced at the collection of almost a dozen different headbands she had made for Hana. "Maybe if you have a sister, she'll like wearing head-bands."

Christy put her hands on her stomach and sat in the rocking chair. *Girl or boy, you will be very loved, little one.*

Hana trotted around her room in her little pink shoes and seemed to be trying to decide if she liked the way her dress poofed out. Christy watched as Hana bent side to side and back and forth, watching the way the broad skirt stuck out no matter which way she moved.

Christy thought about Katie, who was in her third trimester now and going strong. She couldn't imagine Katie with a little pink ballerina running through the green grass and verdant tea fields located near Brockhurst. Weeks ago Christy had cast her vote with Eli and Katie that they would have a baby boy in February. Only a few months remained before they would know.

The sound of the garage door closing below them was followed by the sound of Todd's footsteps coming upstairs. He had taken David out for a last-minute surf session due to a predicted south swell that was supposed to usher in the first of the winter waves.

Hana heard the familiar sound as well and scooted over to the closed bedroom door. She had mastered opening the door by herself, which had been a problem more than once. When she opened it now, her daddy was standing on the other side, still in his wet suit, bending down to meet her at eye level when the door opened.

"Hello, my little Sunshine. Oh, don't you look like a doll." Looking over at Christy he asked, "Where did the dress come from?"

"Aunt Marti."

Todd picked her up and speckled her cheeks and neck with kisses. "I'm not wet, but I hope I don't mess up our little birthday girl's dress."

"I'm sure you won't."

Todd came over to where Christy rested in the rocking chair. He leaned over and planted a warm kiss on her lips. As he pulled back, Christy pressed her lips together.

"Mmm, salty kisses," she said. "My favorite."

Todd grinned and kissed Hana again on the cheek before putting her down. She went over to her toy basket and was pulling out one toy after the other.

"You doing okay?" Todd reached over and fingered the ends of Christy's long hair that she had left down today. She had even put on makeup since the clan was coming over for the Saturday afternoon party.

Christy slipped her hand in Todd's and looked up at him. "I'm better than okay. I'm so happy. God has been really good to us, Todd."

"Yes, He has. I still can't wrap my head around the reality that we now have a two-year-old."

They both looked at Hana and saw the cutest thing ever. She was continuing to go for more toys, Dumpster-diving style. When she bent over the large basket, her bell-shaped dress fluffed up on the sides and popped up in the back and revealed her ruffled pink panties that covered her diaper.

Christy chuckled.

"Thank you." Todd's silver-blue eyes looked immensely deep and sincere.

"For what?"

"For being my wife and the mother of our children. You are a gift to me, Kilikina." He drew her hand up to his lips and planted another salty kiss on the back of her hand. "Not everyone gets this, you know? A family, a home, so much love. I honestly don't know who I would be or where I would be if you hadn't shown up in my life the way you did that summer when you were fourteen."

Christy felt a wave of memories wash over the shore of her heart. She and Todd had shared so many sweet moments over the years. The memories seemed to tumble forward in her thoughts like tiny seashells rolling in the sand. The past and present met and meshed.

In a few months Katie and Eli would have their first baby. In the spring, she and Todd would welcome their new precious cargo she was now carrying. In a few weeks she would go to Jenn's tea party and hopefully see a friendship blossom. David and Fina would continue to be in their everyday lives as they made decisions about their future, and Christy's mom and dad and aunt and uncle were all nearby and very much involved in Hana's life.

The tears came without a sound. Christy remembered how Alissa had said when they were together in Glenbrooke that tears that fall that silently and that quickly always come from the heart. Alissa was right. These tears came from Christy's heart. A heart that was filled to the brim and overflowing with thankfulness. She smiled up at her husband.

Todd leaned in and kissed Christy on both cheeks as if his lips were on patrol, determined to catch all her tears before they fell.

Christy's lips found his, and in perfect unison, they shared a lingering, salty kiss that was brimming with an ocean-full of hopes and dreams for all that was to come.

ABOUT THE AUTHOR

Robin Jones Gunn is the much loved author of the popular Christy Miller series for teens and Sisterchicks novels as well as non-fiction favorites such as *Victim of Grace* and *Spoken For.* Robin's Father Christmas novellas have been made into a 2016 Hallmark Original Movie titled, "Finding Father Christmas". Her 90 books have sold over 5 million copies worldwide. As a frequent speaker, Robin has traveled extensively in Africa, Brazil, Europe, and Australia. She and her husband Ross live in Hawaii where she continues to write from her heart.

RobinGunn.com

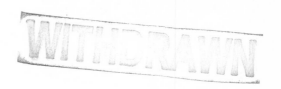

The employees of Thorndike Press hope you have enjoyed this Large Print book. All our Thorndike, Wheeler, and Kennebec Large Print titles are designed for easy reading, and all our books are made to last. Other Thorndike Press Large Print books are available at your library, through selected bookstores, or directly from us.

For information about titles, please call:
 (800) 223-1244

or visit our website at:
 gale.com/thorndike

To share your comments, please write:
 Publisher
 Thorndike Press
 10 Water St., Suite 310
 Waterville, ME 04901